About the author

Jamie Macilwaine was born in Zimbabwe and brought up amongst the wilds of Africa. A hopeless romantic, farm girl at heart, she grew up on various farms around the world as she and her family followed her ex-pat farming father moving from continent to continent. Now she lives in Kent, in England, where you can find her typing away, watching her favorite romance films, and escaping in books—typically with a glass of wine in hand.

ALWAYS, FOREVER

JAMIE MACILWAINE

ALWAYS, FOREVER

Vanguard Press

VANGUARD PAPERBACK

© Copyright 2022
Jamie Macilwaine

The right of Jamie Macilwaine to be identified as author of
this work has been asserted by her in accordance with the
Copyright, Designs and Patents Act 1988.

A CIP catalogue record for this title is
available from the British Library.

ISBN 978 1 80016 264 8

Vanguard Press is an imprint of
Pegasus Elliot MacKenzie Publishers Ltd.
www.pegasuspublishers.com

First Published in 2022

Vanguard Press
Sheraton House Castle Park
Cambridge England

Printed & Bound in Great Britain

Dedication

To all the hopeless romantics.

Prologue

It was a cool autumn morning, winter just around the corner; the air rich with hopes of sunshine. Grey clouds part slowly to reveal the rising sun, doves and pigeons coo gently, in the trees, picking a wild berry breakfast from the branches. A squirrel darts along a green stained wooden fence, lawn mower humming lazily in the distance.

Goosebumps rise along my heated skin, cold air kissing my damp neck, the fresh morning breeze making me dizzy. I blink past the dots in my vision, clearing the watery haze from my eyes.

I want to stop, take a moment to turn my face toward the sun, to let it bathe me in its comforting embrace, to let the cold morning air tell me it was going to be OK. Instead, arm bent painfully backwards, I stumble, pushed from behind, bare feet meeting the morning dewed grass, unkempt and tickling my shins.

Behind me, he smells of fear, damp breath shifting the hair at my neck, fingers digging horribly into my arm, keeping me securely in front of him.

I'm aware of the sharp ache coming from my stomach, but that's the least of my problems. Right now, I simply need to focus on putting one foot in front of the other, to stop my legs from shaking, control the trembling and pins and needles working their way through my arm.

The otherwise beautiful morning glare is like razors on my eyes, as if grains of sand are trapped behind the lids. A sharp gleam bounces off the blade in his hand, and I flinch back, into his bare chest.

His body shakes too, like an addict needing their next fix, deep, velvety voice vibrating through me. He's speaking, but I can't hear the words, unable to listen past the thudding of my heart.

How had it come to this?

I should be listening, trying to think of a way out, trying to hold onto hope, but my mind is numb, like the static of a TV.

I'm tired.

All I want to do was lean back, let him carry my weight, carry me to somewhere warm, where I can curl up and disappear into a dream where none of this is happening.

A sea of strange faces come into focus in front of us—eyes full of fear, worry, concern. Brows pulled together. Lips taut. But I know there's nothing they can do. I know what he's going to do—I know it in the pit of my stomach as if the ache there is pulsing with whispers of what's to come.

Wouldn't it be easier? To give in, tell everyone to go away—I'm where I want to be.

Darkness tells me that I am. Part of me knows it too.

Maybe I've been in denial. Maybe he was right, and I'm where I should be. Why should I ignore that alluring darkness when it would be so easy to embrace it?

Closing my eyes, I imagined wrapping a star flecked blanket around myself, letting go, stop fighting. For a moment I'm suspended as if space has sucked me in, and I float amongst the constellations.

His voice rises, breaking my dream, eyes sliding lazily open.

Maybe I should tell them I want to stay?

Like an angel rising out of the darkness, a light beaming in the black of night, suddenly I see him. The reason I can't let the shadows in.

The reason I don't want to.

My gut squeezes, a lump appearing in my throat, knees threatening to buckle beneath me. Suddenly I'm conscious of the way I look. I've lost weight—from the anxiety and stress, not the lack of food—and I'm acutely aware that I'm wearing another man's T-shirt and nothing but his boxers, thighs exposed.

Pleading with my eyes, I hope he can see the message behind them; *I love you. It's going to be OK. I'm sorry.*

"Ty," the man behind me whispers. "It's the only way, Ty. We'll be together. Always and forever. Forgive me, but I promise I'll follow you." My body tenses, the knife piercing my skin.

I love you. I love you. I love you. My mind whispers across the distance, just as his face contorts into a scream.

CHAPTER ONE
Australia

Everyone has a first love, and Ryan Andrews was mine.

He moved to the house across from ours with his parents when I was six. I remembered peeking through the white net curtain, watching him run up and down from the moving truck with a dog chasing beside him. I later learnt that the dog was a Weimaraner, and they had two that looked almost identical. Toby and Tinker (the dogs) were tall with fur so grey it was practically blue, tails cut low, so they stuck out like sausages.

Mum and dad were quick to drag my sister and me across the field to meet these new neighbours. After all, their house was the only other one of the farm plot, beside ours.

Clinging shyly to my dad's hand, I hid behind his legs when Ryan's mum leant down to greet me.

"Hello, Tyler." Mrs Andrews' voice was soft and kind. I ducked behind dad.

He laughed, "She's a little shy. This is her sister, our eldest, Melanie."

Mel beamed like the little golden sheep of the family that she was, confidently shaking Mrs Andrews' hand. When Ryan sauntered into the room, he politely shook both my parents' hands and even Mel's. I hid even further behind dad when he offered me his outstretched hand, his smile playful yet still somehow understanding, and not at all mocking of my meek behaviour.

In our room that evening, blue dolphin duvet wrapped around my shoulders, Mel and I gushed how 'cute' Ryan was—though, two years my senior, Mel had a better idea of what a 'good looking' boy was. Still, I was eager as ever, nodding vigorously as she described how sweet, kind, and confident he was.

Sweet. Kind. Confident. I grinned at the ceiling in the dark when Mel had turned out the light, heavy breathing coming from her corner of the room. *And he lives just across from us!* My little excited heart couldn't take it. All the girls at school would be so jealous.

It was an innocent kind of excitement; he was the first boy I had ever actually *noticed*—ever thought was cute. The first one I ever felt those first fleeting feelings of a crush.

So Ryan was the boy next door for the next ten years, and Mel and I grew up with him. Our houses sat on the end of a dead-end street, on a no longer used patch of farmland. Tall gum trees lined the road leading to the houses, both bungalows with similar bay windows overlooking sprawling fields around them, peeling white paint flaking from the wood.

A little way at the back of the houses was a large pond where Mel, Ryan and I liked to play. The grass was always tall and unkempt, towering at least an inch or two over me. Once, I'd almost got lost entirely amongst the stalks, and after that, insisted on holding someone's hand every time we ran through it. Mel found this hilarious and would run off without me, cackling as she left me at the edge of the tall grass.

One warm summer day, Ryan was already running ahead in the depths of the golden stalks, when Mel left me behind, shouting over her shoulder that I needed to 'stop being such a baby'.

"Mel!" I yelled; small voice raised as loud as it could go, Mel disappearing amongst the golden sea. "Mel, I want to come!"

Tears pricked my eyes when silence fell around me, and I looked at the grass, tall and menacing as if it held encroaching monsters. Just as I was about to turn and bolt home, Ryan appeared through the curtain of stalks, grinning, chest panting, beads of sweat along his forehead, a hand outstretched. "Come on."

My face split into a broad smile, and I slapped a hand in his. Together, we ran, my little legs pumping as hard as they could beside his, our hands waving awkwardly between us, gripping onto each other, propelling ourselves forward. He laughed about how short my legs were, and I laughed purely because he was.

All too soon we broke through to the pond on the other side, and he released my hand to run to where Mel was balancing on a mossy log at the water's edge.

Mel and Ryan were the same age, which meant that they were in the same class at school, got the same homework, and hung out with the same friends. I always felt just on the edge. But Mel and I were always united in our adoration for Ryan. Though, as we got older, she stopped telling me how cute she thought he was, instead whispering it to her friend Caitlin—I saw the way they looked at him, pink rising in their cheeks, giggling when he left the room. It was the first time I felt threatened that they might take Ryan away from me.

He was no longer *ours*.

The worst part was when Ryan started hanging out with Mel and Caitlin more than me. When he stopped defending me with things like 'We can't leave your little sister at home' or 'She's not that annoying, let her come,' and happily left me longingly watching them cycle down the road, retreating forms disappearing, laughter thinning on the wind.

My first boyfriend was Tom when I was ten. My first kiss was with Alex when I was thirteen. But through all the time, I still looked at Ryan like he was the greatest love of my life. The one I could never get—the one I always wanted. I often prayed that he would notice me more than Mel, but when Mel's breasts came in, I knew I didn't stand a chance.

I used to find excuses to go into Mel's room when he was there; "Mel, can I borrow your hairbrush? Oh, hi Ryan, I didn't know you were here."

Why did she have to be so perfect? Why did she get to be the one with deep chocolate-coloured hair, while I was left with a colour best described as that of muddy water? Why did she get to be the one with the radiant smile, the big hazel eyes, the entirely unmarked skin? I used to hate the small freckles running over my nose and along my cheeks. Hate my too small lips. Flat chest. Hair that wasn't as long as hers.

But the day that truly broke me, was the day that Mel bounced into my room, announcing that Ryan had asked her to be his girlfriend.

I frowned, "He asked you?"

"Yup," she beamed.

"Why?"

She laughed. "What do you mean why? He likes me. Obviously."

I was thirteen but hadn't yet shared that beautiful first sloppy kiss with Alex. I wanted to throttle her with the pillow as she pranced out of my room like an obnoxious show pony. She was only boasting because she knew I liked him.

Lying back on my bed, tears leaked down my cheeks, the homework I'd been working on discarded to the side. My tiny chest shuddered, young heart quietly breaking.

CHAPTER TWO

Jealousy. I'd never understood it until I saw Ryan holding Mel's hand. I was so insanely jealous that it turned into anger. From anger to hatred. Hatred for *Mel*. How could she do that to me? Anger because he'd chosen *her*. Anger because the longer they stayed together, the more it became apparent that Ryan didn't see me as anything other than 'Mel's-little-sister'. I quickly stopped looking for excuses to 'run' into him when they were together, instead, deliberately *avoiding* being in the same room as them.

It wasn't as if they had an overly lovey or physical relationship, the opposite really. But every now and again, when he'd casually drape his arm around her shoulders, or she'd hold his hand, the little dragon in my adolescent stomach would rear its head. I so badly wanted to know what it felt like to be that close to him. Have his arm around *my* shoulders.

Not long after Mel and Ryan got together, I had my first kiss. Alex timed asking me out perfectly. Still raw over the whole situation with Mel and Ryan, I'd started noticing Alex now that Ryan wasn't stealing all my attention.

Alex was sweet with soft brown hair that was long on the top, eyes that slanted in the corners. I liked him more than any of the other boys, and I decided it was time to pop my 'kissing cherry'. My friend Lilly and I had practised enough on the back of our hands, and I was ready—Alex was going to be the one to do it.

It happened in the field behind our house, beneath a large tree hiding us from view of prying eyes at the windows. It was wet and sloppy, but how was I to know that was a bad thing?

When Ryan and Mel broke up, I subconsciously started making reasons why I shouldn't be with Alex. But before I had a chance to break up with him in the hopes that it was my turn with Ryan—my adolescent brain didn't see anything wrong with the notion—he and Mel got back together.

Mel and Ryan were on and off for a long time, and I stayed with Alex throughout. We were even still together when they broke up for the last time. Yet by that point, I had convinced myself I didn't like Ryan any more and was pretty invested with Alex. I liked him a lot.

When Alex and I eventually broke up, it was because he was moving to the northern territory, too far to try long distance, even if we were too young to make it work.

At thirteen, my hopeless romantic-ness had grown. Previously fuelled by Disney love stories, it became grand romantic movies—like the love between Romeo and Juliet, of Rose and Jack on the *Titanic*, of Satin and Christian in the *Moulin Rouge*. I craved a love so deep and pure, so grand and majestic, that people would cry and laugh and love all at once upon hearing the story.

I used to see Ryan as my leading man. But as I got older, I soon realised the bleak truth of my reality; that even if I were a character in a movie, I certainly wouldn't be a Rose or a Satin. I would be the best friend, the side character or supporting actor.

Average. I was average.

My hair was short-cropped around my shoulders because I couldn't be bothered with the effort that came with having it long, and I typically tied it in a half-bun on top of my head. My wardrobe consisted of dull colours; greens, blues, blacks and whites, and the only time I ever wore lip gloss was when I could steal it out of Mel's room.

I was comfortable with my reality. I knew I'd never get a story like my favourite characters, knew I would never look like them either. I was content with my muddy-brown hair, average green eyes, even my unremarkable features no longer bothered me. And I knew, Ryan would never be mine—only in those precious moments before waking every morning, deep in my dreams, when he would smile at *me,* drape his arm around *my* shoulders.

****

By fourteen I'd had a range of various boyfriends and seen Ryan go through a variety of girlfriends. Then suddenly, one day, a miracle happened.

At the pond behind the house, I was sitting in the little broken shack with its crumbling timber walls and musty floorboards, watching a frog swim through the water when Ryan made me jump appearing through the grass.

"You scared me," I held a hand over my heart.

"You shouldn't be so jumpy," he smirked. "Anyway, you should be more alert, wouldn't want those grass monsters catching you off guard." He playfully wagged his eyebrows.

"Ha, ha," I rolled my eyes.

The floorboards creaked under his weight as he climbed the three rickety steps, knowing to skip the fourth, and leapt to the top. Grabbing a dry branch on the way, he sat beside me.

It was a beautiful evening; the sun was setting behind the gum trees, last rays catching on the rippling water, midges zinging over the surface so it looked serenely hazy. The sky was a striking shade of blue blending into soft pinks and yellows. Ryan began pulling off bits of the branch, throwing it into the calm water, creating steppingstones of circular ripples.

Our friendship was comfortable. If I still didn't find him insanely attractive, I might have been able to describe it as that of siblings as we sat quietly listening to the sounds of the croaking frogs and singing cicadas.

"So why are you sitting here all by yourself, Ty?" Ryan asked.

I shrugged a shoulder, feet flicking back and forth below the deck. I didn't feel like telling him I'd fought with Lilly. Then I'd have to explain the reason we were fighting was because she wanted to make a move on *him*. When I didn't have a good enough excuse as to why I'd objected, she'd accused me of being a bad friend. I knew why I didn't want her to make a move, and I think she knew too. I was at the point of deny, deny, deny. Being a teenager with unrequited love left a door open for all kinds of mockery.

"Hey, did you ever hear from Alex?" Ryan asked instead when I answered the first question with a shrug.

I frowned, "Alex? That was such a long time ago. What a random thing to ask," I laughed.

"It just seemed like you two were together for ages," he shrugged. "Thought he might have got in touch after all this time."

"No," I shook my head. "I mean, we messaged for a while after he left. But the Northern Territory is far away, and it kind of, you know, poodled out."

"*Poodled* out?" Ryan smirked, a dimple appearing on his cheek.

I laughed. "Yes, poodled."

"Are you with anyone now?"

"No. You?"

"No."

"Surprise," I snorted.

"Really?"

"Honestly? Yeah. You always seem to be surrounded by a gaggle of girls." And Lilly was part of the gaggle now.

"Remember when you used to like me?"

I raised my eyebrows, giving him a look I hoped was indifference. "What?"

He grinned, both dimples in full effect. "Don't try to deny it." He bumped my shoulder playfully.

I'd never really considered that he knew I liked him. The hopeless romantic in me had hoped that if he did, he would come running, professing his undying love for me too. But then, realising that he did, in fact, know this whole time, a small part of me withered.

"Maybe once," I admitted, eyes trained on the shimmering water at our toes.

"Managed to ditch those feelings so easily, did you?" He was clearly trying to get some sort of rise out of me.

White Ibis's with black heads pecked their way across the grass, long beaks picking at the evening bugs. "Well, you kind of started dating my sister."

"Oh yeah," Ryan laughed, shoulders shuddering as he shook his head.

"As if you forgot about that!" I punched him on the arm.

Brown hair flopped on his forehead as if he hadn't brushed it all week. A shark tooth on a brown leather strap hung around his neck.

"No, I didn't mean it like that!" he protested, hands in the air. "Mel is nice. But you can hardly call it a relationship though, can you?"

"Why would you say that?"

He pursed his lips, the final piece of the branch twirling between his fingers. "We were so young. And when I think about it now, it was just two friends calling each other boyfriend and girlfriend." He chuckled. "Do you think that would stop anything ever happening between us?"

My eyes widened. I shifted back slightly. "What's that supposed to mean? Why are you grilling me like this? It's not very nice, you know."

He laughed, Adam's apple bopping gently.

Ryan had always been kind and gentle with a knack for making me feel comfortable and secure. But now, my skin felt prickly under his questions. I would expect this kind of teasing from the kids at school—but not from him.

He left his comment hanging, a chorus of cicadas rising to mingle with the songs of tree frogs and growing noises of the twilight bush. Just as I was contemplating going back to the house, he cleared his throat and said my name.

"Ryan?" I mimicked, turning to give him a stare that said *back off,* when suddenly, he kissed me.

I don't think my lips even moved. I sat still, spine rigid, muscles tensed, until Ryan pulled back, licking his lips. Then, he gave me a *weird* smile and looked back at the water.

Did that just happen?

"Uh," is all I could manage. "Ryan!" I slapped his arm, "What the *heck*?"

He laughed, shrugging, hands steepled between his legs. "I just felt like it."

"You *felt* like it? Why? What? *Why*?" I shook my head in disbelief.

He was messing with me. He'd found out from someone, maybe Lilly—*that traitor*—that I liked him and thought it would be fun to mess with me. That was it. I'd always dreamt of kissing Ryan. But not like this. Not when he was doing it as a joke. It was so unlike him; my kind, sweet neighbour who always defended me against bullies at school or called out the girls who made fun of me. Who was this cruel boy? Maybe I didn't know him as well as I thought. Maybe our friendship meant so little to him that he didn't care about risking it over... what? A fleeting kiss? My chest squeezed. I bit back the tears burning against my eyes.

How could he?

Leaping to my feet, I jumped to the grass before he could say anything, running across the field, disappearing into the tall stalks which now only brushed my elbows. Ryan called behind me, and I wiped furiously at the tears blurring my vision, dripping down my cheeks. Clearing the other side, his hand wrapped around my wrist, pulling me to a stop.

"Tyler," Ryan panted, eyebrows furrowed into a frown.

"What?" I yelled.

"I'm sorry. I—" he fumbled for words, "I read it all wrong."

I mirrored him, shaking my head. "Read it wrong? I thought we were *friends*. Why did you do that?"

"I'm sorry."

"Are my feelings just a cruel joke to you?"

"What? No! Of course not. Tyler…"

He grabbed for my hand again, but I tore it away, sprinting towards the house.

Burying my face in the pillow on my bed, I let heaving tears rack through me. The realisation that the love of my life didn't care about me at all, not even about the precious friendship I held so close, threatened to tear me in two. Why would he do that to me? Kiss me as if it meant nothing—as if it would mean nothing to me?

It was a miracle he'd kissed me at all. Just not the miracle I'd hoped for.

****

"We have some news we want to share with you two," mum said that evening, all of us sitting around the dinner table. I was pushing beans around my plate, building pancakes with my mashed potatoes when mum and dad smiled between Mel and me.

"What? You're being weird," I said, still grumpy from earlier—I'd hid in my room for the rest of the day until the smell of sizzling sausages teased me out.

Mel frowned at them too when mum grabbed dad's hand. "You're not pregnant, are you?"

Mum laughed, "No, honey."

"Good, because that would be so weird," Mel breathed, bracelets jingling on her wrist, perfectly manicured fingers holding her fork.

"No, we're not pregnant. But I have been offered a new job," dad smiled.

"That's cool," Mel nodded. "Where?"

"Well, that's the thing," mum started. "It's in Jamaica."

"Jamaica?" Mel practically shouted.

"Where's Jamaica?" I attempted to visualise the Australian map and which territory had a Jamaica in it. Geography was not my strong subject.

"Jamaica, you idiot. Like *Jamaica*, next to *America*," Mel shook her head.

"What? It's not even in Aus?" I looked alarmingly between our parents.

Dad put a hand up to calm the rising voices. "Don't talk to your sister like that, Melanie. But yes, you're right. It's between North America and South America. It's a very small island."

"Why would you want to go so far away?" I continued to flatten the mash cakes.

"I won't be moving," dad paused.

"We *all* will," mum finished.

Fork clattering to the side of the plate, my mouth dropped open. Turning my shock on Mel, she sat with her arms crossed over her chest, glaring. The look had 'you moron' written all over it.

"We're *all* moving?" I rotated a finger.

"Yes," mum nodded.

"To Jamaica? All of us?"

"Yes, honey," mum laughed lightly.

After that, the house was in an uproar thanks to Mel. She yelled a few things in a barely legible pitch, before storming to her room, shouting that they would have to drag her to Jamaica kicking and screaming. When dad chased after her, attempting to talk reason through the bedroom door, he swiftly gave up when she cranked up her radio. I, on the other hand, was stunned into silence, like a deer in the headlights.

Staring at mum, I tried to process what the move meant. She waited patiently, until finally, clearing her throat, she asked if I was OK.

Was I OK?

No. Of course not! Why would I be OK with moving to a country I still didn't *really* know where in the world it was? Leave all my friends behind? Leave my school? Leave this house?

My muddled brain couldn't quite get any of that out, so instead, I shook my head before padding (much quieter than Mel) to my room. Thankfully, mum and dad had the sense to leave me alone. Eventually understanding we both needed time to process what they'd sprung on us.

In my room, I Googled Jamaica.

It was so far away!

Later, they dragged us into the lounge, where dad explained it was a job offer he couldn't turn down. He'd already accepted it. The new company had promised a bigger house and would organise places for us in one of the top private schools.

We would be leaving in a month.

By late evening, the idea had finally begun to sink in, when my phone pinged loudly, Ryan's name flashing across the screen.

Ryan.

I inhaled sharply. The thought of leaving him hitting me like a train. Then I remembered the cruel kiss, and I wanted to be mad at him. Maybe I would have stayed mad at him if something so monumental wasn't about to change my life.

Tentatively, I opened his message.

Tyler. I think you got the wrong idea. Can we talk?

With the shock of the move announcement, my traitor heart couldn't think of anything more comforting than being in Ryan's presence. I quickly replied to meet around back. I found him leaning against the fence post when I crunched across the fresh evening grass.

A meagre, and rather scrawny, fence ran between our two properties that started and ended suddenly, as if the previous owners had once tried to separate the gardens but gave up. The porch light spilt an acidic orange glow across the grass, lights from our lounge behind sending shadows dancing across his face.

"Hey," I smiled tightly.

"Are you, OK?" He looked concerned. But it couldn't have been from what mum and dad had sprung on us, so he must mean what had happened by the pond. Biting the inside of my cheek, I contemplated my answer.

I'd always dreamed of kissing you. But I never imagined you would have kissed me for those reasons. "Uh…" the words stuck in the back of my throat.

"Look," he cut in. "I'm not sure what you were thinking earlier. But I just wanted to make something clear—I like you. And I thought you liked me too. But, if you don't, that's fine. I just don't want it to come between our friendship."

I frowned—I was going to have a permanent gorge running through my forehead after today. "What?"

"If my kiss was so horrible it made you cry. I apologise." He laughed awkwardly.

I laughed too, stunned into silence for the second time that night.

He wore a loose T-shirt and a pair of board shorts reserved only for the evenings, light material shifting in the gentle breeze

32

The words slowly sunk in. "Hang on. *You* like *me*?"

He scratched the back of his head. I'd never seen him so adorably awkward. Maybe that was what the weird smile was after the kiss. It wasn't a mocking one, but the look Ryan gave to the girls he *liked*.

"Yeah, I... I've just been watching you lately, and thinking, you know, that I like you more than a friend."

Was this day even real? How was all of this happening? I wanted to run away. Run away and pretend that everything wasn't changing in one night. Why couldn't Ryan have told me this sooner? Why couldn't mum and dad have decided to move later? Why did this all have to happen at the same time, and I had absolutely no control over it?

Ever since Ryan had moved in, I'd wanted to hear him say those words. And now that he finally had, I was leaving. Going so far away that there was no hope of us ever becoming *anything*.

The call of a nightjar travelled overhead, darting across the dark sky. Finally, managing to push past my constricted throat, I croaked, "We're moving. Mum and dad just told us. To Jamaica."

Ryan blinked. "Jamaica? Like, near America?"

I nodded. Glad that his sense of geography was better than mine. I watched as he pieced it together.

"Oh," he stood straighter. "Right. When?"

"A month."

I wanted to cry, but I didn't want him to see me cry again, so I breathed slowly, chest shuddering as it rose and fell.

"OK," he nodded. "But you could have just said you didn't like me like that instead of pulling a Chandler Bing and announcing you're moving to a new country to get away from me. Although, I give you props for Jamaica. At least you have more imagination than Yemen."

A startled laugh escaped my lips. Mel, Ryan and I had obsessively watched every episode of *Friends* together. It was our after-school thing for a while that I always looked forward to, when we would squeeze together on the sofa, share popcorn, and laugh until our stomachs hurt.

"You think I would have learnt from Chandler to pick somewhere a little closer though?" I hiccupped through a laugh. Suddenly his arms were around my shoulders, reaching for me over the fence separating our bodies. Burying my face in his chest, the smell of him so familiar, his shirt soaking up my tears. Resting his head on top of mine, he rubbed a hand gently over my back.

Why was this happening?

We stayed like that for a while. Ryan holding me as I cried quietly into his chest. We'd hugged before, but this time it felt different. He didn't say anything, and I wished I could read his mind. To know what he was thinking, his chocolate eyes staring into the darkness.

Grass rustled gently around us, dim sounds of the TV filtering through the house. Above, the clear sky glistened with a blanket of stars, and from Ryan's chest I looked up, wondering if we'd see as many stars in Jamaica. Our little town was nowhere near big enough to pollute the sky, and constellations shone as clear as if looking through a telescope.

****

I stood in the empty lounge staring at the dark spots in the wood where shadows of furniture were left. Rectangles on the walls imitated ghost-like picture frames, dust motes danced across the empty space. Mum had packed us up in record time.

It was four a.m., the kookaburras were singing loudly in the trees, and I watched from the back of the truck as the only home I'd ever known receded in the distance. With one last look at Ryan's window, I wished he'd appear so I could see him one final time, but his curtains were still drawn—the image of him from the small leaving party the previous night would have to do.

When he'd hugged me, I'd etched the feeling and the woodsy, grassy scent full of sunshine that clung to him, into my brain. We promised to stay in touch. I knew *I* would stick to that promise, and I hoped Ryan would too. But I wasn't so naïve as to hope that it would last. To even hope that this newfound crush of his would span across the Pacific Ocean. I couldn't expect him to want to start anything with me being so far away, so I tried not to take it personally when we fell back into our usual friendship for those last few weeks.

My heart ached, my younger self cried and cried, throwing a tantrum at the fact that I couldn't be with Ryan Andrews. Especially when he was telling me he liked me. The best thing I could do was try my hardest to leave an impression, so that when we met again one day, he would remember me.

Because we *would* meet again. I *would* see him again. I didn't know when, but I would be back.

CHAPTER THREE
Jamaica

Jamaica.

The people were different. The landscape was different. The air was different. The accent was different. *Everything* was different. Everything felt strange and unnatural.

Waking up in my new room felt foreign, even with the dressing table from Australia in the corner, familiar trainers tucked under the desk. My room was big, much bigger than the old one, and mum and dad had agreed to let me paint one of the walls, hoping it would help it feel homier.

My phone became my most prized possession—the only link to the other world, but the sixteen-hour time difference was a killer. I hung onto my old life as hard as I could. Living more there than in the present, vaguely remembering the first few weeks in our new hometown, Kingston.

Ryan and I spoke as often as we could. Regularly, I'd stay up until one a.m. just to be able to talk to him. I think mum and dad felt sorry for me, because they never once complained about having to top up my credit so often. After the second month, Ryan stopped calling. His messages got less and less. Then I found out from Facebook that he had started dating Lilly.

Yes, that Lilly. *My* friend, Lilly.

I tried to be happy for her. But a part of me resented the fact that it should have been me. *I* should be the one he was dating. Not her.

For those first few months, I spent hours and hours on Facebook, trying to be part of my old life. But as people do, my friends began to move on, and a part of me started to slip away too.

That year of my life, there were so many tears. Tears over seeing those first pictures of Lilly and Ryan. Tears for my friends back in Australia. Even tears for our farmhouse—for the pond and the gum trees. I even missed the damn kookaburras.

Mel always managed to make friends easily. Not just that, but she had a way of being immediately popular. As if all popular kids gave off a particular pheromone, and she exuded it. And Jamaica was no different.

Mel slipped into our new school easily, I, on the other hand, couldn't have felt more like a thumb. My biology teacher *asked* Ashley from my class to look after me. And as much as she tried, it was obvious she only talked to me because she had to. I sat with her group a few times at lunch, but they had a way of making me feel small, and I found myself falling into an awkward, quiet persona—like the Jamaican me was this unsure, timid creature.

Nothing felt right. At least, not until I met Beck.

Beck and I weren't immediate friends. She had a grunge rocker look; remnants of black liner around her eyes, constant bed hair, leftover dark nail polish spotting her nails. But one day we got talking, and the rest was history.

"Fuck those prissy little, know-it-all's," she said, talking about Ashley and her friends. "All they do is talk about Jacob, Jimmy and Brendon and how they're getting As in every class."

"They actually do that!"

"Of course, they do," Beck snorted.

Sitting beside her pool, it was a Saturday, the first time I'd been invited to hang out with someone on the weekend. Mum had tried to smother her excitement in the car on the way over, but I could tell she was just as thrilled about it as I was.

Making fun of my accent was everyone's favourite pastime. They made me repeat certain words over and over, bugging me until I complied, then laughed themselves hoarse. I didn't miss the fact that no one made fun of *Mel's* accent, though.

"Don't worry, when I first moved, they made fun of my accent too." Beck was Pilipino.

"But you moved when you were in preschool?"

"Yeah, and they still made fun of me *then*."

That was just another thing that made me feel oddly out of sorts—most of my classmates had been together since *preschool*. Beck even said she had once been friends with the queen bee of our grade, Ally, and all I could think about was the whole *Mean Girls* scenario, with Janice Ian and Regina George.

Lying on the hot cement, a foot hanging in the clear water, black hair spread around her, Beck smiled at a message on her phone. "Keegan," she explained, tapping away at the keys.

Keegan was the only grunge guy in our class, with long black hair that swept across his forehead and was always in his eyes.

"OK," Beck snapped her phone shut. "So, I don't want to be basic or anything, but is there anyone you have a fancy for?"

I smiled at the typical teenage girl conversation I'd missed for so long—it wasn't as if Mel and I talked about these things any more. "Justin and Jimmy are cute, I guess."

"Justin? As in flaky Justin?"

"He's cute,"

"Yeah, I guess, but he's a major waste-man."

"Waste-man?"

"Yeah. You know, someone who is just a bit of a waste."

Justin very rarely turned up to classes. When he did, he'd slink in on the cusp of the bell, sitting in the back, spending most of it doing who knows what except the

40

teachers kept glaring at him. To me he was shrouded in alluring mystery, his voice deep and raspy but rarely heard, his smile gorgeous but hard to come by.

"I can kind of understand Justin. But Jimmy? Really?" Beck raised her raven eyebrows.

"He's sweet."

"He's short and a pain in the ass. And his biggest turn off, he's part of *that* group."

"I'm not saying I'm going to make a move or anything."

"Well, let me know if you do. I want to be there," she scoffed.

Finding a more comfortable place with Beck, I soon joined her group of misfit friends, feeling more relaxed than I ever had with Ashley and her group. Without the ever-present black cloud of discomfort over my head, I finally began to appreciate the new culture—how rice and peas were a staple meal in the canteen, that peas were actually red kidney beans, and when trying to explain something, I had to run through every variable of the word until they understood—boot, back of the car, *trunk*, until I felt like a walking encyclopaedia. The canteen ladies wouldn't sell me a small bottle of water until I'd pronounce it the 'right' way: *likkle wata*, which always had them in fits of laughter. For them, I didn't mind obliging, their broad, warm smiles always teased a giggle out of me too.

As it was coming up to our first year of being in Jamaica, I'd just started to find my footing and settle in, when one day, I got an unexpected call from Ryan.

"Hi, Tyler." His crackling voice came from the other side of the line.

Squinting at the clock on the bedside table, I rubbed the sleep from my eyes; it glowed three a.m., light wane of the brightening morning just starting to glimmer around the sides of my curtain.

"Ryan? Is that you?"

"Yeah, it's me you hooligan," he laughed.

Ah, that sweet sound, the familiar part of my chest sighed. Suddenly I'm transported to those chilly evenings on the farm, surrounded by loud bird song, the scent of sunshine and trees filling my nose.

"Did you change your number? It didn't come up with your name."

"Yeah, I changed it a while ago. How are you?"

"Fine," I rubbed my eyes again and yawned. "Bit tired. You do realise it's three o'clock here?"

"Oh, sorry. I didn't try and work out the time. I just remembered this was about the time we used to talk."

I chuckled, not caring that he was about two hours out on that calculation. "So, how're things on your side?" I asked in a low voice.

"All good thanks. The ball is a few months away. Everyone's going over the top." There's a whoosh of wind, the sighing of heavy branches and grass crunching under foot coming faintly from his end.

42

The ball. I'd forgotten about it. It would be his leavers this year.

"Oh yeah, that'll be fun." I wanted to ask who he was going with, but even now, the words stuck in my throat. "How's the farm?"

"It's all good. Got some new neighbours, but they're nothing like you two."

"I should hope not," I snickered.

"How's Jamaica?"

"It's good. Taken some getting used to, but I'm getting there."

"Been offered any weed yet?"

I chuckled quietly, gentle noises of the early morning risers in the garden seeping through the open windows. "Not yet."

"All right, well I'll let you sleep. It was nice talking to you, Ty. Drop me a message now that you have my new number."

"I will," I smiled, head dropping back onto the pillow.

The prickly foreign feeling washed over me again, like I wasn't where I was supposed to be, and I quickly added Ryan's new number to my phone, vowing to message in the morning. Rolling over, I fell asleep with a smile on my face.

****

43

"Do you know Luke?"

Beck and I sat on a bench below the cafeteria beside the sports field, eating our chicken, rice and peas with gravy out of white, Styrofoam containers

"Luke?"

"Yeah, he's in your sister's year."

"Um…"

"You know; short black hair, brownish skin? Really good looking, but don't tell Keegan I said that. Come on, Ty!" she rolled her eyes when I continued to look dumbstruck. "*Luke*," she said again as if it would help. "He carries this faded blue backpack."

"With a tennis ball-thing hanging on the zipper?"

"Yes!" Beck clapped.

"Oh, yeah," a vague image of him appeared in my head. "I've only spoken to him a couple of times, though." Most of which was when Mel was around, and he'd actually been talking to her.

"Well, you must have made an impression those couple of times," Beck wagged her brows suggestively.

"Why?"

"Because he likes you."

"You don't know that."

"I do! He *kind of* told me."

I glared at her. Beck's new hobby was getting me a boyfriend. She'd been on a mission ever since sparks hadn't flown between her friend Rob and me.

"What does 'kind of told you', mean?"

"He was with a group of people I was talking to yesterday, and you came up. He said—without me even asking—that he thought you were cute, and that he liked your accent!"

I still found it strange when people said they liked my accent. *I* was the one surrounded by weird accents. "Why?"

Beck laughed. "What do you mean why? It's not that weird that a guy would like you, you know? You're not that bad on the eye now that that bob of yours is growing out!"

I threw a piece of chicken at her, instinctively brushing fingers through the chest-length hair hanging over my shoulders.

After lunch, we were on a mission to find this *Luke*. But after a few unsuccessful rounds of the various school buildings that dotted the open campus, and on our way to Spanish class along the crowded lower corridor, Beck tugged me to a stop, gaining a few groans of protest from people behind us. "Oh, calm down," she hissed to the boys swerving around us. "There," she whispered, eyes wide, a mischievous grin pulling at her lips. "Don't make it obvious you're looking."

As casually as I could manage, my eyes went to the balcony above the Spanish room.

Oh, now I remembered.

Luke had a kind face. One that seemed like he was always happy, even when he wasn't smiling, whilst still somehow looking like a model at the same time. Plus, he didn't look half bad in the blue trouser and white shirt uniform—the white bringing out his caramel brown skin.

Looking back at Beck, she was grinning.

"What?" I sucked in my cheeks.

"Oh, I see that look. Finally!" She spun and shouted, "Luke!"

"Beck, no," I whispered, but it was too late. Luke's eyes dipped towards us.

"Beck?" His forearms rested on the railing. "Hey, Tyler," he nodded.

"Hi," I said pathetically. "I've, uh, got Spanish. See you later." I waved awkwardly, ducking into the Spanish room—he didn't know Beck and I had Spanish together, so hopefully didn't see through the absolute pathetic attempt to get away from him and the awkward situation Beck was no doubt about to create.

Flopping in a seat, throwing my bag between my legs, Beck bounced in a few minutes later. "We're going out tonight," she declared.

"We are?"

"Yup, there's a party, and we're going."

"What party? You mean the one all of *them* are going to?" I dipped my head towards Ally, Ashley and their group lining the front of the class.

"Yeah, but normal people are going too. Luke will be there."

"You did *not* just agree to go to a party just to make me talk to Luke?" I was partly mortified, but the other part—the bigger part—swelled with happiness that Beck cared enough to do such a thing.

CHAPTER FOUR

It turned out Mel was going to the same party, so mum talked her into letting me catch a ride with her and her friends after *a lot* of protesting. Jamaica had worked the opposite on Mel—she was thriving, the last thing she needed was her awkward, younger sister tagging along, those days were supposed to be behind her, she'd said.

In the bathroom, I stared nervously at my reflection. *You can do this*, I told myself. My stomach had been in knots since getting home, barely managing to force down dinner.

I'd painted my nails an electric blue that winked brightly as I faffed with my hair, which was at an awkward in-between length that didn't necessarily look better this way or that, so I'd settled for straightening it. I'd decided on a good pair of jeans and a 'nice' top, though Mel disagreed with the 'nice' part.

"You can't wear that," she said bluntly when I walked into her room to wait for her to finish applying yet more mascara. Heavily black-lined eyes sized up my reflection in the mirror, perfectly waved, auburn curls bouncing against her shoulders.

"Why? What's wrong with it?"

"You don't think they already make enough fun of us being country bumpkins? And you want to go to a party in a khaki green shirt?"

"It's my *nice* khaki green shirt. And look, I tied it, so it's not all baggy," I pointed proudly at the knot on the side.

Shaking her head, Mel threw open her cupboard. A second later, a hoot came from outside, and mum shouted that our lift had arrived. She threw a sparkly red top in my hands. "Put it on," she instructed, grabbing a ridiculously small handbag off her bed.

I'd seen her wear the top before and doubted I'd be able to pull it off. But she hurried me along, and before I knew it, I was stumbling out the door, pulling at the front of the slinky top. She was right of course, it looked far more 'party-acceptable' than my khaki one, but I'd never had so much cleavage on display—it felt as if at any moment a nipple might pop out.

Parked in front of the house was a large Land Rover. Black and grey paint shone primly in the early evening light, the few trees surrounding our house reflected in its mirror-like surface. Sparkling alloy wheels made it look as if it had ever seen mud before, but even more shocking than the lavish truck, was the individual driving it: Luke.

"Mel, wait," I whispered, but she was already climbing in the open passenger door to two squealing girls.

"Tyler," Luke smiled warmly, arm hanging casually out the window. "Come on, jump in."

What are the odds? I huffed, sliding over the expensive leather seats beside Mel. I'd never been in such a fancy, *clean* car before, mostly because the people who lived in our little town in Australia owned sturdier trucks made for dust and covered in scratches. I imagined Luke wouldn't like the idea of driving this thing through the bush.

Jo was in the front, Lianna on the other side of the back seat—both in Mel and Luke's year.

"Aw Mel, you brought your little sister!"

"That's so cute!"

I rolled my eyes. *Great.* Maybe Luke's fondness for me might be gone as early as this car ride.

I had quickly become 'Mel's-little-sister' to everyone at school, and still wasn't sure if I was grateful for the recognition or annoyed at the label.

Jo passed around a silver flask as we pulled away, and they took turns sipping, wrinkling their noses and shaking their heads. When the container reached me, Mel paused.

"Oh, go on, she's not that young," Lianna encouraged. "I remember being drunk every weekend at her age."

"Fine. But not a word to mum. And if you can't act sober when we get home, I will kill you," Mel handed me the flask.

Not even sure I wanted any, but after all the fuss, it would have been embarrassing not to, I cautiously sipped. The alcohol burnt its way down my throat, though I was determined not to make a face like the others.

"Oh, looks like she's done this before," Jo teased, tapping Mel's knee.

Coughing quietly into my hand, I looked up to find Luke watching me in the rear-view mirror. Managing a small smile, my cheeks warmed. His eyes crinkled in the corners, and he winked.

If I wasn't sitting down, I think my knees may have melted. My cheeks burned red hot, and I put a hand to one of them, quickly turning my gaze to the window. If I didn't think Luke was attractive before, that wink had suddenly catapulted him onto the *hot* Richter scale.

The drive was only around fifteen minutes, and we pulled up to a three-story, pristine white house on the edge of a cliff face that was all windows and minimalist modern angles. From the tall, automatic gate, a driveway slanted from the road towards the house. Lights glinted from every direction. Music flowed from the building onto a sprawling lawn, and my jaw dropped when we climbed out of the truck.

The house was perched on the edge of a cliff overlooking the city of Kingston below, twinkling like millions of fireflies. Bodies spilled onto the lawn, and to my relief, I already recognised some faces from school. Still, there were more that I didn't recognise, and unwanted chills climbed over my skin. Wrapping arms protectively around my exposed chest, Mel and her friends immediately made their way inside, arm in arm, heels clicking on the stone driveway.

Scanning the strangers for Beck, and with no sign of her, I was just contemplating climbing back in the truck, when Luke's voice cut across my thoughts, "Are you OK?" He stood a few feet away, hands casually in the pockets of his blue jeans, strong musk of cologne floating under my nose.

"Uh, yeah, fine," I pulled consciously at the crimson top.

"It's all right. You'll be fine," he smiled warmly as if reading my mind.

The kind look in his brown eyes already had my pulse slowing, and I loosened a nod. "I'm OK." Or at least I was going to attempt to put on a brave face. Hiding in the truck was out of the question.

"OK. Well, come and find me later."

Luke vanished into the house too.

Heading to the garden, I pulled my phone from my jeans, feeling prickly and awkward.

"Hello?" Beck answered on the fifth ring.

"Hey, I'm here. Where are you?"

"Leaving in a minute. See you there."

Slapping the phone shut with more force than I'd intended, a frustrated huff escaped my lips.

Arms crossed over my chest again, I walked further onto the lawn, eyes transfixed on the bright horizon. *You wouldn't get this view on the farm,* my traitorous mind cooed.

The city was the biggest I'd ever seen. Roads wound between buildings, bright sparks of green puffing up here and there. How could people live so close, yet so far from each other? Atop this mansion on the hill, I felt on top of the world, imagining the sprawling landscape below the views of birds. The mesmerising kaleidoscope of red and yellow car lights weaved along the roads, streetlamps dotted through the city. Descending dusk threw sharp oranges across the sky, sun tucking itself below the horizon.

"Tyler?"

I spun to find Jimmy, Ally and Ashley approaching.

"Hey," I rubbed my arms.

"Wow, country girl at a party! It must be about to snow," Jimmy teased. Ally and Ashley snickered too.

They each held a clear plastic cup filled with different coloured liquids. Jimmy's sloshed from side to side, stumbling towards me, flinging an arm around my shoulders.

Playfully rolling my eyes, I hunched to accommodate his small frame. "I've been to parties before."

"I don't think I believe you," he said in my ear, breath smelling sweet and spicy. "First piece of evidence—that you don't have a drink in your hand," he slurred.

53

"Leave her be, Jimmy," Ashley scolded. "Did you want a drink, Tyler? There's some inside." Ashely had always been kind.

"Thanks, I'll get one in a minute."

Jimmy began to sway back and forth, and I shifted my footing so we didn't fall.

"Hey Jimmy, let her go, man. You're going to get your drink all down her." Luke's voice boomed across the grass.

Pulling his arm from around my neck, Jimmy held up his hands. "Whoa, all right there, Lukey. Didn't know you had dibs."

Balancing two drinks in his hands, Luke pretended to kick Jimmy. Jumping away, Jimmy fell hard on his back, liquid from his cup spilling across the ground. He laughed hysterically. Ally and Ashley rolled their eyes, throwing Luke a flirty smile before turning towards the house.

"Hey! Wait for me," Jimmy stumbled after them.

"He's harmless," Luke extended a cup.

"I know."

"I thought you might want one." I took the drink from his outstretched hand.

"Thanks," I sniffed at the contents.

Luke laughed. "It's rum and coke."

"Thanks," I repeated. "I thought you were driving?" I pointed at his cup.

"Just a coke for me. Want to test it?" he offered.

"No, I believe you," I laughed, pushing it back.

Knowing Luke's potential feelings made me feel strange. Like I had something to live up to. But he didn't know me, not really. What happened if he didn't like the real me?

Awkwardly, my eyes shifted back to the view.

"Pretty awesome, isn't it?" Luke turned too.

"Yeah," I breathed. "Who lives here?"

"Ren. From my year."

"Oh yeah, I think I've met him. Do you think he'll mind me being here?"

Luke laughed, stopping suddenly. "Oh, you're serious? Of course, he won't mind. I'm guessing he probably doesn't know half the people here."

"Do you know many of them?"

"Yeah," he shrugged. "I've been to a lot of parties."

I'd never really admired the beauty of a man before, but Luke was glowing under the golden hue of the setting sun. His biceps humped against the cuff of the Ralph Lauren polo he wore when he brought the drink to his lips, his physique athletic.

"You play tennis, right?"

"Yup." He had full lips, ones that women envied for.

"Are you any good?"

He chuckled, "I hope so." On his wrist was a heavy, and expensive-looking, silver watch.

What was I doing? There was no way a guy like Luke liked me, Beck must have got her wires twisted. I was so far out of my league it was laughable.

A cheer echoed its way across the lawn from inside, the music was turned up, booming through the air. Suddenly, everyone began to move, to dance, even the people meandering outside. The song had a bouncing beat to it, and they jumped up and down, singing along—girls bending in front of the boys with an impressive grinding motion.

My eyes widened.

"Do you know it?" Luke asked, amusement in his tone, watching the shock skirt across my face.

"No," I shook my head. "What's the dance called?"

"The dance doesn't go specifically with *this* song. It's called Soca. Like… carnival music."

"Right. So, what's the grinding thing everyone is doing?"

"The dutty wine." His accent bent around the words.

"*Dirty wine?*"

"No, d-u-tty wine," he said slowly. "Want to try?"

"No, no," I shook my head. It seemed so intimate.

Even little Miss goody-two-shoes, Ally, was 'dutty wining' away with a boy two grades up—hands on her knees, bent in front of him, pushing her backside into his pelvis, grinding impressively with the music.

"I wouldn't even know how to."

"It's easy. I can show you."

"Maybe another time," I laughed awkwardly, not entirely against the idea—it looked fun.

"That's OK, I'll get you to do it one day," Luke winked again.

When Beck finally turned up, it was over an hour later—so much for 'leaving in a minute'—and I was sitting with Luke in a plush garden seat under the wrap-around veranda. Maybe it was because I'd looked like a lost chicken without her brood, but whatever the reason, I was grateful for his company.

"How nice of you to show up," I mocked Beck, tugging Keegan behind her.

"Sorry! Sorry!" she held up a hand. "Looks like you're fine though," she raised her eyebrows at Luke sitting in the armchair.

"I've been looking after her. Someone has to with that top," Luke smirked. My jaw dropped in shock, slapping his arm.

Rubbing the spot, he pretended I'd wounded him, before pulling himself out of the chair. "I better go, or people will get suspicious."

His hand lingered on my shoulder before disappearing into the packed house, where a loud 'Luke-eeeeeeey' roared over the music.

"You work fast," Beck beamed, sitting beside me on the two-seater.

"Nothing happened. Unlike you," I eyed up her messier than usual hair.

"Keegan liked my outfit," she faffed, giving Keegan bedroom eyes, who had wondered to a group on the grass.

As the night wore on, I found myself glued to the chair, even when Beck and Keegan joined in on the dutty wine. Going to grab another drink, I almost choked when I caught sight of Mel dancing with some guy. She was doing a version of the dutty wine—still sexy—but nowhere near as practised as the other girls.

Luke and I somehow ended up talking again, and already it felt as if we were old friends. I hadn't felt this way with anyone since we'd moved, and it was nice.

When darkness blanketed the sky and drunken bodies sprawled by the pool, on the grass and chairs, Luke offered me a lift again. Mel wanted to stay longer, perched on the knee of the same guy she had been dancing with, and as Luke and I left together, Beck made obscene gestures at our backs. I stuck out my tongue, trying not to let my excitement show.

In front of the dark cab, Luke roared the engine to life, acidic light of the radio flashing on, Fall Out Boy playing from the speakers. I grinned. "This one I know."

"Well, turn it up," Luke twisted the volume until 'Memories' blasted.

We sang at the top of our lungs, and when the song ended, he turned the radio down and grinned. "So, how are you liking JA?" he asked.

"JA?"

"Jamaica," he chuckled.

"Oh, right," my hands fidgeted nervously. *Stupid.* "It's all right. Different to what I'm used to."

"Yeah, you lived on a farm or something in Australia, right?"

"Sort of. It wasn't exactly a working farm, but the town was, like, really small. A lot quieter than here." I stared distantly out the window. Streetlamps zoomed past, people dotted along the sidewalks, even at this hour.

"I can imagine. My dad helps farm the sugar they put into the Appleton rum."

"The rum we were drinking tonight?"

"Yeah."

"That's cool."

I couldn't help the sheen in my eyes at the thought of our little farmhouse.

"Well, I'm glad you moved here," Luke said.

Blinking away the thoughts, tucking the past into a box, I forced myself to focus on the here and now. "And you?"

"What about me?" he leaned casually as if he'd driven these roads thousands of times before.

"Where are you from?"

He laughed lightly. "Isn't it obvious?"

"I guess."

"Jamaican born and bred. My family have always been here," he clarified anyway.

Jamaica was nothing like I'd imagined.

In his fancy car, I felt the weight of my position in, as dad had called it, one of the top private schools. Even in Australia, I could only ever have dreamed to drive a truck like this or go to lavish parties in mansions on the hill. Maybe my parents were right, and in Jamaica, all the things we could only have dreamed about were possible.

I was embarrassed when we pulled up to our house now, but if Luke cared about our modest family home, he didn't let it show. Considering my apprehension at the beginning of the night, it surprised me that I didn't want it to end.

CHAPTER FIVE

At school on Monday, Luke caught me near the entrance gate, and we swapped numbers. He messaged that afternoon when I was in art class; something about the art teacher which made me laugh aloud, earning myself a menacing glare. I was surprised how quickly my feelings grew for Luke: from not giving him a second glance, to being all I could think about within the space of a few days—that was fast, even for me. But Luke made me feel comfortable, which was something I hadn't felt for such a long time.

And somehow, it seemed that Luke *did* feel the same about me.

It started with small things; surprising me at lunch with a hand on my shoulder, waving through the open door to the class I was in as he passed. Then came the touches as we passed in the hallway, the private smiles from across the courtyard, butterflies erupting in my stomach.

When he finally kissed me, it was behind the cafeteria next to the swimming pool changing rooms.

The stench of chlorine was thick in the air, gentle sounds of lapping water not far off. I'd just finished PE, an embarrassing, sweaty mess, when he caught my arm, pulling me to a secluded side of the building.

"Your face matches your shirt," he joked, flicking the material, before running a finger gently over my flushed cheek.

I groaned, knowing that when they'd assigned me to the red team it was a bad idea.

His black hair was wet and sticking at angles—he'd just been in the pool—and there was a bedroom look to his heavy brows and dark eyes. I cringed, covering my face; this wasn't exactly how I wanted Luke to see me, but he chuckled, pulling my hands away.

He was only slightly taller, a heavy, silver chain offsetting brown skin around his neck, buttons of his shirt undone so the striped, blue tie all the boys wore was loose.

Hands in his pockets, he closed the gap between us, those full, cool lips finding mine. I sighed gently against his mouth—at the feeling of his skin, hands at my waist pushing me against the scratchy brick wall. I'd never been kissed that way before. Never felt the fire in my belly, the tingling running across my thighs. When a hand brushed the hem of my shorts, I instinctively lifted a leg, then the other, until I was propped between his body and the wall. My breaths were short and heavy, skin feeling as if it was on fire.

When the bell echoed overhead, I cursed the blasted thing, and he laughed into my neck. "There's lots of time for kissing," he whispered, aching when he pulled away to disappear back to wherever he'd come from.

It turned out Luke was popular—I couldn't believe I'd never noticed it before—but everywhere he went, people greeted him. Boy's slapped hands with his, girls lilted sweet hellos through their eyelashes.

Fingers entwined as we walked the hallways, I soon became 'Luke's girlfriend' instead of Mel's-little-sister, a title I preferred much more.

By his side, my awkward piece had finally found the part of the puzzle it was meant to match to. With Luke, my old self came out more and more.

For the first time, he had me excited about the differences that Jamaica had to offer, showing me all the incredible cultural diversities that I hadn't yet experienced, even after being there for a year.

I discovered the unique flavour of Patty King patties, tasted fiery jerk chicken, and he introduced me to all the mesmerising sounds of Soca music.

We spent most weekends at his massive house, hanging out by his pool, or watching movies in the pool house. He, like most of the kids in our school, lived a life filled with all the things I'd only ever seen on *MTV Cribs*. We never went to mine, even though he said he didn't mind the small bungalow my parents rented in town.

One day, Luke threw a party at his house, and I felt like the VIP. Everyone knew my name and talked to me.

Not once did I feel uncomfortable like that time at Ren's party.

That night, confidence zinging through my veins; I attempted my first dutty wine.

I had made my rum and cokes stronger than usual all evening, but finally, wading through dancing bodies, I found Luke at the centre of the throng. His skin was slick, hair plastered to his forehead, beads slipping down his cheeks. The humid Jamaican night air was tight with the need for rain, and skin brushed skin amongst the thrashing bodies huddled under a thatched pergola beside the pool.

Music bounced and wound its way through me, Luke's dark eyes on mine, watching the way my body curved and swayed to the rhythm. With one hand, he pulled me against his body, where we danced face to face, his shirt damp and open to show a chiselled chest. A clap of thunder echoed through the night, though no one acknowledged it, and I turned slowly, until my shoulders rested on his chest, hips moving with his. I waited until the fast-paced reggae was coming to an end, the chorus building in a series of bouncing drums, and then, as if perfectly coordinated with the music, I bent forward, slapping my hands on my knees, and began to wind.

"Woooooow," he and the others shouted around us, our bodies moving, crowd clearing in a circle to ogle at the foreign girl dutty wining to the beat.

For all I knew, I looked ridiculous, but when Luke's hands fell onto my hips, he guided me with his—slow, slow, round, round, then fast, fast, fast. The dance still felt incredibly intimate, and I was in no hurry to do it with anyone else, but with Luke, it was something bringing us closer.

Rain began to fall, clattering over the paving stones, splashing into the pool water like midges bouncing above the surface. The party shouted in glee, worshipping the downpour, and to the sound of Soca and rain, Luke and I danced and danced until early dawn crested the sky.

****

I experienced a lot of firsts with Luke. Not like the firsts of trying patties and jerk chicken, but *firsts*. After a few months, he asked me to go to the prom with him.

"Prom?"

"Yeah, it's the senior prom next month. Your sister's going, isn't she?"

Timothy asked Mel to go—to the absolute jealousy of all the other girls, of course—and she'd planned her outfit down to every last sparkling detail.

"You want me to go with you?"

"Yes," Luke laughed. "Of course, I want you to come. I couldn't imagine going with anyone else." He placed a tender kiss on my forehead. I beamed from ear to ear, leaping into his arms.

Though I was nervous to tell Mel that I'd be going to *her* prom, mum was so excited that evening that she quickly spilled the beans for me.

My parents loved Luke—or at least my mum did. Dad was still the ever-protective father when it came to boys and his daughters. Mel threw a fuss as expected, but Luke was my *boyfriend,* and it was his prom too, so that weekend, we set off to find a dress.

Scouring the shop mum took us to, and after a bunch of 'this one is nice' and 'this one, looks just as nice', I finally laid eyes on *the* gown. It was a bright, silky yellow reaching my toes, a small rhinestone belt around the middle, with a ruched, sequined top. The store assistant then brought out the most perfect, sparkling peep-toed gold shoes, and my outfit was complete.

****

When prom day finally arrived, sleek, straightened hair fell over my shoulders, mum's pearl earrings dangled from my ears, and even Mel helped with my makeup. When Luke stepped out of the Land Rover, a yellow tie to match my dress, orchid corsage with misty white petals in hand, tears burned in my eyes. He looked handsome in his suit, dark hair brushed neatly to the side.

I grinned from ear to ear, like a blushing bride, when he slipped the corsage on my wrist, kissing me tenderly. "You look gorgeous," he whispered in my ear.

At the hotel, Luke helped me out of the car, handing keys to a valet. We followed the stream of students and bouncing reggae music to a large hall decked out in tinsel, lights and disco balls.

A DJ booth was at the head of a changing, coloured dance floor. Plush roll-arm sofas in deep navy and purple were dotted around the room, a large photo booth in the corner, a professional photographer station complete with comedic props in the other.

The girls looked as if they'd stepped out of a glamour magazine in their expensive sparkling gowns, makeup, hair and nails done by professionals, diamond-looking jewels that I had no doubt were the real thing hanging from their throats and wrists.

"You look perfect," Luke whispered, sensing the turn of my thoughts, a warm, reassuring hand in mine.

Mel was like a mermaid in her aqua dress, silver heels on display at the front where the hem ended higher than the trail. There were a few other girls from my grade attending, and Ally and Ashley smiled warmly when Luke and I approached.

"Wow, your dress is so pretty, Tyler," Ally ran a French manicured hand over the material, a Pandora bracelet sparkling on her wrist.

"Thanks," I blushed. "Yours is, wow," I breathed.

It was the kind of simplistic beauty that cost more than an elaborate gown, with its silky white material and gentle lace.

I weirdly felt more connected to the girls than I ever had, and we danced together under the watchful gaze of our dates. When the DJ announced it was the last song, hours later, moans came from the students, and Luke set out inviting everyone back to his for an after-party. Before the final song had ended, the hall was mostly empty.

Teenagers in ballgowns and suits flooded Luke's home—his parents disappeared to the furthest wing of the house to give their son and his friends their privacy—and rum was quickly procured from who knows where. One thing I'd quickly learnt—there was never a shortage of rum in Jamaica, no wonder Luke's family was so loaded.

Once the music started, everyone danced, and soon ties and heels were flung to the side.

Luke and I snuck down the garden stairs to the secluded pool house at the bottom of the garden where we spent so much of our time. The air was warm and comfortable, solar-powered lamps dotted along the path igniting our way, my heels in one hand, the hem of my dress in the other.

Sounds of night fought against pounding music coming from the main building. Luke's tie hung loosely around his neck, jacket discarded somewhere inside, sleeves of his white shirt pushed to the elbows.

Reaching the lower level, and with the main house now far behind us, the songs of tree frogs finally broke through the night.

Mirror-like pool water glistened under a full, silver moon, and at the edge, Luke pulled off his shoes and socks, and we sat with our feet in the cool murky depths.

"Tyler," Luke's gentle brown eyes looked deep within mine.

"Mhm?" Our fingers, entwined between us, moved constantly with gentle caresses.

"I love you."

My heart stopped, goosebumps rising along my arms. "I love you too," I whispered without hesitation.

I'd never said the words to anyone my whole life.

I loved Luke.

I loved him with everything I was.

His smile was broad and infectious, his kiss deep and full of glee.

Breaking apart, he shouted into the air, "She loves me!" before leaping to his feet and diving into the pool. Water sloshed over the edge, spilling onto my dress, dampening the bottom where I sat on the warm cement. Swimming to the edge, Luke craned up to kiss me, lips peppered in droplets.

"Luke, no!" I squealed as he gently pulled me forward, chuckling into my mouth until my body was in the water, cradling me so my head didn't go under.

The pool-house was dark with shadows when we padded inside, clothes dripping on the expensive porcelain tiled floor.

"Leave it off," I said when Luke reached for the light switch.

Moon light shone through mahogany Venetian slats at the side of the room so that our bodies were striped with shadows. In a second, we clashed together, but this time, the kiss was deeper, hungrier.

Luke's hands travelled up and down my dress, and I wanted to pull him as close to me as possible. I wanted more of him. I wanted all of him.

Slowly, I slipped off the straps of my dress.

He paused, chest heaving.

"Tyler," he whispered. My heart squeezed at the gentle concern in his voice.

"Shhh," I kissed his temple, his neck.

"Are you sure?"

I nodded into his skin. "Do you have a," I paused, "*condom*?" I whispered with an embarrassed chuckle.

He laughed gently, disappearing into the en-suite bathroom.

By the time he returned, my dress was a wet, crumpled heap on the floor, and I was left in only in my strapless bra and knickers.

What would be the point in waiting? The moment couldn't have been any more perfect. *Luke* couldn't have been any more perfect. I wanted to give everything I had to him.

****

It was coming up to two years of being in Jamaica. I'd finally found my place, starting to settle down, when our parents gathered Mel and me around the dining table once again.

Mel was due to start University, the company dad worked for wouldn't fund it like they did our schooling, and he had been offered yet another job.

The catch was—this time, the new job was in England.

They explained they'd thought long and hard about the decision. It was in all our best interests that we moved. Again.

"We can't move again!" I shouted, chair scraping loudly, jumping to my feet.

Mel sat calmly, nodding along to their words. She turned her calm eyes on my crazed expression. "Don't be so dramatic, Tyler. It's not about you, OK?"

"How can you want to go? We've just started our lives here! I've got friends. A boyfriend," my chest hiccupped.

"We know it's been hard, honey, but this will be the last move. I promise," mum said in a kind voice. "There's so much more there for us. This job for your dad is exactly what we need, and Mel's at a critical point in her education."

71

I tried to protest, but they'd already made up their minds. It looked like we were moving again. Like I had to leave someone behind. Again.

Luke and I spent every moment we could together, and mum and dad even agreed to let him join our last family trip to Ocho Rios on the coast where we spent the time wrapped in each other's arms. Though no matter how much we tried to enjoy every second, weighing heavily on our hearts, was knowing that it would all be over in a few days.

Sitting on the beach, listening to the sounds of the waves, wind blowing hair around my face, Luke's warm hand in mine, I bit back tears.

"It'll be fine," he said gently, a tear escaping down my cheek. "I'll come and see you as soon as I can. I promise."

He gave me his graduation ring, a massive silver thing made for a man's hand, looping it through the chain hanging around his neck, before slipping it over mine.

"So, I'm always with you."

I managed a weak smile, wrapping a hand around the warm metal.

As the sun set on Jamaica, I thought something I never thought I'd ever think; I'd miss it.

This once alien island had somehow become my home. I couldn't bear the thought of leaving it. Not just leaving Luke, but Beck and Keegan, who I'd finally found a genuine friendship.

When the weekend was over, and we dropped Luke at his house, we clung to each other tightly, praying it wasn't the last time we saw each other—praying that we'd come back together one day.

CHAPTER SIX
England

Cold. It was the first thing I thought as we stepped off the plane in England, face hit by a gusting, icy wind. England was bloody cold.

Mum tried to prepare us, though now, I wished I'd taken more of her advice—the thin blue sweater I'd worn hardly doing anything to keep the spikey chill away as we wheeled our suitcases to the train station, where the sight of the Underground map had my already frazzled nerves ready to explode. Leaving mum and dad to attempt to figure it out, I hugged my arms around my body, trying not to get trampled on.

Hordes of people walked briskly in every direction—it was amazing they didn't crash into each other, expertly weaving between one another. I'd never seen such a diverse range of people as in London Victoria Station. People from all over the world, so many different cultures, languages, and accents all mingled together, many dragging suitcases or hauling backpacks.

Amongst the ones like us, were the obvious locals—the woman in a knee-length, chequered grey dress, sky-high red stilettos and only a simple red coat with matching red lips, moved like liquid through the throng. Two guys in blue trousers, finely pressed shirts, one in glasses, the other in a beanie, laughed as if they navigated this hell every day, and enjoyed it.

On the Tube—when we eventually found the right one after hauling our heavy suitcases up and down multiple flights of stairs—was not much better. We stood shoulder to shoulder, packed like sardines while even more people climbed impossibly on the already full train.

Finally, hiking the stairs to the outside, inhaling the fresh air, I quickly decided the cold was better than the squishy Tube, even as my body shuddered, breath turning to white mist.

A train ride and two long bus journeys later, we arrived in the dead of night at our new hometown, Gloucester.

Our house was nestled in a quaint cul-de-sac, a centre terrace, with orange coloured brick walls. Inside, on the first floor, was the lounge with a little fireplace, kitchen, and small dining room overlooking a modest garden. It was the first double-storey we'd ever lived in—three bedrooms on the top floor with a shared bathroom.

Bright sunflower yellow adorned all four walls of my room, while Mel's was green, and our parents' pink. Mum had already said I could paint over it as soon as we got settled, and I knew I wanted to paint it the same shade as my crimson wall back in Jamaica.

Remembering the shock at the bustling city of Kingston, compared to my brief experience with London, *that* now seemed calm.

We didn't have a car, so took the bus and trains everywhere, which always made me feel like my personal space was being violated in some way. That if I stuck my arm out at any moment, it was at risk of being torn from its socket.

People walked briskly, heads down through the cold, never making eye contact, noses buried in their phones, books, or newspapers. I couldn't blame them—getting out of the cold was now my priority too.

The first few weeks were tough for many reasons, the cold being one. I layered on every piece of clothing I owned just to keep out the chill, until, finally, mum took us to a second-hand store, where she beamed like a kid in a toy shop at the prices.

My parents struggled to find the money to buy us the new clothes we desperately needed, and even the furnishings for the house. I could see how hard they were trying—how hard the move had been on them too. So I resolved to at least *attempt* to be the humblest, and most accepting daughter, I could be, only crying when I knew they couldn't hear, and hiding my phone so they didn't feel obliged to top up my credit so I could talk to Luke.

Just like those first weeks in Jamaica, I struggled to exist in the present—living in my old school sports T-shirt, hand instinctively going to my neck and the chain there every few minutes and dreaming every night of reuniting with Luke.

You'd think I would have learnt the first time—to not hang on to my old life, to embrace the change. I tried, I really did. But it all felt so wrong that all I wanted was to curl in a ball in my bed and hide away from the cold grey skies.

We'd only been there a few months when it was time to start school again. Not school this time though—I was starting college, Mel, was going to university.

I'd be attending Cirencester College, and mum had painstakingly planned my route; the ten-minute walk from the house, up to the main road where the college bus stopped. From there, it was a forty-minute bus ride.

On Monday, handing over a yellow piece of card with my name and the 'Number 20 Bus Pass' printed across the top, a tight hug from both mum and dad, the front door slapped behind me, icy air hitting my face. Pulling the grey scarf I'd recently purchased tight around my neck, I began the walk I'd practised a few days before.

Other hooded figures walked quickly along the street, and I wondered if any of them were on their way to the same bus stop. Hoping that maybe the kind-looking girl I passed would be the first person I talked to. Or even the guy with the gentle eyes, but he looked far too dressed up for college.

I'd contemplated my outfit the night before, but no matter what I did, there was no getting away from the bulky jacket, woolly scarf or boots.

How did anyone even wear anything *nice* in this kind of weather?

Surprisingly, the sky was cloudless, so at odds with the icy nip that stung my exposed nose and ears. As the morning sun washed over my face, I stopped on the pavement, closing my eyes, revelling in the way it felt. If I focused hard enough, ignored the sounds of the cars rushing by on the road, the prickling cold, I could almost imagine sitting in the garden in Jamaica.

You'll be fine, I inhaled deeply.

Opening my eyes, I bit the inside of my cheek. No number of positive mantras would alleviate the pressure on my chest, or the tears stinging my eyes. I promised myself I wouldn't cry today; I could do this. I'd done it before; I could do it again.

England marked the third country I'd lived in during my short sixteen years.

I. Could. Do. This.

When the bus stop came into view, my heart dropped—there was no one else waiting at it. Had I got it wrong? Had I somehow taken a wrong turn? Had mum got the bus stop incorrect?

Panicked flutters worked in my chest.

Pulling the backpack tighter around my shoulders, I checked the time on my phone—twenty-minutes early, there was still time.

Taking a spot at the side of the stop, it had a small red roof, a transparent plastic wall, and a tiny seat running the length of it, holding my breath at every person that passed. Finally, after ten agonising minutes, a girl and a guy approached.

The guy had blond, curly hair that flopped around his head, a scarf pulled tightly around a bulging neck, jacket half hanging off one shoulder, jumper pulling tightly against a vast belly. The girl, who looked like she was floating rather than walking, wore a piece of material tied around her head, with a pair of grey, patterned tights, and a green flowy dress. Around her shoulders was a knitted jersey three sizes too big.

Swallowing past the nervous lump in my throat, I averted my eyes across the street. They stopped a few feet from me, continuing their conversation.

"I know right," the girl laughed. "Kate was furious with me. But I didn't have anything else to wear!"

"That's hilarious," the guy said in a strong accent, flipping the hair from his forehead. Both had cigarettes. "Hey," came the guy's voice. My spine stiffened. "Hey," he called again. "You."

"Me?" I squeaked with a dumbfounded, doe-eyed look.

"Yeah," he smiled. "Are you going to Cirencester College?"

I nodded.

"Cool." His smile was friendly, the girl's eyes crinkling in the corners too with a drag from her cigarette.

"I'm Hattie," she nodded. "This is Matt," she poked the guy in the stomach before adding, "He's gay."

My eyes widened, but Matt just laughed, shoving her shoulder. "Thanks, Hattie! I'm sure it was obvious anyway." Matt popped a hip and grinned.

"I'm—" I cleared my throat against the cold. "Sorry. I'm Tyler," I bobbed my head with a smile I hoped was more confident than I felt.

"Ty-ler," Matt copied. "Oh, I love the way you say it! Where are you from?"

The million-dollar question I knew was going to haunt me; where was I from? Or where had I *just* come from?

I settled with the former. "Australia."

"Oooh," Hattie and Matt said together, turning surprised looks on one another.

"That's *so* cool," Hattie chimed in a sing-song voice. "I'd love to go to Australia."

"Ya, me too," Matt nodded vigorously, blond curls bobbing.

"How long have you been in the UK?" Hattie asked, eyes roaming over my outfit.

I tugged consciously at the scratchy blue patterned jersey under a large maroon jacket. "Not long," I laughed awkwardly. "About two months."

"Two months!" Matt's mouth dropped open dramatically.

When more people began to loiter at the stop, Matt and Hattie moved closer. Matt shouted to a guy named Joe that he waved over with a big nose and sandy blonde hair sticking in the air. "Joe, this is Tyler, she's from Australia," Matt said proudly.

"Oh, Aus, that's interesting. I'm Joe."

Just as I was beginning to worry Matt would pull another unfortunate bystander into the conversation, a white bus stopped in front of us, the number 20 flashing across the front in bright orange lights.

"This is us," Hattie smiled.

With one last drag on her cigarette, she and Matt shuffled in front of me, and we flashed similar bus passes to the driver, filing on.

The back of the bus was already full. Hattie and Matt headed that way, and I decided on a pair of seats a few rows from the front.

Placing my backpack on the empty seat beside mine, I hoped the bus wouldn't fill up enough that I'd have to sit next to someone. Within seconds, the door closed with a *whoosh,* sealing in warm air flowing from the heaters running along the side of the chairs.

We made one other stop about twenty-minutes up the road, before heading for the college. The seat next to me was still empty, and I sighed with relief, relaxing into the chair, pulling my knees up to rest against the back of the seat in front.

My fingers brushed the lump beneath my jersey, where Luke's necklace sat tucked beneath the layers. Closing my eyes, it pulsed warmly, as if he was there, reminding me of the feeling of the setting sun on my face as we sat on the beach, his arm around my shoulders. Outside the window, trees and fields whizzed past, warmth of the heater defrosting my already frozen toes, the bus winding its way along country roads.

A radio played on the speakers overhead, though I could barely make it out over the loud voices coming from the back of the bus. Now and again, I thought I recognised Hattie or Matt, but nerves kept my eyes glued forward.

The first day of college was a blur of bodies and faces. Though, unlike that first day in Jamaica, almost everyone was starting the new term too.

I met our class leader, who introduced himself as Gideon—which I found strange at first, but as the day wore on, I learned that all the teachers went by their first names. In Jamaica and Australia, teachers were either Mr so-and-so or Mrs so-and-so, or Sir and Miss.

It was also the first time I didn't have to wear a school uniform, and it was strange and distracting to see everyone in different attires; from casual jeans to overly dressy pant suits, underdressed sweats and hoodies, to gothic blacks and purples. Most girls wore heavy makeup, hair either teased, curled or straightened, and dyed all kinds of colours.

This was definitely no strict private school.

In the toilets later that day, a group of girls were 'touching-up' their makeup—although it still looked newly applied to me. I tried not to eavesdrop, but their conversation echoed through the room—though they might as well have been speaking a whole different language for all I could understand. For a moment, my ears strained to hear any familiar foreign words, but my heart raced when I realised they were speaking *English*.

I left as quickly as I could, afraid they might speak to me, and I'd have no idea what they were saying. Although the Jamaican accent was strong, and in some cases had its own dialect, I could always somehow understand.

After the incident in the toilets, I suddenly noticed all manners of accents. Some with long rolling R's, others so strong it seemed like talking was difficult. Some were soft and gentle, others harsh and loud.

How could all these accents come from one country?

I was surprised to find I enjoyed my classes. The campus was easy to navigate, and my class schedule was clear and precise that I managed to find my way around easily.

Lunch was the worst.

Following the signs weaving between buildings to the cafeteria, I eventually found it overlooking the sports field and the walled entrance. Small, metal tables dotted the inside, though all of them were occupied, loud voices intermingling in the air. Swallowing down rising panic, I shifted awkwardly in the walkway, feeling as if eyes were turning on me, frustrated bodies pushing passed me—a boy shouted some obscene comment to me about standing in the way, though I had no idea what he said, which probably made me look even more stupid.

Stop being paranoid, I told myself, finally walking across the building to doors on the other side leading onto an outdoor paved area. It too had tables and benches, and like the inside, all were occupied. Suddenly I missed Mel and the easy way she made friends—at least if she were here, I could sit with her.

With not much option, I joined the small groups lounging on the grass of the field. Mum had made sandwiches *and* given me money—we weren't sure what kind of facilities the college would have, so prepared for any scenario. I made a mental note to thank her when I got home, relieved I didn't have to try and find my way to the food—that would have been another disaster waiting to happen.

The clear day had turned gloomy grey, clouds blanketing the sky. White and grey gulls called from the air, picking across the field with black crows in search of discarded food scraps. Pulling my scarf tighter around my neck, tucking my feet beneath me, I scoffed down the sandwiches as quickly as I could.

Unfazed by the cold, students milled outside in outfits I would barely even wear indoors in this country; short skirts with tights, polo necked tops and flimsy cardigans. A group threw a rugby ball at the end of the field in only T-shirts, and I shivered just looking at their exposed skin.

Art was the last class of the day, and I arrived early, eager to get inside where there were heaters. Taking a seat at one of the large tables towards the back, a familiar crocheted bag slung across the table.

"Hey," Hattie beamed. "Tyler, right?" She said around a lollipop hanging from her mouth.

"Uh, yeah," I smiled back.

My fingers and toes were still trying to warm up, tingling as feeling returned to them, when a man with a thinning mohawk and moustache that stuck out and twisted up at the ends clapped his hands at the head of the class.

"Welcome," he began, eyes scanning over the students. "I'm Albert, and this is A-Level Art!"

"Urgh, I love Albert," Hattie pulled a sketchbook from her bag.

"Sorry?" I frowned, trying to divide my attention between Albert, still speaking at the front, and Hattie.

"Albert," she pointed her lollipop. "He's the best. I'm so glad I got him and not snobby Sarah. She's the worst," Hattie rolled her black-rimmed eyes, electric blue eye shadow sweeping across her eyelids—each nail was painted a different colour.

Pulling a pencil from her case, she started sketching before Albert had finished his speech.

There was something about art that soothed me, and I relaxed into the familiarity of it while Albert talked us through our first assignment. Art was something that, judging by the few minutes I'd already been in the class, was the same in most countries. Where a different viewpoint was cherished, not made fun of or laughed away. Seeing the world uniquely was a cherished trait to a creative, the art room in Jamaica similarly becoming my place of solitude, just as this room with Albert was already starting to feel like.

When class was over, Hattie and I walked to where the bus dropped us off with a steady stream of chatter. The bus station, Hattie called it—though it was nothing like a typical bus station at all—was a semi-circular, tarred area where buses lined along the sidewalk, each with different numbers flashing over the front.

"Each number represents a different area," Hattie explained, pointing to the other numbers. "Ours, twenty, is for the Gloucester and Cheltenham, and everywhere in between. They always stop here. But," she leaned on her tippy-toes to peer over the ever-growing crowd of students, "I'm not sure if it's here yet." She craned her neck. "Oh, wait, there it is!"

Climbing inside, I took the same seat as that morning, but Hattie stopped in the aisle, "Come sit with me, Ty." Her face was warm and open, and I immediately slid from the seat to follow.

"So how was your first day?" she asked.

I took my seat on the aisle beside hers, tucking my backpack between my legs.

"It was all right."

"It sucked, didn't it?" she giggled, the sound a bit like a cartoon character.

I couldn't help smiling at her contagious grin. "A little."

"Don't worry, it always does. It'll get better."

"How come you know so many people already?"

"I did my GCSEs here. So, I've already been here for two years. Where did you do yours?" she added.

"I, um, I did them in Jamaica," I said timidly.

"Jamaica!" she said too loudly, jaw dropping dramatically as if I'd just told her I had a secret tail. "I thought you said you were from Australia?" She baulked like an actress on stage.

I laughed at the absurdity of my own story as I recounted it briefly to her.

"Wow," Hattie breathed. "That is *so* cool. So, you've travelled a lot?"

"Not really," I shrugged. "Just Australia and Jamaica, and now here I guess."

"That is still insanely cool," she nodded. "So why did you come here?" She pulled a bag of sweets from her purse. In Jamaica, they called it *candy*, but I'd never got comfortable using the phrase.

"My sister was starting Uni."

Hattie scrunched her nose in disapproval. "But why here? No offence, but beautiful, sunny, cultural Jamaica is so much nicer than mud-island."

I'd asked the same question so many times and still didn't know the answer. I pursed my lips, which Hattie understood, shaking her head. "That's crazy."

"Tell me about it," I muttered.

A bag flew painfully into my shoulder then, bouncing me back into the seat.

"Oh! I'm sorry," a boy that had been passing in the aisle put out a hand.

"That's OK," I rubbed the tender spot on my shoulder where it felt like I had been skewered by a bookend.

"Urgh, Oliver! Be careful!" Hattie threw her wrapper at him.

"Who's your friend, Hattie?" Oliver shifted his weight, green eyes bearing into mine.

I couldn't help the blush that rose to my cheeks— he was remarkably handsome. His eyes were big—doll-character big—with green and gold irises. His dark brown hair gelled into spikes, a small fringe pulled down at the front, with full pink lips.

I quickly looked away.

"This is Tyler," Hattie presented.

"Nice to meet you, Tyler. I'm Oliver," he smiled. The British accent was so alluring on him. "Sorry again about the bag. I'll be more careful next time."

"It's all right," I tried not to blush.

"Is that an accent I hear?" he paused mid-turn.

"Yeah," Hattie cut in. "She's from Australia."

I nervously tucked a strand of hair behind my ear, heat rising from under my jersey.

"Oliver!" Another female shouted, "Are you going to sit down or what?"

A few feet in the aisle behind was a gorgeous girl with mocha-coloured skin, fringe sweeping across her forehead and down the side of her face.

"Christina, this is Tyler," Oliver introduced.

Christina looked as if she couldn't care less who I was. "Yeah, hi. Can you move now please?" she shoved Oliver, and he laughed.

"Chris?" came another familiar female voice from this morning.

Behind Christina was another gorgeous blonde— *why were they all so damn good looking*? Except she had long, straight hair reaching to her waist, eyes slanted in the corners and rimmed in smoky black.

"What's happening?" the girl asked again.

"Oliver is holding everyone up while he *flirts*," Christina raised a pierced eyebrow.

I wanted to disappear.

"I was not!" Oliver laughed again, finally making his way to the back of the bus.

Christina followed, and when the blonde girl reached my seat, she smiled.

"Hey, I'm Emily," her voice was a husky feminine.

"Tyler," I nodded before she joined the others at the back.

Hattie smiled warmly as the bus filled, the door finally closing.

"So, where do you live?" Hattie asked when we turned onto the motorway.

"Around the corner from the bus stop."

"Oh, that's good. I live outside the town centre, so I have to catch *another* bus after this."

The world had already begun to darken outside, I checked the time—it was just after five. I couldn't imagine catching another bus on my own, let alone at night.

At Gloucester, I walked with Hattie to the next bus stop, where we said our goodbyes and I turned down my road, the chatter of voices disappearing behind tall hedges before heaving a sigh of relief.

I'd survived my first day.

Mum and dad grilled me about everything as soon as I walked through the door. Over a dinner of spaghetti Bolognese that evening, gas fire flickering behind its grate, the world outside the conservatory windows like black curtains, I told them about Hattie and her hippy style, about Matt and the others on the bus, then I told them about the teachers and how we get to call them by their first names.

"I'm so glad it went well, sweetheart," dad beamed. "Sounds like you'll fit right in."

I nodded tentatively, hoping he was right.

The first day had been smoother than that in Jamaica at least. Maybe it was because I was older, maybe it was because I'd done it before, either way, I was glad it had been easier.

Crawling into bed later that evening, I was exhausted. Counting the time difference off on my fingers—it was five in the afternoon in Jamaica, Luke was probably just finishing for the day. Like Mel, Luke graduated, but moved to a senior school in Kingston that taught Btec.

My first day had pleasantly surprised me. Granted, most of it played out how I had expected, but the bus journey home was an unexpected development. I liked Hattie and her eccentric style, even if she did ask a lot of questions.

Plus, she called me her *friend*.

I smiled at the unbelievable possibility that I'd made a friend on my first day, *and* with someone I truly seemed to get along with.

My phone vibrated, and I grinned at a message from Luke.

Luke: *I hope you had a good first day. I missed you.*
Tyler: *It was ok. I'd rather be there though. Miss you too.*
Luke: *I would prefer it if you were here too. It must be late there now?*
Tyler: *Yeah, I'm about to go to sleep. Meeting new people is exhausting!*

Luke: *I can imagine. Sleep well. I'll be dreaming of you.*
Tyler: *I'll be dreaming of you. Love you.*
Luke: *Love you too.*

We knew we couldn't keep going the way we were; speaking every day, saying how much we missed and loved each other. But I wasn't ready to stop, not prepared to lose him completely. I still looked forward to messaging him every day. And in one filled with strangers, it was a comfort knowing there was someone out there who really knew me.

Before turning out the light, I scrolled through Facebook, liking a picture of Beck and Keegan sprawled out by the pool, before coming across a picture of my friend Lilly from Aus.

Pausing, I stared at the picture for a moment—it was a lifetime ago that I was crying over leaving Australia. Though, every so often, there were still those emotions simmering under the surface, for that other place, that other world that hardly seemed to be part of me any more. A place that didn't even seem real in so many ways. I'd folded and tucked that box of emotions neatly away, with a label that read *'do not open'*, gathering dust in the corners of my subconscious attic.

But from the box slipped a single thought, like mist under a door: what was Ryan doing now? Were he and Lilly still together?

On impulse, I scrolled through the pictures on my phone, near the bottom, to find an image of Ryan and me, taken a few days before we left.

Holding the phone in front of us, his long arm extended out—we were both grinning like goofballs.

My chest ached.

Ryan, like that life in Australia, was some crazy fantasy now. Like something I'd dreamed up.

The boyish grin, wind mussed hair, thick dark lashes. He had the beauty of an actor, but more rugged, free, as wild as the field we stood in. His grin sang of open fires, his skin of days spent in the sun, calloused fingers telling stories of mud castles, tree bark beneath his nails.

What would he look like now? I tried to imagine a man, but all I could see was the boy that pulled on my heartstrings, teasing a smile to my lips.

I was so much younger in the picture, looked so different. If I ever saw Ryan again, would he even recognise me? Would I recognise him? Who had he grown up to be? Was he still kind and thoughtful, quiet and contemplative? Did he still love the outdoors? Did he still go fishing in his spare time?

I had no idea.

For all I knew, he'd taken up smoking and drinking, gambling the nights away in dingy bars. Or maybe he was already married—he'd always had an old soul. I could imagine him proposing to his high school girlfriend, making an honest wage by working on a farm, or maybe with animals, anything outdoors.

CHAPTER SEVEN

My face was puffy the next morning. I must have fallen asleep crying again—I really shouldn't look back on old pictures—but I was determined to make a better impression than the day before. After seeing how gorgeous the girls at college were, I had a hot shower before digging out my straighteners, meticulously ironing my hair until it fell in a sleek line around my shoulders. After layering on foundation and mascara, I smiled at my reflection.

Hattie oohed and ahhed when I arrived at the bus stop—which only confirmed the state I must have looked yesterday—and Oliver, Matt and even Emily talked to me on the way.

By day three, Hattie invited me to sit with her and her friends at lunch. By Friday, I already knew my way easily around campus, people stopped in the halls to say hi, even inviting me to sit with them at lunch. Only once more I had to sit on the field for lunch, but this time, it was because Hattie and her friends wanted to 'soak up the sun'. They laughed when I'd bundled up like an Eskimo whilst they shed every layer, pale skin exposed.

Mel called home Friday evening. She was staying in the dorms at Uni, and of course, she'd already made plans to go out that evening, and the next, cutting the conversation short when her friends arrived, leaving mum and dad beaming proudly.

On Saturday morning, sun pouring through the kitchen window above the sink, giving the false impression of a summer's day, I poured cereal into a bowl, still in my pyjamas, rubbing sleep from my eyes.

My phone vibrated on the kitchen counter. Dropping the box of cornflakes, I hit answer.

"Hey Aussie," Hattie said.

I rolled my eyes at the nickname she'd latched on to. "Hey, Hattie. What's up?"

"Nothing. What are you doing today?"

"Nothing."

I'd just planned on calling Luke and watching TV.

"Want to meet me in town? I'm in dire need of a new dress."

"Yeah, OK," I grinned. "Hang on, which town?"

"Gloucester town centre? Have you been yet?"

"Uh, yeah," I scrunched my forehead, remembering when we'd gone with mum.

"OK, meet me in front of *Boots* at eleven, all right?"

"Yeah, OK. See you then."

Cereal forgotten, I took the steps two at a time to my room, glancing at the clock.

It was already ten, and I had no idea how to get into town. "Mum!" I yelled, pulling clothes from my drawer. "*Mum!*"

"What? No need to shout," she appeared magically, like mothers do, at the door.

"I'm going to meet Hattie in town, is that OK?" I pulled on a pair of jeans over the top of my leggings, not missing the glimmer in her eyes.

"Yes, of course, that's fine. Do you know how to get there?"

"No," a worried crease formed between my brows as I wiggled into the jeans.

"Right, maybe dad can take you," she disappeared.

I groaned.

Dad had only just picked up our new Citroen and was still getting used to the roundabouts. But getting a lift was better than trying to figure out the buses.

Pulling a long-sleeved shirt over a thermal top, topped up with a jersey and scarf, dad wandered into the room, looking over the top of his glasses. "Mum says you want a lift. Where to?"

"Into town, if that's OK?"

"Yeah, that's fine."

"I have to be there for eleven. When do we have to leave?"

He looked at his watch. "When you're ready. It only takes about fifteen minutes."

I grinned. "Thanks, dad."

In the car ten minutes later, I laughed as dad cursed at every roundabout, slapping a hand over my mouth when he virtually ignored a pedestrian crossing. Miraculously, we made it safely into town, though ended up in a bus lane, and I jumped out to angry honks coming from the big double-decker buses.

Checking my watch, it was ten forty-five, *where the hell was Boots?*

Just as I'd turned to walk down the corridor lined with buses, Hattie called, and she breezed off one of the buses wearing a multi-coloured crocheted jumper made of different patchwork squares, easily standing out like a spark in the darkness amongst the muted colours of the crowd.

"Hey," I beamed.

She bounced to my side, a feather hanging from the braid in her hair. "Did you just get here?" she asked.

"Yeah, only just."

"Did you catch the bus?"

"No," I laughed. "My dad dropped me off."

"We'll have to get you comfortable riding the buses soon," she giggled, looping her arm through mine.

"So, where are we?" I looked around, "And where is this Boots place? I thought you said you wanted a new dress?"

Hattie laughed hard, a hand over her mouth. "Oh, my goodness, Aussie, you have so much to learn. This," she pointed behind us, "Is, like, the main bus terminal. If you caught the number ten from your place, it would bring you here."

My mouth formed an 'O'.

"And this," she continued, sweeping her arm dramatically as we rounded the corner, "Is the High Street."

The small pavement opened to a large, bricked area, flanked on either side by grey, cement buildings. Each had tall glass windows, high arched doors, and varying assortments in the windows.

"And that," Hattie indicated, "Is Boots," pointing to a store in front of us. On the corner of where the buses were, a blue and white sign indicated '*Boots*'.

"So, it's not an actual *boot* store?"

Hattie giggled, "No. But I don't want to go in there anyway." She tugged me down the High Street.

Pigeons walked confidently among thundering feet, people weaved this way and that, everyone in their secluded bubble where no one except them and their party existed.

Town was busy, I'd never seen such a grand and crowded High Street, and Hattie would never understand my relief with her arm entwined with mine, keeping me grounded. Without it, I might have floated away amongst the sea of bodies.

"First thing you have to learn," Hattie continued, weaving effortlessly through the throng of people, "Is the best, and I mean *best*, place to shop—is Primark."

"Primark?"

"Yeah. It has the most amazing things, at a fraction of the price!"

"I thought that's what second-hand shops were for?"

"Oh, so you do know a little," she winked. "Second-hand shops are my *favourite*, there's one on the corner down there we can go to." She pointed a purple-painted finger covered in rings. "But I'm looking for something a bit newer today."

Not far down the High Street was the shop Hattie had talked about, and through the doors, a breath of heat blew down my neck, making me shudder.

"So, what are we looking for?" my fingers ran over the soft materials.

The store was large with an escalator at the other end leading to another level of Men's and Kids, indicated by a sign. Rails of clothes stretched to the back wall, weaving around the corner to another section of the store.

"A dress," Hattie shifted through hangers scraping loudly against metal rails. "There's a party tonight at the park."

"The park?"

"Gloucester Park. It's not far from here." Her eyes widened, "*Ohmygosh*. Do you want to come? You're already here, so you don't have to catch the bus, and your dad can just pick you up from there? I can't believe I didn't think about it before!"

"Uh, a party?" my cheeks flushed.

I didn't think I'd be invited to a party so soon. It had taken months before I went out in Jamaica.

"Come on," Hattie begged. "It'll be fun!"

"I won't know anyone."

Standing in the middle of an aisle; people pushed past with annoyed grimaces, but Hattie hardly seemed to notice.

"You'll know me, and I'll introduce you to everyone. It's the best idea. I can't believe I didn't think of it sooner," she knocked the palm of her hand to her head.

I wasn't sure if I was ready for a party, but Hattie was excited, and I was eager to please my new friend. "Why not then."

Hattie squealed, jumping up and down. "We have to get you a dress too."

"Oh, no, thanks. I'll just go in this."

Dad had only given me ten pounds, and I wanted to save it for just-in-case. Plus, if this party was really in a park, *outside*, there was no way I would survive in a dress. If anything, I was contemplating buying a few more layers.

Hattie's lower lip popped out. I laughed. "Don't worry. We can still find you something. How about this?" I pulled the dress my hand had been lingering on.

"It's perfect!" she tugged me into the changing rooms.

Hattie tried on so many dresses I lost count, but I didn't care—I was having the most fun I'd had since arriving in the UK.

She ended up buying a red dress that hung loosely to her shins to show off her Doc Martins, small yellow sunflowers patterned all over.

My nerves had relaxed, and with Hattie as my guide, she confidently navigated us up and down and around the High Street.

We bought hot chocolates from Costa Coffee—which she swore was better than Starbucks—and giggled as we ate the cream off the top sitting on a bench beside a small patch of green where a one-legged pigeon hobbled around a bin.

"*Ohmygosh*!" Hattie exclaimed by late afternoon, "I need to get back so I can change. You'll come to mine, and we can go to the park together, right?"

I nodded—definitely not wanting to be left alone around here when it darkened.

Making our way to the bus station again, Hattie pulled me behind her onto a bus, touching a card to a yellow machine before walking to the back.

I stopped, unsure what I was supposed to do.

"Where to, love?" the driver said through a clear plastic window separating us.

"Uh," I looked for Hattie.

"Oh, sorry!" she tumbled back, "Sorry, she's not from here. Bristol Road, please."

I laughed as the man said, "One pound fifty, love."

Handing over the ten-pound note, he returned my change on the little plastic tray in front of him, and I followed Hattie upstairs, where she took two seats at the front of the bus on the left, so I sat on the right.

The double-decker had rows of seats on either side, with blue-patterned material, a dappled blue aisle running down the centre between the seats. Every two sets of chairs, a yellow pole ran from the floor to the ceiling, with a big, red button saying 'STOP'.

A large, curved window provided an unlimited view of the street below where Hattie and I sat at the front. It was both spectacular and a little scary.

Checking my phone, there were no messages from Luke, so instead, I opened a message to dad, telling him I was going to stay a bit longer.

He replied quickly, saying it was OK.

"Boyfriend?" Hattie raised an eyebrow.

"What? Oh, that," I smirked. "No, I was just messaging my dad."

"Oh, OK. But *do* you have a boyfriend?" She asked with a curious twitch of her brow.

Not quite sure how to respond, she took my hesitation as answer. "Oh, you do! Who is he? Is he here? Is he in Jamaica?"

"No," I shook my head, smiling at her endless enthusiasm. "I mean, yes, he's in Jamaica. But we're technically not together. It's not that easy to make it work this long-distance," I laughed, attempting to lighten my tone.

"Did you have to break up for the move?" she asked softly, knowing eyes roaming my face.

"Yeah."

"What's his name?"

"Luke," I smiled. "Do you have a boyfriend?"

"No," she sighed. "Not yet anyway," she wagged her eyebrows.

There was something about Hattie... Maybe it was her never-ending optimism, or endless well of enthusiasm, but whatever it was, she was helping plaster over the wound in my chest, and I silently thanked whatever lucky stars there were for bringing me a friend so quick after the move.

The bus ride was short. Before I knew it, Hattie was pushing the STOP button, and I followed her back down the stairs.

On the icy road, we walked down a street lined with streetlamps, buildings tall and tightly packed side by side. Hattie's house was like the Weasleys' from *Harry Potter*, flanked on either side by matching three-storey buildings. Inside was like the Weasleys too—bits and bobs lying here and there, the small entranceway flanked by a pile of well-used shoes and jackets, coats piled one on top of the other. Pushed up against the staircase was a random jumble of items; a miniature piano, a cricket bat, a pair of red peep-toed heels and a discarded purple scarf.

Barely through the door, two small boys rushed past, screaming at the top of their lungs, and a girl yelled from a nearby room. Hattie shouted at the boys, quickly introducing her two younger brothers before indicating her sister in the other room, two years younger than her.

"Hattie," her mum sighed, appearing from what I assumed was the kitchen at the back of the house. Her hair was knotted messily atop her head, and she wore a pair of breezy patterned trousers with a yellow tank top.

"Hey, mum," Hattie beamed. "This is Tyler. Tyler, mum. We're going upstairs to get ready," she tugged me behind her, and I shouted a quick hello over my shoulder.

Up the rickety stairs to the third floor, Hattie's room was exactly as I would imagine—Indian-patterned sarongs draped from the roof and around a desk, over her bed, and across a cupboard with no doors. Wind chimes and dreamcatchers hung from the ceiling. Crystal chimes caught the lights as they turned. On the wall, and draped here and there above the bed, were white fairy lights setting off an ethereal glow.

If I didn't already know Hattie, I could have perfectly gleaned her personality from this room.

Smiling, I sunk into an amethyst chair at a desk, the air smelling of burning incense.

Hattie immediately pulled off her clothes. "Can you pass me the dress, please? Oh, and take the tag off."

From the bag, I pulled her new dress, and with it tumbled various pieces of jewellery I'm sure I hadn't seen her buy. "Hattie," I frowned.

She looked over her shoulder, then down at the jewellery on the floor, giggling mischievously with a hand over her mouth.

"Shhh," she whispered, snatching the dress from my hands.

I was still digesting the thought that Hattie had quite obviously *stolen* the items, when she appeared, twirling in front of me.

"Ta-da." She looked every bit a flowy, boho princess; long, strawberry-blonde hair twisted into a braid hanging down her back, loose tendrils snaking around her neck.

Within another ten minutes, Hattie had layered on blue mascara, slathered on purple, shimmering lip gloss, and shouted goodbye to her mum as we headed out the door, towards the bus once more.

She pulled a cigarette from her bag.

"Do you smoke often?" I asked.

"No," she shook her head, pulling the cigarette from her mouth in a plume of smoke. "Only on the weekends and after college. Never at college. That's my rule," she said sternly. "Want some?"

"No thanks," I scrunched my nose. "So, who do you know that's going to be at the party anyway?" I asked when we were back on the same bus as before, thrumming towards town again.

"Callum, James, Nicky, Hannah, Adam… everyone!" she counted on her fingers with a giggle.

A nervous, sickly feeling sat in the pit of my stomach that I just couldn't shake.

I'd only just built up the courage to dance in Jamaica. Dancing like that here made me nauseous. How *did* they dance here? Did they have their own particular dance that I'd have to learn again?

From the town centre, we walked in the opposite direction of the High Street this time, passing corner shops and dingy alleyways until turning into a park.

It was already dark, and there were no streetlamps, the almost full moon bathing the ground in shimmering silver through ghostly trees, lighting our way. Shadows were deep and endless, and Hattie and I clung tightly to each other until flickering light broke through the dark ahead.

"There they are!" Hattie squealed, an open fire coming into view.

A few bodies were dotted around it, sounds of crackling wood and voices drifting in the air.

"Hattie!" came a voice before the owner barrelled towards us and into Hattie's arms.

"Hannah, this is Tyler. Everyone, this is Tyler!" Hattie announced.

The five loitering strangers mumbled their hellos, and I wondered if more would join; otherwise, Hattie's idea of a party and mine were very different.

Releasing my arm, Hattie leapt into the arms of a guy with long hair, her dimpled smile giving away that this guy was probably the reason she'd wagged her eyebrows at me when I'd asked the boyfriend question.

"So, Tyler," Hannah's voice came from beside me. "Hattie says you're from Australia?"

I rolled my eyes playfully, blowing warm air into balled hands, jumping lightly on my toes, "I think it's her favourite thing about me."

"It is pretty cool, to be fair," Hannah said, nose ring glinting in the flames of the fire. "Want a drink?" She pointed to a pack of beers on the floor.

"No thanks." I'd never liked the taste of beer, which had been a bonus in Jamaica, because all they drank was rum.

The fire pit was simply made with wood scavenged from the park, crisp leaves still burning on the branches. Make-shift log seats flanked either side that couldn't have been found just for this occasion. No grass grew around the fire patch, proving it was a well-used, off-the-grid party spot. Not a house or streetlamp in sight.

Around the fire was a cocoon of darkness my eyes couldn't penetrate. Nothing existed except these strangers and me in a bubble of icy air and tongues of flames.

The roar of an engine tore through the night, an orb of light cresting a nearby hill, a black motorbike pulling to a stop a few metres from the group, almost entirely camouflaged with the shadows. The figure that dismounted was cloaked in misty darkness, black clothes blending with the shadows, raven helmet reflecting against the fire.

Hannah had taken up conversation with a guy on her other side, which left me to freely gawk at the black-clad newcomer.

He removed his helmet to reveal dark, shoulder-length hair tied half up, and immediately, my pulse rose. I smothered a laugh—*really, Ty? Bad boy biker? Can you be any more of a cliché?*

Yet my eyes strained to see more of him standing just outside of the flickering fire light.

With two easy steps towards the group, the newcomer clapped hands with one of the other guys. Looking across the fire, I quickly glanced away, swallowing passed the panic thrumming in my ears.

"All right, Adz," someone shouted.

I desperately tried to ignore the pull on my gaze.

"Hannah," a velvety voice came from nearby.

Biting the inside of my cheek, I finally looked towards the voice. Towards him.

"Hey, Adam," Hannah cooed, popping a hip and twirling a piece of hair between her fingers.

I smothered another smirk.

"Who's this?" his shadowy eyes slid lazily to mine.

He was breath-taking.

"This is Tyler," Hannah filled in.

An earring glistened in one of his ears, another in his brow. When he opened his mouth to sip the beer in his hand, I quickly glimpsed another sparkling in his tongue.

"Uh, hi," I managed pathetically.

Adam's lips turned into a smirk. My body thrummed.

"Where are you from, Tyler?" The way his accent bent around my name sent a shiver through my stomach.

"Australia," I croaked.

He quirked an eyebrow, swigging casually from his drink, as if he met people from Australia all the time. Who knows, maybe he did.

"What are you doing here?" he asked bluntly in a way that was borderline rude.

"Family."

Who was this guy, and why was he turning me to jelly just by looking at me?

A dark ring glinted on the middle finger of the hand holding the beer, an inked mark peeking out from under the shirt at his neck. His other hand rested in the pocket of his dark jeans.

"So how do you like England?" Adam asked when Hannah dashed to the other side of the fire to where another girl arrived.

"It's cold," I laughed.

He quirked a side smile. *I'm in trouble.* My stomach squeezed again.

"Yeah, but it's not so bad once you get used to it."

Blowing air in front of me, it quickly turned to white mist. "Probably not any time soon."

"Adam!" Hattie bounced across the circle; the long-haired boy attached to her hand. "I see you've met our new resident Aussie. Cool, isn't she?" Hattie gushed. My heart swelled.

"She's all right," Adam smirked.

"You don't have a drink!" Hattie looked at the hands tucked deep in my pockets.

"I'm not a big beer drinker," I confessed.

"You should have said." From his jacket, Adam pulled a small, clear bottle.

"There's Coke over there," the long-haired guy attached to Hattie pointed to the other side of the fire.

"Oh," I looked between the two. "Go on then."

"Yay," Hattie grabbed the bottle from Adam, pulling me across the circle.

Handing me a plastic cup, Hattie poured the vodka.

"Whoa," the clear liquid almost filled half the cup.

"Oh shush," she cooed, opening the Coke and filling the rest. "Cheers," she raised the glass bottle.

"So, who's the guy?" I lowered my voice, pointing across the fire to the guy now talking with Adam. The alcohol burnt its way down my throat, warming my insides deliciously.

"Callum," Hattie smiled dreamily, I could almost see the hearts popping around her head.

"I thought you didn't have a boyfriend?"

"That's 'cos I don't," she rested an elbow on her knee, chin in her palm. "But I'm working on it," she smiled wickedly.

111

Hannah joined us on the log, then Gareth—I was told was his name—sat on the floor on the other side of the fire with James and Nicky—the other two I hadn't spoken to yet.

When the burn of the alcohol became a soothing tingle, head already feeling light, I took sip after sip, and before I knew it, I was staring at the bottom of the cup.

"Need a top-up?" Adam's voice appeared close to my ear; my eyes darted to where he was supposed to be across the fire.

"Yes please," I reigned in the urge to giggle for no reason.

Had I eaten at all today? Hot chocolate and whipped cream could barely count as food.

Crouched behind me, Adam took my cup, unscrewing the red lid of the small bottle. Chewing my bottom lip, I begged my body to stay upright, even if all it would take to touch him was a slight movement to the right.

Shadows danced and curled around him. His eyes endless when he handed me the drink, watching until I lifted it to my lips. Those hooded eyes dropped to my mouth, a flicker behind them when I licked the droplets along my bottom lip.

My pulse rose, heart thudding in my ears, heat curling up from under my jersey.

Hattie's scream tore our contact, she and Hannah squealing, legs curling under from a small frog leaping in front of them.

"Aww, Hattie, no!" I shouted when she tried to kick it.

She and Hannah hung on to each other as if their lives depended on it, squeezing as far away from the little amphibian as possible. "Ew! Take it away then, Tyler!" Hattie moaned.

Resting my drink on the ground, I cupped my hands around the frog's slimy body, before pretending to throw it on Hannah and Hattie, earning even loader screams.

Beneath a tree, under the cover of leaves and shadow away from the group by the fire, I let the frog leap happily to the ground.

"There you go, little guy."

Looking back at the group, I noticed that Adam was missing, when a flickering orange ember caught my eye from where he leaned against his bike, the firefly-like glow of a cigarette igniting his features. Before my mind had a chance to comprehend what I was doing, my feet took me towards him.

Wiping palms on my jeans, his lips curled into a smile around the cigarette as I approached, blowing smoke from his nose. Those penetrating eyes watched me again.

I'd never met anyone like him, perhaps that was why I was so drawn to him—curiosity, my mind reasoned.

Smiling awkwardly, I wrapped my arms in front of me.

"Do you have a boyfriend?" Adam asked bluntly, smoke escaping his lips.

"What?"

"You heard."

"Uh," I faltered. He was trying to hold back a smile. "No, not really."

He quirked an eyebrow, "Not really?"

"Not really."

"I'll take that," he nodded gently.

I frowned, although it probably didn't come off as menacing as I was aiming for.

Maybe it was the alcohol. Maybe it was just Adam. Whatever it was, thoughts of Luke slid away. From the corners of my mind came the words; *traitor*, *cheat*. But I had every right to feel the way I was. If I had any chance in hell of getting over Luke and moving on, I needed to accept that. Plus, it didn't hurt that there was a hauntingly beautiful guy standing in front of me, possibly even flirting with me.

Shaking the thoughts away, Adam watched silently.

"We'd better get back," he pushed off the bike.

By the fire, Adam sat next to me this time. The warmth from his body sent shudders through mine, and suddenly I was aware of how cold I was, even though my face somehow felt like it was burning.

As the night wore on, eventually Hannah and James left. Nicky and Gareth ended up draped over each other, the waning fire flickering over their kissing faces. Hattie and Callum disappeared somewhere into the dark, and a chill climbed up my spine, body trembling in the fading fire.

"You're cold?" Adam asked.

"A little," I tried not to let my chattering teeth give away just how cold.

"Come here," he wrapped an arm around me. Snuggling under his arm, holding one of my hands, he brought my frozen skin to his warm lips. My chest hiccupped. "You're as cold as ice," his breath danced across my hands.

Taking both in his, he lifted his shirt, placing them on his hard stomach.

We inhaled together.

Looking to where my head rested on his shoulder, he smiled. "Better?"

His breath smelt of cigarettes and beer, possibly the worst combination. Still, somehow there was a hint of something else, something that made me inwardly groan, thighs squeezing with my hands still touching his skin.

His eyes flickered to my lips again, and I was grateful when he finally dipped his head, lips grazing across mine. Closing my eyes, I surrendered to him, his tongue snaking through my lips, jumping at the sensation of the ring brushing across my tongue.

Wrapping a hand around my neck, the other coming to my hip, my body trembled for a completely new reason. Adam smiled knowingly against my mouth.

It felt like only minutes had passed when my phone rang, and Adam sighed, breath shifting the hair at my temples.

"Sorry," I pulled the phone from my pocket, dad's name flashing across the screen. "Shit," I rubbed a hand over my eyes, pressing the answer button. "Hey, dad."

"Tyler? Are you OK? It's late. I wanted to head to bed, are you ready to be picked up?"

No, leave me here all night. "Yes, I'm ready," I tried to calm my shaking breath.

"OK, where are you?"

I imagined his frown, a deep groove between his brows from years of squinting in the sun, as it dawned on him that he had no idea where I was.

"I'm at Hattie's house, it's beside the Gloucester Park," I lied quickly, earning a lazy smirk from Adam. "I'll meet you on the road in front of the park, that'll be easier."

"OK, I'm leaving now."

"I have to go," I turned to Adam, tucking the phone back into my pocket, the metal already turning cold.

"I figured."

Forcing my legs to move, I stood, Adam doing the same, pushing stray hairs from around his face behind his ears.

"It was nice to meet you, Tyler," he smiled.

I bit my kissed swollen lips. "You too."

With a brushed kiss on my forehead, Adam turned to his bike.

Making my way in the opposite direction, to the edges of the park and main road, I struggled to reign in the smile threatening to tear at my cheeks.

"Hattie," I whispered into the dark, "Hattie, I have to go. I'll message you tomorrow." I shout-whispered blindly into the air.

Her soft voice drifted from within the shadows. "Bye, Tyler, talk tomorrow!"

With one last look over my shoulder, Adam was straddling his bike, pulling on the helmet.

Tearing my eyes away, it was only a few minutes before dad's maroon car pulled in front of me, and I climbed in the gloriously warm cab.

CHAPTER EIGHT

My head ached when I peeled my eyes open on Sunday, tongue feeling like sandpaper.

Water, my mind pleaded. Grabbing the glass off the side table, I gulped deeply, slumping back on the pillow.

Goosebumps rose along my arms at the memory of the guy with the dark hair and dark eyes—*had I really kissed him?* Maybe it was the high of making new friends, or the lingering pleasure of having such a good day with Hattie. Or maybe just a *little* bit to do with the vodka.

Opening a message to Hattie, she replied almost immediately:

Tyler*: Hey Hattie, did you get home OK?*
Hattie*: Yeah, Callum took me home.*
Tyler*: Where did you guys get to?*
Hattie*: Got a little frisky under the tree!*

I slapped a shocked hand over my mouth.

Tyler*: Hattie!*

I could just imagine her giggling into her pillow.

Hattie: *You were a little preoccupied with Adam.*
Tyler: *I can't believe that happened...*
Hattie: *Are you OK?*
Tyler: *Yeah, I guess so. Just feel a bit weird. I don't usually kiss guys I've just met...*
Hattie: *Well, Adam is a hottie, so it's OK.*

Already feeling better, I absently wondered if I should tell Luke, though I knew I didn't need to—shouldn't.

My hand went to the ring around my neck. With a sigh, I pushed away the nagging feelings of betrayal. We hadn't spoken much this week. Maybe that was all the sign I needed that he was moving on too.

The thought twisted in my gut, and I shook it away.

Opening Facebook, I hesitated for only a moment, before typing in Hattie's name. The profile picture of her sitting with crossed legs, an apple balancing on her head, came up. Searching her friends, I typed 'Adam', quickly finding a side profile of someone with dark hair wearing a beanie, ring glinting in his eyebrow.

My heart hammered, clicking the image.

Surprisingly, there wasn't much on Adam's Facebook wall; a picture of his motorbike, a few tattoo pictures (were they all his?). Finally, I came across a picture, and my pulse raced again.

He was as beautiful as I remembered.

Had I really kissed this gorgeous human last night? I'd never been into tattoos and piercings, but there was something about Adam, even now, that drew me in.

Finger hovering over the 'Add Friend' button, I hesitated.

Would he even want to know me after last night? Was he the type of guy that did that kind of thing regularly? Would I look like a naïve little girl if I added him the next day? The obvious answer, of course, was yes. A guy like him would have girls throwing themselves at him. Who was I but a shy new addition to the group, and, really, the only one left after everyone had paired off?

Shaking my head, I closed the app, throwing my phone across the bed.

****

That evening, after spending the day mooching around the house in my pyjama's, nursing my hangover—which, to my parents, was only a result of being out in the cold all evening—my phone pinged with an incoming notification.

When the screen lit up, my heart stopped. 'Adam Wisley has sent you a friend request'.

Tapping it open, I almost squealed pressing 'Confirm'.

Oh, my eyes widened.

Was that too quick? Too eager?

I smacked myself on the head, but before there was too much time to overthink it, the message box flashed.

Adam: *Hey.*

I took a breath.

Tyler: *Hey, yourself.*
Adam: *What are you doing?*

He was talking to me like we were old friends.

Tyler: *Not much. You?*

I waited.

Adam: *I'm at the pub. Want to come?*

My eyes widened. Did he just invite me out?
I wanted to say yes, but it was already seven p.m., and with college in the morning, I knew my parents wouldn't allow it.
How old was he anyway?
I contemplated my response.

Tyler: *Can't. College tomorrow.*

I waited.
And waited.

And waited.

I'd blown it. He'd finally realised my age and he'd made a grave mistake.

Adam: *Cirencester College, right?*

I jumped at the message with a mental fist pump.

Tyler: *That's the one.*
Adam: *Maybe I'll see you tomorrow then.*

What? What did that mean? I was about to ask, but the little green symbol showing he was online turned red.

****

On the bus the next morning, I told Hattie about my conversation with Adam. She assured me that I shouldn't worry; being mysterious was part of his charm.

She said he was nineteen, working full-time at some garage in Gloucester. I felt like I was being nosey but couldn't help myself. Plus, Hattie was happy to answer the questions, so I didn't feel too much like a stalker.

The day was a blur from class to class, and I couldn't help checking my phone to see if Adam messaged, but when my final lesson was over, and with nothing from him, I thought maybe I'd overthought what he'd said.

On my way to the bus, Hattie ran towards me, almost knocking me over, skidding to a stop, using my bag as her anchor.

"Tyler!" she panted.

"What?" I laughed at her frantic expression.

"You… have… to come with me!" she said between breaths.

"Why? Hattie, where?" but she was already pulling me behind her.

Stopping on the cemented area in front of the cafeteria, Hattie grinned, pointing at the road. My eyes followed her finger, to where, standing on the road, leaning against his motorbike, was the tall, dark form of Adam.

Heat rose hotly to my cheeks, my mind slowly leaking images of him from the other night.

"What?" I whipped towards Hattie.

"Yup," she grinned. "He came to see you! I saw him on my way back from English and said I'd come and get you."

"Why is he *here*, though?"

"Who cares? Go, go, go!" She nudged me.

Stumbling on the stairs, over my shoulder, Hattie gave a quick thumbs-up, before turning to run to the buses.

"Hey," I smiled tightly, a few feet from Adam.

"Hey yourself," he drawled.

In the light of day, even with the sun dipping towards the horizon, scattered hues across the sky, Adam was still swathed in shadows. His eyes, which were an incredible mix between steel grey and blue, were penetrating. His features devilishly angelic. That mouth...

"Uh, what are you doing here?" I managed.

"I told you I'd see you today, didn't I?"

"Yeah but... I didn't think you meant *at* college. I need to catch the bus," I pointed to where the buses were, hoping the number 20 hadn't left yet.

A few students still milled around, walking to the bus stop, and I felt their eyes on us.

Adam laughed. "I'll give you a lift." His head cocked towards the bike.

"On that?" It looked like an intimidating wasp, and a little scary, but adrenaline at the thought of riding on it, with *him*, zinged through me.

"I even brought you a helmet." He unstrapped a black and green helmet from the back.

Shit. Shit. Shit. I can't. My parents would go nuts. I swallowed the lump in my throat. "Uh-," I started, but he cut in.

"Come on, Ty. It'll be fun."

I pursed my lips. "Fine," I smiled.

He grinned, throwing a leg over the side, kicking up the stand to catch the weight between his legs.

"Oh," I stopped.

He turned, his own black helmet in his hands. "What?"

"Uh, nothing. It's just going to be seriously cold," I shuddered, tugging at the flimsy cardigan I was wearing.

"Ah, I thought of that too," he pulled back the seat so it opened to a small compartment, where he procured a black jacket.

I grinned. "Perfect."

Dropping my backpack on the ground, I shimmied into the jacket. It was far too big, but the inside was warm and fleecy, and I zipped it to my neck, the smell of his musty cologne floating from the material. I fought not to let my eyes roll back.

Pulling the helmet on and bag over my shoulders, I swung a leg, fastening my feet on the footholds either side, before wrapping my arms around his waist.

"Ready?" Adam shouted back.

"Hell, yes!"

The key turned, bike roaring to life. The foot resting on the ground kicked up, and we lurched forward, cold wind whipping at my hands as we sped down the road and out of the college entrance with an exaggerated rev of the engine. Adam was a guy used to people looking at him, and he welcomed it.

Expertly manoeuvring through traffic on the main road through Cirencester, passing one of the college buses, I wanted to bury my face in the back of his jacket, hoping it wasn't the number 20.

Stopping at a set of traffic lights, he twisted his head, shouting back to me, "If your hands are cold, tuck them in my pockets."

Not needing to be told twice, because they already resembled popsicles, I tucked them into the warm, woolly pockets of his black leather jacket.

When the light turned green, we sped off again.

Once town was behind us, Adam didn't take the motorway, instead, green fields of the countryside whipped past, fallen leaves floating around our feet as we shot through them. Rays of the setting sun felt gloriously warm on the black of the jacket I wore, and Adam turned down lane, after lane, until I had no idea where we were or where we were going.

Trees zipped past, and we laughed at sheep in the fields and when he had to pull the bike to a stop because a large pheasant with bright brown and orange plumage refused to clear the road.

Wind whipped past my face where it sat snugly in the helmet, squirrels darted amongst the branches of the trees.

The roads were nauseatingly tiny, and I cringed at every car we came across, but Adam was a natural, and I felt safe tucked into his back.

Eventually, we slowed, and he guided us over a small mound off the most recent dirt road, opening into a clearing.

The ground was flat with a jumble of dirt and grass, flanked by tall trees. In front, there was a sudden drop, the ground bowing to a sprawling town below.

I inhaled sharply at the patchwork of houses, streets, trees and fields, going on and on as if it had no end, until the pink-hued sky met the green earth.

"Like it?" Adam watched as I stared, climbing off the back of the bike.

"It's beautiful," I breathed, helmet tucked under my arm.

"It's Gloucester."

"Really? I didn't realise it was so big."

"It's not that big compared to some of the others. But it's not that small either, I guess."

Unlike Kingston, or even London, the Gloucestershire countryside had a quaint beauty to it where houses and roads worked in harmony with beautiful fields. Farmer's borders were edged with hedging so the landscape was like a puzzle, the countryside preserved so that civilisation and nature worked together to create the beautiful city.

I remembered flying in from the air and admiring the unique patchwork of land that made up England, disappointed when we were met with city smog and hustle and bustle of London.

But now, looking over the sprawling landscape, I could barely describe this strange and beautiful land.

My body still hummed from the thrum of the bike, feeling strange after being on it for so long, and Adam kicked out the stand, pulling a box of cigarettes from his pocket.

"Where are we?" I asked when he flicked a lighter, hand over my eyes in search of a sign.

"Birdlip," Adam said with an inhale.

"I know where that is. Sometimes the bus takes it as a cut-through."

Adam was quiet, smoke tendrils escaping from his lips, swirling into the air.

My eyes watched the horizon, but my mind was now purely on Adam, and the gaze I felt turning the skin of my face to blisters. I wanted to pull a hand through my hair, hoping the wind and helmet hadn't turned it into a bird's nest.

When I couldn't take it any longer, I slid my gaze to his.

"So, Hattie tells me you're a mechanic?" I asked, desperate to fill the silence.

"Yeah."

"You didn't want to go to university?"

He scoffed, "Not a Uni kind of guy."

I was acutely aware of how much older Adam was and couldn't help the tickle of intimidation that climbed up my spine. I was by no means a child—I'd be eighteen in a few months, an adult by UK laws—but somehow Adam seemed so… experienced. I blushed at the thought, wishing it had never crossed my mind.

Leaning back on the bike, flicking his unfinished cigarette to the floor, he extended a silent hand.

His fingers were long, the tell-tale signs of tattoos curling around his wrists. "Come here."

My body responded on its own, walking slowly towards him until I was only a few feet away. He closed the distance by tugging on my jacket, so I stood between his legs.

A faint scar ran across his eyebrow, the one without the black ring, and finally I noticed that his hair wasn't black, but a deep, dark, chocolate brown.

Musky cologne filled my nose, and as he licked his bottom lip, his tongue ring peeped through.

The memory of it on my lips sent shivers of pleasure through me, my pulse continuing to quicken until I was afraid that my heart was beating so hard, he might be able to feel it where our chests almost touched.

Tired of his teasing, of this *almost* touching, I lifted a hand to his neck to end the torture, closing the last bit of distance between us.

The kiss was slow, sensual. Soft lips gently brushing over mine, tongue skimming my bottom lip. I greedily wanted more, but he kept the slow, agonising pace.

When he pulled back, I moaned from the loss of contact.

"What is it about you?" he spoke quietly.

"What do you mean?"

"I've only known you for two days and already… fuck," he sighed again, pushing hair behind my ear.

I knew what he was trying to say. At least, I hoped I knew because I felt it too.

The hunger. The need. I'd never felt it like this before.

A yellow VW Beetle crunched slowly over the gravel nearby, coming to a stop at the other end of the clearing, three girls inside.

"Do you do this with a lot of girls?" I asked before I could stop myself.

Adam's body tensed, he frowned, pushing me back as if I'd just slapped him. "Why would you ask that?"

"I just... I don't know," I stammered, not sure why I'd asked it either. It was a fleeting, paranoid thought that managed to slip past my lips before I could think about what I was saying.

"It doesn't matter if I do this with other girls," he bit out harshly. There were the sound of slamming doors, the girls getting out of the car, their voices high pitched in the small distance between us. "Obviously, I've done this with other girls. I'm not a bloody monk or something."

"No, I know. I didn't mean..."

His eyes flicked over my shoulder, and I turned to where one of the girls was staring pointedly at us, unashamed that she'd been caught.

Another car pulled in behind them, this one filled with four guys, music blaring from the flashy silver and purple car.

"I should get you back," Adam pushed me away, swinging a leg back over the bike.

"Uh, OK," I stammered, climbing tentatively onto the back.

The girl staring at us smirked when Adam revved loudly like a preening male peacock, sand and gravel flicking behind us.

I tried to think what I could say to bring back the moment before I opened my stupid mouth. But the way the girl watched Adam, and how his gaze flicked, however briefly, to hers, had my mind telling me I was right to ask the question, no matter how unfair it was to voice my insecurity out loud, especially in this early stage.

Stupid.

Guiding Adam to my street, I asked him to stop a few blocks from my house, and as I climbed off, he asked, "This your house?"

His eyes scrutinised the house to our right. Part of me wanted to say it was because it was much nicer than ours.

"No, that's mine, number twenty-four," I pointed down the street.

"Ashamed of me or something?"

I shook my head quickly, "No. It's just that my parents probably wouldn't be too happy if they knew I rode on the back of your bike."

"Right," he scoffed, the tender guy who had picked me up and kissed me on the hill, gone.

I desperately wanted to get him back.

"Look, Adam, I—"

"I have to go; see you around," he flicked the engine on again, voice lost to the loud rumble.

I watched him disappear down the road, into the darkness that had now descended, the orange glow of streetlamps flickering across his helmet until he was out of sight—engine echoing across the night like the roar a lion.

Sighing, I dropped my face into my hands.

What have I done?

The door had barely slapped shut behind me when my phone vibrated with a message. My heart skipped a beat, but I waited until I was safely locked in my room to pull it out, hoping to see Adam's name on the screen.

But it was Luke's instead, and a different feeling washed through me.

I opened the message:

We need to talk.

****

Pacing a path into the carpet in my room, I tried to think of what I was going to say.

I felt guilty.

Guilty to the pit of my stomach. For kissing Adam. For hoping it was Adam that had messaged. I told myself that if Luke were around, I would never have even looked twice at Adam.

But he wasn't here. He was thousands of miles away. I had every right.

Didn't I?

Then why did it feel so wrong? The butterflies in my stomach weren't from the anxiety that came with cheating. No. These were nervous balls of energy from knowing it was over. That it was *really* over. Because I knew—deep down—I knew that I didn't want to go back to Luke.

A sick feeling settled in my gut as the butterflies turned to rocks.

Who was I?

When the phone rang, I answered with a shaky breath.

"Hey Tyler," Luke's familiar Jamaican accent was comfortable, suddenly I wanted to crumble to the floor in tears.

"Hi Luke," I managed to croak out.

His breathing was heavy and raspy, as if he'd been crying. "How are you?"

"I'm OK. How are you?"

He sighed, "Not great."

A few seconds of awkward silence passed. I couldn't bring myself to speak.

"Tyler, is everything OK?"

My heart pounded. "How so?"

"I haven't heard from you in a while… we haven't been talking like we used to. I feel like…"

His sentences kept dropping off. I got the feeling he didn't want to say what he was thinking. Hell, I didn't even want to say what was going on.

"Luke, I'm sorry." My voice cracked.

"Oh. Right," he sighed, like everything that had happened the last few days were laid bare with those few words.

Tears trailed down my cheeks.

I didn't want things to end with him, but they had to. I knew they had to. I couldn't keep hanging on to the past. Not like I did before. I missed so much because I refused to move on, and Luke didn't deserve that either.

Luke sniffed quietly on the other end, and we silently cried together for a few moments. He knew what had happened—in a way, he knew.

"OK," Luke said eventually. "I understand, Ty. Please know how much I understand."

"Thank you," I sobbed.

"I love you. Just remember that."

"I love you too," I said, and the line went dead.

Throwing myself onto the bed, I hugged a pillow to my chest, letting tears soak through the fabric.

When Adam appeared that night, I felt the first sense of pulling away. Like I *could* pull away. That there was a life without Luke—that there *could* be someone else.

As bad as I felt about it, there was no point in wasting months and months, living in the past again. Leaving Ryan was one of the hardest things I'd ever had to do. I'd hung on to that old life for too long. Missed so much. Part of me, as much as I loved Luke, didn't want to do that again. Not when standing right in front of me was a guy that I was finding myself falling fast and hard for.

Ryan.

His name echoed through my chest, a blooming warmth filling the ache left by Luke's words.

I hadn't thought about him in so long.

Luke, Adam, Ryan; each made me feel differently.

For Luke, I felt the open, pulsing wound of losing him.

And every thought of Adam had my blood rising.

But for Ryan… I felt… home. And the pulsing ache I felt now was the ache for that friendship, for the boy I left behind. All I wanted was to talk to him. If I could just hear his voice, the pain might go away.

Wiping a hand under my sniffling nose, tears drying on my cheeks, I found Ryan's number and hit call, but a monotone voice said that the number was no longer in use.

Instead, I opened Facebook—the link to all my other worlds.

My stomach squeezed in longing ache at his profile picture, standing by the pond at the farmhouse, shorts dirtied with mud, cap askew, a fish he'd caught dangling from his fingers.

I smothered a laugh.

There were no new updates on his page, so I opened a message.

Hi stranger, I was just thinking of you and how we haven't spoken in a while. I tried calling, but your number seems to be disconnected. Did you change it again?

Here's my quick update, we've moved to the UK. Only been here a few months, so still trying to get used to the cold. I miss the long hot summers in Aus, please send some my way. Mel's in Uni, I'm in college. The people here are nice.

Love, Tyler xx

Hitting send without another thought, I held the phone to my chest, where my heart beat slow. Not the thudding beat that Adam elicited earlier, but more of a sad, soft *thud, thud, thud,* in the final realisation that it was over with Luke.

Instinctively, rubbing the small mound under my shirt where the ring still sat snugly against my chest, I wondered if I should take it off, anxiety fluttering through my veins.

At the dresser, lifting the chain from my skin, the necklace dangled in front of me, ring spinning slowly, winking its goodbye before I tucked it safely in a drawer.

CHAPTER NINE

I hadn't heard from Adam in a week, even though I crumbled and messaged him—though now I felt stupid that it had been two days and he still hadn't replied.

By Friday, Hattie had hatched a plan to 'accidentally' run into him.

"So, what's the plan again?" I frowned while Hattie applied lip gloss to my lips, the number 10 bus bouncing us into town.

"We are meeting Callum, then going to the cinema, and we just so *happen* to walk past Adam's garage," Hattie smashed her lips together, indicating that I should do the same.

"Don't you think he'll see through it?" I picked nervously at the skin around my nails—a habit mum always scolded me for.

"I don't think so. And that's why Callum will be there. As a buffer."

Hattie's confidence in our plan calmed my nerves. Slightly.

I wanted to see Adam.

I wanted to take back what I'd said the other day. To feel the energy zinging in my veins again from his touch. He was all I could think about, day and night. I was going mad from it.

I *had* to see him.

I didn't want to lose what we'd started. He'd admitted he felt drawn to me too, that day on the hill, so why was he so adamant about keeping his distance? I hoped this plan of Hattie's worked.

Disembarking the bus before it reached the town centre, Callum was leaning against the bus stop, hands in his pockets when we arrived. The three of us began the walk to the cinema, and when Callum questioned why we weren't taking another bus, Hattie shushed him, saying it was a beautiful evening to walk.

Autumn was descending, the air crisper, nights longer. Trees were beginning to turn from green to colours of a campfire, and somehow, it was only going to get colder—Hattie warned.

Night was already falling when we padded along the pavement, sloppy fallen leaves turning to brown mush. The sign for the garage Adam worked at flashed harshly in neon blue lights in front of us.

I wanted to stop. *This was a bad idea.*

It seemed like such a sound plan when Hattie and I had spilled over the details at lunch. But now, with him possibly only metres away, I wanted to turn and run.

I didn't want whatever it was between us to be over. But I also didn't want the hard and callous guy that dropped me off at my house. I wanted the boy from the park, the chocolate-haired guy that had kissed me on the hill.

Nearing the shop, mechanical sounds of drills and lifts echoed from the open-plan room. Cars sat on stilts to one side, others with the bonnets or doors open on the other, the smell of oil thick in the air, a radio blasting The Prodigy through the room.

"Hey, Adam works here," Callum pointed when we arrived flush with the open garage-style entryway.

Hattie looked at me, rolling her eyes. I giggled quietly. "I wonder if he's here?" Hattie said suggestively.

"Adz!" Callum shouted into the workshop.

My heart hammered while we waited.

Within a minute, Adam strolled from the back of the shop, a bandana fitted around his head, a pair of dirty blue overalls tied at the waist with a white sleeveless top covered in grease stains. His bare arms were long and muscular, and finally, I could see some of the tattoos that covered both, twisting and winding before becoming shadows under his shirt.

He spotted us quickly, a bored look on his face when he strolled over, clapping a hand with Callum's, "All right, Cal." Those steel eyes shifted quickly over Hattie and me.

"You still working, bro?" Callum asked.

I looked away, not wanting to give him the satisfaction of seeing my disappointment.

"Just about to finish."

140

"We were heading to the cinema, want to come?" Callum asked.

Hattie practically bounced proudly beside me; her man was playing right into our plan.

"Nah, I've got plans."

My heart sunk.

"Oh yeah, you're going to that party, right?"

"What party?" Hattie straightened. "You never said anything about a party," she slapped Callum's shoulder playfully.

"I didn't think you'd want to go. I'm not that bothered," Callum shrugged.

"Is that where you're going?" Hattie turned her big, innocent, non-meddling eyes on Adam.

He shrugged, "Yeah."

"Well, I'd *love* to go to a party," Hattie overdid it just a tad. "How about you, Tyler?" She continued the charade.

"Sure," I managed an I-don't-really-care-either-way shrug.

Hattie bounced up and down happily.

"Well, I've got my car if you guys want a lift?" Adam wiped his hands over the overalls.

"Even better!" Hattie grinned, "We'll wait here."

Adam nodded, walking back the way he came.

Hattie turned, eyes full, lips pursed in victory.

I raised my eyebrows in a look that said—*yes, but did you notice how uninterested he was of me?* Hattie shook her head with a look that said—*don't be silly.*

We only had to wait five minutes before Adam pulled in front of the garage in a midnight blue car with black leather seats. The car was pimped out so it looked angry, its body low, sharp rims glittering with every turn. Callum climbed in the front, Hattie and I slid in the back.

Adam had changed his clothes, the pungent smell of cologne in the cab. Now he wore a pair of dark blue jeans, a black top hugging all the right places and pushed up at the elbows, with a beanie over his head so tendrils of his hair peaked out the bottom.

"Where's this party anyway?" Callum asked, the muscles under Adam's shirt working as he steered onto the road.

"Christina's. She goes to college with you, doesn't she?" Adam looked in the rear-view mirror at Hattie and me.

"Oh yeah, she catches our bus," Hattie nodded.

Great. I rolled my eyes.

Christina had never warmed to me like the others on the number 20, though admittedly, neither had I to her.

"What, lost your tongue tonight, Tyler?"

I jerked suddenly. "No," I scowled, "Just not much to say." I crossed my arms over my chest defiantly. Two could play this game.

Adam chuckled. I bit the inside of my cheek to stop myself from joining in.

Light from the radio bathed his face in its glow, the ring in his eyebrow glinting with the streetlights, long fingers tapping the rim of the steering wheel.

When the song changed, Hattie shouted "Turn this one up!" diving through the middle of the chairs to yank up the radio so that Katy Perry's '*I Kissed a Girl*' filled the cab.

Adam scowled, shaking his head, but Callum laughed, gazing adoringly at Hattie as she sang along.

"You ever kissed a girl, Tyler?" Adam asked over the music, those steel eyes meeting mine in the rear-view mirror.

"No," I smirked.

His eyes crinkled in the corners.

"Why not?" It was Hattie that asked. "I have. You should try it."

"You have?"

"Yeah, of course," she smiled.

"Yeah, Tyler, you should try it," Adam said without looking at me this time.

Hattie's response was innocent and playful. Adam's, daring and erotic. His tone holding a hint of humour.

I sucked in the sides of my cheeks. Hattie bumped her elbow with mine.

Pulling up to a house at the end of a street, it was big with a spacious front garden, which I already knew was a rare benefit that only wealthy individuals could afford. Cars were parked haphazardly along the road, in front of neighbours' houses, thumping music flowing from the walls.

Hattie and I threaded arms, walking up the stone path, and Adam didn't bother to knock, swinging the door open, noise hitting us like a wall.

People sat on sofas in the lounge or on the floor and lined the walls. A stereo pounded music from the corner. I followed the others through the house to a dining room and into the kitchen.

"Adam!" Christina's voice carried across the room, bouncing toward us in a slinky, silver dress to wrap her arms around Adam's neck. He returned the hug with a slack arm around her waist.

"Oh, hi guys," Christina didn't even try hiding her scowl when her heavily false-lashed eyes roamed over Hattie and me.

Tugging Adam's shirt, a seductive smile played on Christina's lips, and I wondered if they'd slept together?

He didn't stop her when she led him into the kitchen, offering him a drink from the row of glass bottles lining the counter, where she poured Adam a whiskey, swaying seductively in front of him.

My blood boiled. Adam's eyes watched her.

Callum graciously poured drinks for Hattie and me, and when Christina was practically rubbing up on Adam, I couldn't take it any longer, pulling Hattie towards open doors leading to a garden.

"Don't worry," Hattie faced me outside on the patio. Fairy lights draped along the side of the house caught the glitter in the blue-winged liner on her eyes.

"I'm not."

But I was.

Why had I hoped he'd push her away? Just because he was flirting with me in the car.

Of course, Christina would be interested in him. I just wish I'd been more prepared to deal with the fact that he was interested in her too, and *maybe* they'd already slept together.

I shook my head as if I could physically shake the emotions away. I was not this girl. Possessive and jealous wasn't me.

Surprisingly, I recognised a lot of faces from college, and Hattie and I threw ourselves into the party, mingling among the other attendees. I forced myself not to look for Adam, and not to be disappointed as the night wore on, and still, there was no sign of him.

I ended up sitting with Oliver, from the college bus, on a brick wall of the patio, a playful grin etched across his face.

"It's not like a porcupine!" he whined.

"It *so* is! It looks like you could draw blood on those tips," I teased, pointing at the hair that usually fell across his forehead but was now gelled into spikes.

"I dare you to touch them," he bent his head forward.

"No way!"

145

"Go on. Just once."

"No. They might put me into a coma like Sleeping Beauty."

"Comparing yourself to Sleeping Beauty? Don't flatter yourself," he winked mischievously.

I slugged him in the shoulder.

"Tyler." Came a familiar, velvety smooth voice.

Both Oliver and I swivelled to find Adam standing behind us.

"Hey Adz," Oliver smiled over his shoulder.

"Come," Adam said, ignoring Oliver, turning towards the house.

"*Come*," Oliver imitated.

I hit him again but didn't think twice before pulling myself up.

Adam had already retreated into the house. Not once did he look back, and I began to wonder if he'd meant for me to follow him. I kept a few steps behind, weaving through the crowd. Maybe he'd been talking to someone else?

He took the stairs two by two to the second floor, picture frames hung along the wall, a pink carpet leading to a spacious landing. At the top, there was a moment before Adam opened a door, dark eyes briefly catching mine, before he disappeared inside.

Pausing, I chewed the inside of my cheek, feeling like Alice chasing the white rabbit.

What was behind that door?

Wonderland, my mind whispered.

Every nerve in my body felt the pull, like a magnet to steel, wanting me to follow.

The phone vibrated in my hand, and I glanced at it quickly to find a message from Ryan.

I smiled, glad he'd *finally* replied. Tucking it in my jeans, I made a note to read it later.

With a breath, I pushed the handle of the door, eyes met with darkness.

"Adam?" I whispered—the beat of music below pulsed distantly through the floor.

A window at the end of the room bled light along the floor, bulking shadows of furniture here and there. But there was no sign of Adam.

Was there another door?

I stepped hesitantly in.

A warm hand wrapped around my arm, the door slammed shut, and I spun until my body bumped into the chest of another.

I knew it was Adam, purely from the scent of him.

He pressed his mouth hungrily against mine, as if I was the air and he was drowning, and he pushed until my legs bashed into something hard, sending something else tumbling to the floor.

Adam didn't stop, continuing to press until my back hit a wall, body crushing over mine, my face in his hands.

Kissing him was like being in the ocean during a storm; he was the waves, crashing, consuming, engulfing, his hands the frantic, powerful water. I couldn't breathe, but I didn't want to.

His lips were as impatient as his hands; I curved around him, fingers entwining in his hair, pushing the beanie from his head. He tasted of whiskey and smoke.

His fingers left trails of burning fire where they ran over my skin, hips moving tauntingly against mine. I'd never felt a hunger like this before. Not even with Luke.

Nipping at his bottom lip, I smiled in victory. I wanted Adam. I wanted him with everything I had.

My hands pushed under his shirt to a hard stomach, where his muscles were long and lean. I hadn't realised how much taller he was, not until now, with his neck craning to kiss me, body shifting to move his lips down to my chest.

My hands clumsily fumbled over his shirt, snaking towards the buttons of his jeans, when he grabbed both wrists, pinning them to the wall above my head.

I inhaled sharply at the force, at the pressure of one of his large hands easily holding both my wrists.

"Tyler," Adam purred into the crook of my neck, other hand caressing the skin on my tummy, above the waistband of my jeans.

My body shuddered in response. The sound of my name on his lips had me groaning.

"See," he nipped at my skin. "You don't want to be down there with Oliver."

"No."

Fingers travelled further up my shirt.

"You want me?" his breath was hot on my skin.

"Yes," I panted, pushing my hips against his.

He chuckled, a sound from deep in his chest. A sound that sent both goosebumps along my skin and ignited a fire in my tummy.

Letting go of my wrists, my shirt was swiftly pulled over my head before he effortlessly lifted my body so my legs straddled his stomach. Burying his face in my chest, he tilted me backwards onto something soft, lying on top of me.

Sitting up to pull off his shirt, I opened bleary eyes in time to see light from the window dance across his body. A chain glinted around his neck hanging over a patchwork of tattoos webbing their way over almost the entirety of his torso to meet with the ones on his chest and arms.

We were on a sofa, under a window, and he pushed a hand through his hair before reaching into his jeans pocket, pulling out a small, foiled square.

I knew we should be taking it slow. But I didn't want to.

I wanted him.

Right here.

Right now.

"You want me?" he said again as if reading my thoughts.

His eyes raked up and down my body. I squirmed under his gaze, wanting to cover myself with an arm, but he pinned both to my sides.

"Yes," I breathed.

"You don't want Oliver?" The shadows in his eyes were endless, the hunger mirrored in mine.

"No."

"You're sure?" A hand crept under my bra. I bit my lip with a nod.

His fingers expertly unbuckled the buttons of my jeans, and I wiggled as he pulled them down and over my toes, throwing them carelessly to the side. Pulling off his own, then his boxers in one swift move, my eyes widened at the sight of him towering over me, ripping the foil between his teeth.

His eyes, in the darkness of the room, looked like the deepest parts of the ocean, like the eye of a storm, never leaving mine; watching as I drank in the sight of him, confidence oozing from every pore.

He chuckled. "Have you done this before, Tyler?" He tugged at my pants, and my hands came down to cover me.

I nodded.

Of course, I'd done this before. But this felt *different*.

My body trembled at his feral gaze. At the pure animal thirst. His skin was soft, like butter under my tongue, half his face covered in shadows, the other half ignited just enough so that the pupil of one iris turned to an iridescent, glimmering opal. Phantom wings with dark membranes stretched between his blades, dancing along the roof, expanding to mingle with rippling lights that turned the roof to a glimmering night sky.

"Good, so I don't need to be gentle," he thrust, my eyes rolled back, my inhale swallowed by the darkness.

****

Adam sat on the sofa beside me. Sweat glistened on his back, my chest still heaving. A tattoo of a compass was on his ribs. On his bicep, curling round to his back and shoulder, was a phoenix with intricately inked feathers that I could see even in the near darkness.

My body shivered, slowly coming back from release, heat gradually fading as my skin cooled.

I didn't know sex could feel like *that*.

Adam pulled on his jeans, finding mine on the floor and handing them to me.

He hadn't yet made eye contact. Not since discarding the condom, tying the top and chucking it into a nearby bin. Not as he put his jeans on, then sat on the side of the small sofa.

My chest squeezed as I pulled on my jeans, the familiar pressure of tears pushing behind my eyes. I swallowed them back.

Luke had never been this cold. Never this distant. He would always let me lie with my head on his chest, arm wrapped around my body, burying kisses in my hair. But then again, he loved me. What we shared was something special. I barely knew this boy of shadows sitting next to me. And right now, I felt like nothing more than one of his conquests—another notch on his belt.

"Are you, OK?" he asked, head-turning, chin resting on his shoulder.

I nodded, not trusting my voice. Not knowing if I opened my mouth whether my voice would hiccup with tears, or croak in pleasure.

The long muscles on his back shifted, he turned, then those eyes *were* looking at me, hooded in pleasure, hair mussed.

"Scooch."

"What?" I baulked.

"I'd like to lie down too," he smirked, pushing me into the corner of the sofa, lowering his body beside mine.

I was preparing my heart, building a wall of adamant around it, for him to leave; to grab his shirt and disappear out the door with a casual "That was fun" thrown over his shoulder. But I hadn't expected this. Hadn't expected him to lie beside me, light from the window catching his lashes to throw long shadows down his face.

Lying on his back, tucking an arm behind his head, one long leg hung off the side of the too-small sofa.

My eyes wandered to his torso.

I'd seen the tattoos earlier, but I wasn't focused on them then. Now, I saw just how many there were. Only a small section on his stomach remained untouched.

Even his arms were covered in ink, exact pictures unrecognizable under the dim light, except for a rose that sat near his elbow.

"You have a lot of tattoos," I said quietly, a gaggle of giggles and shrieks erupted from the party below.

"Yeah," he ran a hand over his stomach where the tattoos stopped. "Do you have any?"

"No. I've always wanted one though."

"Maybe we can add that to our to-do list," Adam smiled deviously.

The way he said *our* sent a flurry of butterflies erupting in my stomach.

I scoffed. "We'll have to at least wait until I'm eighteen for that. And even then, I'll have to talk my dad into the idea."

"He doesn't like tattoos?"

"Not that he doesn't like them, only that he says it's a permanent mark forever, so *you have to be sure*," I lowered my voice, imitating dad's. "Do all yours have a meaning?" I trailed my fingers along a piece of ink that looked like it belonged to a mandala.

"No," he laughed, "most of them were just because I fancied it at the time."

"My dad will *love* you," I chuckled sarcastically.

Rolling onto his side, face only inches from mine, lashes almost grazing against my cheek, it was his turn to lift his hand, finger trailing lazily along my arm then up to my neck, over my chin until it rested on my lips.

"I like your lips," he said.

My body squeezed.

"What?" I'd always thought they were too small—even more so now after seeing the plump lip fillers that so many of the girls had.

"I do," Adam nodded, eyes half-lidded.

We stayed in our little cocoon for who knows how long, hours maybe, until Hattie's voice calling drifted upstairs.

"I think Hattie's looking for us," I sat up.

"They're ready to go," Adam's voice was heavy with sleep.

"How do you know?"

"Callum messaged earlier."

"He what? Why didn't you say?"

"Because I wasn't ready to leave."

His words did crazy things to my already frenzied heart.

When we rose from the sofa, our skin stuck together. Downstairs, the house was almost empty, littered in bottles and cups, bodies asleep on the floor and in every available chair.

We found Hattie and Callum quickly, and when Hattie gave me a questioning look, I whispered that I'd fill her in later.

This time, I sat in the front of Adam's car, sloppy kissing noises coming from Hattie and Callum in the back. Adam made a face that elicited a giggle from me, then turned up the radio, resting a hand on my thigh before entwining our fingers.

I would never have guessed how the night was going to end. I had *hoped,* but never would have been able to have predicted Adam's softness, compared to his indifference in the beginning. Hopefully, this Adam was here to stay, not the one that could have me on the verge of tears at any minute.

Outside Hattie's house, Adam pulled me across the console and onto his lap. Between the four of us, the windows steamed up within minutes.

The irrational part of my mind didn't care that Hattie and Callum were there—even if they weren't paying attention to us—because I *wanted* Adam again.

Rocking my hips back and forth over his jeans, he smiled against my lips.

"So greedy," his voice was gravelly, nipping my bottom lip. "But now is not the place," he pulled back, holding my face between his long fingers.

When Hattie and I finally stumbled into the house, the rumble of Adam's engine disappeared down the road, and we ended up in a love-drunk heap on the floor of her room.

My veins zinged with energy.

I felt so alive.

CHAPTER TEN

The next day, Adam and Callum picked us up around midday, having only crawled out of bed by eleven. The four of us spent the day walking around town, where Hattie convinced me to buy a box of dark brown hair dye with both Adam and Callum agreeing how much darker hair would suit me.

Adam led us to a small pub for lunch with low lights, the walls painted a deep, bottle green and covered in pictures of famous bands. It was girls versus boys at pool, and Hattie revealed her hidden talent, thrashing the boys. Adam leaned over me at the pool table, his body connecting with mine, fingers brushing the hem of my skirt to send shivers across my skin.

"Foul play!" Hattie shouted, my cue going wide, barely touching the white ball. Callum and Hattie quickly disappeared when Adam lifted me onto the side of the table, legs either side of his hips. The upper level with the pool tables was empty, and I barely thought twice when Adam's fingers found their way up my skirt.

That evening, Hattie covered her hair in the usual reddish colour, before sitting me down, wrapped in a towel, in front of the bathroom mirror to spread liquid through my hair. The air was full of the stench of chemicals, a nervous thrill tingling through me.

Bending over the bath around thirty minutes later, dark brown water disappeared down the drain, excitement sparking in my veins at the thought of a new me.

By Sunday evening, I finally returned home with shiny new hair, and a brand-new sense of excitement for the future.

Mum and dad weren't mad about the dye, as I'd been afraid they would be—both agreeing it looked very natural, though I could see the happiness behind their eyes that I was finally settling in.

Tucked in bed later that night, my mind still buzzed at how perfect the weekend had been. Hattie. Adam. All of it. Opening Facebook to do my usual social media scroll, I noticed the little red number indicating a message.

Ryan.

I'd completely forgotten he'd messaged.

Eagerness had me clicking quickly into my inbox, where I was happy to find a decent length message:

Ty,
I can't believe we haven't spoken in so long. So much has happened! Firstly, and you're not going to believe this, but I'm in the UK too!

My spine went rod straight. I scrambled to read further.

Whereabouts are you? I'm in London, in a place called Greenwich. Would be so cool if you were somewhere nearby. What are the odds that we'd both end up in the same country?

What college are you going to? I'm in University in Plymouth but stay with my parents in Greenwich out of term time. Ryan xx

Quickly pulling up Google Maps, I typed 'Greenwich, London', chest rising and falling in anticipation.

Three hours.

He was three hours away from me.

Ryan Adams, the boy I had been in love with since I was six, the boy who was torn away from me just as something was blooming, had been in the same country as me; no, not just the same country, *but three hours* away from me for months, and I had no idea.

The thought of seeing him sent shivers of excitement through me. I never thought the day would come.

Pressing reply quickly, my fingers flew over the keypad:

You're in the UK? I can't believe that! When did you come here? Why have you not told me before?

We live in a place called Gloucester; I go to Cirencester College.

I still can't believe we're on the same continent. It's going to take a while to sink in xx

Hugging the phone to my chest, I waited for him to reply, mind whizzing with the idea of seeing him again.

The excitement I felt wasn't the same as the feeling I'd got about seeing Adam the day after the party. No. This kind of excitement, for Ryan, was... My mind struggled to piece it together. It wasn't lust, but an age-old feeling that was born once we'd left Australia. Once I'd finally moved on, with Luke, and now with Adam.

Ryan was a constant to me. Something rare and special that burrowed its way deep into my heart that I just knew would always be there.

No matter how far apart we were.

Although now, it seemed as if that distance was about to get a whole lot smaller.

With thoughts of seeing him running rampant through my mind, I struggled to sleep, waking the next morning groggy when my alarm sounded off at six-thirty.

Ryan still hadn't replied.

"Mum guess what," I bounded into the kitchen, dropping my backpack beside the breakfast bar where she had already laid out a spoon and bowl for my cereal.

"Good morning to you too," she smiled from the sink.

"Ryan is here in the UK!" I blurted.

"Ryan? As in Ryan Andrews, from Australia?"

"Yes, can you believe it?"

"His parents used to talk about coming here, I guess they finally did it. How long have they been over?"

"I don't know. He hasn't replied yet," I shrugged, pouring cereal into the bowl.

"Well, isn't that nice? We'll have to try and see them at some point."

My eyes brightened.

Ryan didn't reply for most of the week, but I was so preoccupied with Adam that I barely noticed.

Adam and I texted every day. When the college days were over, I found him waiting for me in the car park on either his bike or in his car.

He took me places I'd never been, showing me the sights of Gloucester, touring Gloucester Cathedral, walking Cheltenham High Street or just hanging at his house, which he'd inherited from his grandad.

It was big as ours, old fashioned on the inside, his grandad's things still spotted here and there in the rooms—but it screamed Adam. I couldn't imagine him redecorating or contemplating what sofa would best suit the room; like the thought of a rocker in a furniture store. His only addition: a drinks trolley that held some expensive-looking glass decanters.

We went on double dates all the time with Hattie and Callum—who had officially asked her to be his girlfriend—and ate at the Chinese place around the corner from the cinema almost every weekend.

It was a few weeks before Adam asked me to be his girlfriend, and I was so giddy that I leapt onto his lap, kissing him with my answer.

Winter had finally descended. The leaves and grass glistened with frost that turned the world into an icy wonderland. Ryan and I messaged back and forth often, regularly talking about meeting up, but I'd been too busy with college and Adam to find the time.

He told me that he had a girlfriend, Sarah, who he went to university with, and I was surprised when there wasn't that familiar pang of jealousy that always used to follow me around when it came to Ryan. Just further proving my theory; I was finally out of my Ryan Andrews' infatuation stage.

Trying to convince Adam of that was another story, though. He often saw the messages coming in from Ryan, and as much as I tried to reason with him that Ryan was *just a friend*, he wouldn't believe me.

As weeks turned to months, I found myself quickly telling Adam that I loved him. When he said it back, a flurry of butterflies erupted in my stomach. By spring, the bare trees began to show first signs of renewal, the air finally warming when Ryan said that he wanted to come and visit.

Without hesitation, I said yes. My parents and Mel were eager to see him, often asking when he was coming, so I jumped at the opportunity.

It wasn't until we were deep into plans for his visit during one of my boring Sociology classes, and I'd offered him the sofa at our house for the night, that he asked if Adam would mind.

I paused.

Yes, the answer was yes. Of course, Adam would mind. How could I be so stupid?

I already knew Adam didn't like me talking to Ryan. So much so that I'd begun hiding Ryan's messages and lying when Adam asked. I felt bad about it, but there wasn't anything going on between us. Plus, I was reluctant to let go of our newfound friendship, no matter how much Adam disapproved.

Once, when Matt from college messaged me, Adam flew into a rage, accusing me of chatting up other guys. We were in town at the time, which resulted in a very public screaming match. But I didn't care. I was furious that Adam would think I was interested in other guys. Furious that he thought I wanted anyone other than him.

How *dare* he?

"He's gay!" I had yelled, by that point, people were stopping and pointedly staring at us.

"I don't fucking care, if he's gay!" Adam seethed. "He probably has a thing for you and is just hiding behind being gay."

There was no reasoning with him when he got something in his head. We could go around in circles for hours.

Eventually, I'd stormed off, even though I knew he was following—seething, but following, nonetheless. He never let me walk off alone, no matter how angry were at each other.

Finally, after an hour of stomping through the High Street, we ended up at the docks, calls of gulls overhead, stench of seaweed on the wind, sails flapping in the breeze, when I stopped. Adam was a few feet away. I had my arms folded defiantly over my chest, but my breathing had returned to normal. When our eyes met, I knew he was sorry, just as I was, and we rushed to each other, starved of one another's touch, crushing our mouths together.

"I'm sorry," I whispered against his kisses.

"No, I'm sorry" he shook his head, lifting me until I wrapped my legs around his waist, carrying us to an empty alleyway.

With my back against scratching brick, Adam's fingers snaked under my skirt and around my knickers, his body shielding us from onlookers.

That was how we were.

It was all fire and desire with Adam. One minute we could be screaming bloody Mary, the next we were making love against the wall of a deserted alley. I hated our fights, but I loved the making up. I loved how Adam made me feel alive.

Though now, having already made plans with Ryan but worried Adam would blow a gasket about him visiting, I didn't know what to do. I couldn't take back the offer. I'd even messaged mum and asked if it was OK; she was delighted he'd be coming to visit.

Adam will just have to deal with it, I thought, a surge of confidence swelling through me.

I'd never told Adam how I'd felt about Ryan in Australia. Adam already hated Ryan simply because he messaged me often, and I didn't want to give him another excuse to order me to stop talking to him.

I knew I didn't still feel that way about Ryan, and that was what mattered.

Adam was waiting in his usual spot in the car park at the end of the day, exhaust fumes pouring out the pipe when I climbed into the warm cab.

"There she is," Adam smiled, leaning over for a kiss. He wore a black beanie with a navy-blue sweater, the smell of cologne and oil mixing in the heated air.

I wanted to change my mind about Ryan. I didn't want to upset Adam. I loved him.

Hands wringing together in my lap, we headed for Gloucester, and I attempted to put a sentence together that was the least likely to upset him.

"You're quiet," Adam observed, warm hand resting on my thigh.

I smiled tightly. "I am? Sorry, just thinking."

"What about?"

It was now or never.

"Remember I told you about my friend Ryan? The one I knew in Australia?"

Adam snorted. "Yeah, the dickhead that keeps messaging you. What about him?"

His tone was already clipped; I swallowed hard against the lump in my throat. "Well, um, he's going to come and visit."

"He what?" A frown split down his face, he wrenched his hand away from my thigh, leaving the skin cold. "Why?"

"Well, because we, um, haven't seen him in ages, and Mel and my parents would like to see him again," I said quickly, throwing in the others as a buffer.

Adam shook his head, sighing loudly. "I don't know why you need to see him. You're barely even friends any more."

"We kind of are," I defended in a small voice.

"Have you been talking to him?"

I got the feeling if I said yes this already barely held-back Adam would explode. His grip was tight on the wheel, knuckles turning white as he waited for me to answer.

"No, not much," I lied.

"So why does he fucking think he needs to come and see you?"

"He's coming to see Mel and my parents too," I said again.

Adam laughed; it was a cruel sound.

How was I supposed to tell him that Ryan was going to be sleeping on the couch too?

I decided not to mention it. There was a week before Ryan was coming. A week to get Adam comfortable with the idea. A week to convince him that Ryan wasn't a threat.

We sat in silence for the rest of the journey. Adam was barely holding his anger together, and I wanted to do anything I could to make him happy again. Guilt twisted in my stomach. I shouldn't have said yes to Ryan. I knew Adam wouldn't like it.

Instead of going to Adam's house like we usually would, he pulled up in front of my mine.

"Adam," I pleaded.

But he didn't look at me, his stern gaze focused out the window, shaking his head in a small, continuous movement.

"Adam, please. It'll be fine. It's only for one night." Stretching out a hand to move the hair that had fallen across his forehead, he slapped it away.

"I just don't understand why you need to see him. Why do you want to see him so badly? Is he more important than me?"

"No," I breathed, shocked that he would even think it.

"Well, it seems like it right now, Tyler."

"I can't..." I sighed, really considering if I could cancel with Ryan. "I can't tell him not to come now. My parents are already expecting him."

Adam shook his head again, palpable anger radiating from him. His eyes clouded, like a thunderous sky.

"Come inside?"

"No."

"Please?" I desperately wanted to calm him the only way I knew how.

Waiting in front of the door, I watched as he raked a hand through his hair, in a movement I had come to recognise meant he was upset.

Tossing the beanie into the back, Adam finally got out, throwing the door shut loudly before slamming a fist into the roof.

Jumping at the impact, the sound of the metal groaning under his fist, I waited patiently for him to stop pacing back and forth. He came at me fast; I barely had time to register when he grabbed my arm, pulling me into the house.

"Are your parents' home?" he seethed under his breath.

"Mum? Dad?" I shouted through the echoing house. There was no answer.

Adam pulled me up the stairs. I didn't protest, knowing he was trying to keep calm. I just had to wait.

In my room, shoving the door closed behind him, I finally yanked my arm from his grip, spinning to look into his eyes before thrusting my mouth over his.

His hands were at my shoulders fast, as if to push me away, but he hesitated. For a moment, I thought he was going to do it, but then his fingers dug into my skin, mouth opening suddenly to an almost painful kiss.

Holding me so close against him, it was tight moving my hand to the buttons of his black jeans, rubbing over the fabric. He moaned against my mouth.

"You're mine," he said breathlessly.

"Yes."

"All mine."

"Yes."

An hour later, we lay on my bed, his hand lazily tracing patterns along my back, my head resting on his chest. His breathing had returned to normal, and I hoped, however naively, that would be the end of the argument.

At least until Ryan arrived.

****

A few days before Ryan was due, I still hadn't told Adam about where he'd be staying. Part of me was hoping Ryan would change his mind and book himself into a hotel. Or better yet, not come at all. But my traitorous mind couldn't help the zing of excitement to see him, or the sadness of him not coming, and I felt shameful for both thoughts.

For the first time, it felt as if I was cheating on Adam by being excited to see Ryan.

It was a Thursday evening. Adam and I had driven to the Chinese restaurant to meet Hattie and Callum.

Adam gelled his hair, so it had a wet look, and he looked devilishly handsome in a leather jacket, black V-neck tee and dark jeans. Hoping to impress him, I'd worn a tight black skirt with a white crop jumper, hair curled at the ends.

Out of the car, Adam came around the side, eyes wide at the bare skin on my thighs.

I smiled triumphantly.

"That's a bit short, don't you think?" He tugged at the bottom of my skirt.

"No, it's not," I giggled, slapping his hand away, walking in front of him to sway my backside seductively in his view.

"Fuck, Tyler," he groaned, looking around as if worried someone else was looking. "You shouldn't wear such revealing clothes in public. This," he cupped a hand around my bum, "is all mine. I don't want anyone else looking at it."

He kissed me deeply before we entered the restaurant, where we found Hattie and Callum at our usual table.

"Wow, nice skirt," Callum raised his eyebrows.

I blushed, catching Adam's eye as he sent a livid look at Callum.

Tugging him down next to me, I whispered in his ear. "Don't worry. He's just playing."

"Well, he can fuck off if he's going to say shit like that."

I'd become so used to Adam's swearing that I barely even noticed it any more.

"Adam?" came a female voice.

A waitress had paused beside our table. She looked older than us. Her dark hair pulled into a messy bun, black coal liner smudged around her eyes, looking at Adam as if she'd found a long-lost friend.

Adam looked momentarily confused, frowning at the girl before his brow relaxed.

"Jemma, hey." The apple in his throat bobbed.

"Wow, it's been ages!" She walked to him, wrapping her arms around his shoulders. "How are you? Where have you been?" she ignored the rest of us at the table. "Are you still working at that garage? I'll have to pop by and see you sometime." She bit her full bottom lip.

Adam didn't look at me. In fact, it was as if he was actively avoiding my gaze and nodded. *Nodded* his head? Did that mean he *wanted* her to stop by?

"Uh, well I better go," this Jemma said, seeming to realise we were customers, and she was at work. "See you later," she squeezed Adam's shoulder, nails covered in black nail polish, before finally looking at the rest of us, offering a smile before carrying on past the table.

"Who was *that*?" I'm glad Hattie asked.

"Just someone I used to know," Adam shrugged, absently placing a hand on my leg under the table.

Hattie and I locked eyes.

170

She pursed her lips, eyebrows raised. The look on her face said she caught the *tone* too. I wanted to ask him how he knew her, but I could already guess.

With Adam, I always felt my inexperience tenfold. Anger, jealousy, and irritation always came with running into his exes—which happened more often than not. Sometimes, I thought it would be nice if the tables were turned and we ran into one of my exes for a change. But with Luke being my only real ex, that was unlikely to happen.

Throughout dinner, I caught Jemma's eyes on Adam every now and again, and I couldn't help myself, pulling him for a kiss when I knew she was watching.

Back in the car after dinner, my phone beeped with a message. Pulling it out of my bag, Ryan's name flashed across the screen.

"Who's that?" Adam asked, eyes flicking to the screen. "*Ryan*? What does he want?"

I bit my thumb. *Stupid*, I could have smacked my head.

Adam snatched my phone, reading the message. "What does he mean is it still all right to stay at yours?" His voice was already rising.

"Um," *shit, shit, shit*. "Uh, he's going to sleep on our couch."

"No fucking way," fire erupted behind his eyes. "He is *not* sleeping on your fucking couch."

"Adam, it'll be fine!" My own anger rose. How could he be angry about Ryan when *Jemma* was blatantly throwing herself at him?

"Fuck this for a joke. No way Tyler, tell him to fuck off." Venom dripped with every word, and in my head, I saw a black viper rearing up, fangs exposed, oily skin glinting purple around a coiled body.

"And what about *Jemma*?" I crossed my arms over my chest. I knew it wasn't a good idea to prod a viper ready to strike, but anger swelled within me like a pregnant volcano, so I shifted from that timid white mouse in his path.

Adam frowned, face contorting as if I'd brought up plans for next weekend or what was for dinner tomorrow. "What about her? Don't try to change the subject."

"I'm not changing the subject. She is *very* relevant to this subject. You're worried about Ryan, a *friend*, when slutty Jemma was just draping herself all over you at dinner?"

"She doesn't mean anything to me."

"She doesn't?"

"Don't be stupid," Adam snorted. "Ryan isn't staying at your house. End of story."

"I don't know why you're so worried about him!" I shouted. "He's just my friend. It's not like he fancies me or anything."

"How do you know?"

"What do you mean, *how do I know*? Because I know."

"That's bullshit. He wouldn't be coming all this way if he didn't fancy you."

Dropping my head back against the headrest, "You're ridiculous," I sighed.

"Your parents won't let *me* stay over, but somehow, they're OK with this dickhead sleeping on the couch?"

"He's not just *someone*. Our families go way back. I bet you'd like him if you met him."

"I guarantee you I won't. But I *will* meet him. I'll be there the whole time he is," he shoved the car violently into gear,

Rolling my eyes, I knew it wasn't even worth fighting him on it.

It wasn't quite a clean win, but I'd take it.

CHAPTER ELEVEN

Mid-Saturday morning, dad and Mel headed to the train station to pick up Ryan. Adam came to the house early, waking me with a tormenting kiss, hands slipping under my T-shirt, then pulling away with a wicked smirk.

"That's mean," I scowled, peeking from below sleepy lids.

"Just reminding you what's waiting when this horrible weekend is over."

"It won't be so bad. You'll see, it'll be fun."

He snorted.

Adam waited in my room while I showered and washed my hair. Then watched as I picked my outfit. I tried not to let my nerves show, knowing he'd take it as a sign I was excited to see Ryan, and I was desperate to keep him calm. I'd even gone so far as to plan my outfit the night before so that Adam wouldn't see my nervous faffing.

At my dressing table, just about to put on make-up, Adam asked why.

"Why what?" I frowned at his reflection draped on the bed, the yellow walls far too cheerful for his glum expression, my blue dolphin duvet looking immature and comical below his dark form.

"Why are you putting make-up on?"

"Because I always wear make-up."

He raised an eyebrow as if he didn't believe me but kept silent.

I calmly breathed past the frustration; he knew I wore make-up every day and it was just his insecurity speaking.

I didn't want to argue. Not today.

My palms were sweating by the time Adam and I sat in the lounge, nestled on the sofa, waiting for the others to return. When dad's maroon car pulled into the driveway, voices drifted from outside, my heart raced.

This was really happening.

The door opened, Mel's laugh echoed through the hall, then dad said, "Come in, come in. No, don't worry about your shoes."

"Is that our Ryan?" came mum's voice from the kitchen before she appeared in the hall to undoubtedly pull him into a hug.

Adam's hand formed a fist where his arm draped around my shoulders. My heart ached for him.

I knew how badly he wanted my parent's approval. They had taken one look at his piercings and tattoos and made up their minds. I hated them for it. Hated that they had judged him in that way. I could only imagine how he must feel now; my parents fawning over a so-called nobody.

"Hi, Mrs Blake."

Goosebumps rose over my skin at the familiarity of the voice. It took everything I had not to leap off the couch and run into the hallway.

Instead, I swallowed, smiling reassuringly at Adam.

When footsteps finally made their way to the lounge, I used that as my cue to rise.

"Tyler," Ryan beamed, a warm, wide smile covering his face.

He'd grown. He wasn't tall like Adam, but where Adam was all long, lean muscles, Ryan was built like someone who grew up outdoors. His skin was still tanned and olive, despite the lack of English sun, and he wore a white Superdry polo shirt with blue-washed jeans, six o'clock stubble running along his chin.

My grin mirrored his, and Ryan reached out, pulling me into a hug.

Suddenly I was back running through the grass, songs of cicadas and melodies of kookaburras. The smell of meat sizzling in the open air, the stench of muddy earth and fish around the pond. There was the ghost of sunshine on my face, dirt under my nails, the cool air as the sun set, heat of the day retreating.

Nostalgia twisted around my senses, stomach leaping into my chest.

Adam cleared his throat too soon behind us, and I pulled myself out of Ryan's all-to-comforting embrace.

"Ryan, this is my boyfriend, Adam."

Adam stood, towering over us both, a hand outstretched. "All right, mate."

"Hi, Adam," Ryan smiled, grabbing his hand. "Nice to finally meet you."

"Likewise," Adam nodded gruffly.

I pleaded with my eyes for Adam to loosen up, but then Ryan draped an arm around my shoulder. "Wow, can't believe it's really you, Ty. It's been so long." He squeezed my arm.

How was it possible that years had passed, we'd changed so much, but somehow, he still seemed so... the same, familiar?

"This is so nice," mum beamed, entering the room, followed by Mel and dad.

Ryan was ushered onto the couch beside Mel and dad, Adam and I took our seats once again, and mum briefly disappeared into the kitchen before returning with a tray of mugs and a pot of tea.

Dad shot question after question at Ryan; asking about his parents and what they were up to, what kind of work his dad was doing, and where he was working. Mum cooed over his achievement at going to Plymouth University. He and Mel shared stories of their campus and study schedules.

Adam and I had barely said a word, though I was just happy listening to Ryan's familiar accent, his deep, rumbling voice that was the same yet different. Thankfully, Adam had relaxed beside me; maybe he'd been won over by Ryan's calm nature—something he hadn't lost with time.

"And Tyler," Ryan eventually turned his russet eyes on me when there were only a few sips of tea left in my mug. "I can't believe how much you've changed." Pink rose to my cheeks. "I remember when you were this big," he gestured with his hand to when I was about six, the height of the grass stalks when they towered over me. "How old are you now?"

"Seventeen," I smiled. "Eighteen in a few months."

"Of course, I should have remembered that."

"Well, what's the plan for this evening anyway?" Mum asked the room.

I shrugged and looked to Mel.

"I thought maybe we could go out if you don't mind?" Mel's eyes darted between our parents.

"Of course not," dad exclaimed. "I'm sure you youngsters don't want to be stuck hanging out with the old folk. Go. Go out. Catch up."

It had just started to get dark outside by the time we finished, and I ran to my room to grab shoes and a jacket, Adam following me in.

"See," I slipped my hands under his jacket, stepping into his embrace. "It's not that bad."

"If you say so," he dipped his head to kiss me.

Mel and Ryan were already waiting for us outside, Adam pulled car keys from his pocket.

"Oh, don't worry," Mel said. "I thought we could just walk down to the pub?"

"Sounds good to me," Ryan smiled.

"OK," Adam shrugged.

"So, Adam," Ryan fell into step beside him. The cul-de-sac was quiet, sharp streetlights pouring over the pavement. "What do you do?"

Mel looped her arm through mine, pulling me close, a few steps in front of them. "So?"

"So what?" I chuckled.

"What do you think?"

"He still seems pretty much the same."

Liar.

"Yeah, but so much hotter!"

"Shhh!" I shushed her quickly, the steady stream of their conversation following behind.

We lapsed into a fit of giggles like we used to when we were younger, whispering about the same Ryan.

"All right, I guess you're not allowed to say he's a fitty because you have a boyfriend," Mel rolled her eyes.

"Exactly," I nodded with a sly smirk.

Ryan held the door open for us when we reached the Greyhound pub on the corner, the room filled with warmth coming from a crackling fire in a grand fireplace.

The pub was packed, but we managed to find an empty booth in the corner, draping jackets and scarves over chairs. Adam and I slipped side by side into the booth. Mel and Ryan offered to head to the bar.

"What are you drinking, Ty?" Mel asked. "You can have a drink if you want, I doubt they'll ID," Mel shrugged.

"I'll have a cider please."

"Fosters for me," Adam said when she asked him too.

Placing her hand on Ryan's back, they made their towards the bar, I rolled my eyes at Mel; I guess some things never changed.

"So, what do you think?" I turned to Adam.

"Of?"

"Ryan, obviously."

Adam cocked his head. "He's all right."

I smiled, nudging his shoulder. That was Adam talk for 'he's nice'.

Fingers entwined in his lap, he brought the back of my hand to his lips.

When Mel and Ryan returned, the conversation was easy—Adam even cracked a smile—and I finally allowed myself to relax, slumping into the cushions of the booth.

"My round, is it?" Adam indicated the already two deep worth of empty glasses littering the table.

"I'll help!" Mel bounced to her feet again, leaving Ryan and me at the table this time.

"So," Ryan turned, the other two lost amongst bodies crowding the bar.

"So," I smiled.

The crackling glow from the fire in the grate warmed my already flushed skin, hot, stuffy air making me dozy. There was even a pink tinge to Ryan's cheeks, which made me wonder that perhaps the manager should turn down the heating a notch, or at least crack a window.

"This is a bit weird, isn't it?" he scrunched his nose.

I laughed lazily. "A good weird?"

"Definitely." His eyes lingered on my face, and I looked away. "I missed you," he said gently.

When I turned to look at him again, his eyes were soft.

"You have?"

He nodded. "It's so weird seeing you again."

Weird. He'd said that twice now.

I tucked a piece of hair behind my ear. He reached out a hand, catching the strand, rubbing it between his fingers.

"And your hair is long. You always had it short. And darker?" He let it float to my shoulder.

"Changes are inevitable."

"Some things never change, though."

What?

"Your accent has changed," he brushed swiftly past the last comment. "Is that a Jamaican twang I hear?" he put a hand to his ear.

"No way," I chuckled. "I'm glad to hear you still have yours."

"Well, I didn't leave as early as you. Kind of stuck with it now."

"Good," I couldn't stop smiling. "When did you leave Australia then?"

"Four years, now."

"Wow, so you're practically British."

"Yeah, yeah," he laughed lightly.

"How come you never said anything?" I hadn't realised how hurt I was that he'd never mentioned it before. Not four years ago, or even that time that he'd called when I was in Jamaica.

Shaking his head, he scratched the back of his neck. "Not sure. No reason. I guess I just thought you'd moved on and wouldn't be interested."

Sitting back in his chair, there was no insult intended in the statement. A rock settled in my chest at the realisation that he thought I could ever have forgotten about him or wouldn't want to hear from him.

"Ah, it's about time," his contemplative eyes turned to Mel and Adam returning with the drinks.

It was well after eleven when we finally made our way back to the house, and I stood with Adam at the door, others already inside. I could tell it was taking everything he had to leave.

"Be good," he said with a final kiss to my head.

"Don't be silly," I scoffed when he eventually climbed into the car.

Mel and Ryan were in the lounge when the door shut behind me, a blanket draped over their legs, Cadbury's bar being passed between them.

"Come sit," Mel motioned, holding up the blanket so I could slip in beside her.

The couch was big enough to hold three comfortably, but I was glad not to be the one squeezed up beside Ryan. His words were still fresh on my mind, Adam's kiss lingering on my lips.

The fire in the grate was lit, buttery warmth spilling into the lounge, and when Mel disappeared to put popcorn in the microwave, tension slithered its way up my spine.

Ryan was on his phone, and I slid a cautious gaze to him from under my lashes. My heart beat so hard that the cider in my stomach began to curdle with the chocolate, and even with the distance between us on the couch, I felt where the blanket over our legs connected us. As he shifted, it brushed gently over my thighs, as if he was touching me.

I was glad when Mel returned.

We decided to watch Crocodile Dundee for old times' sake, ending up in a fit of laughter the whole way through. When it finished, my eyes were heavy, and I made my way up to bed, Mel helping Ryan throw a duvet and pillows over the sofa.

That night, I dreamed of Ryan like I'd never dreamed of him before.

Dreams of him used to be as regular as the sun rising, but they were the innocent dreams of a young girl. Now, when I woke the next morning, I felt the ghost of dappled sunshine through leaves, tall, green grass swaying around my vision, and Ryan's lips on mine, the lingering touch of his hands on my stomach, the press of his skin.

The dream caught me by surprise, and I lay in bed, staring at the ceiling for much longer than usual, mulling it over.

I was so sure that any romantic feelings I had for Ryan were gone. Sure, that him coming this weekend wouldn't change anything. That I wouldn't *feel* anything except the love of seeing an old friend again. So, what was with the dream? What were the *feelings* now twisting in my gut? No. This couldn't be happening...

Shaking myself, I pulled the covers off, shoving my feet into slippers.

I was being ridiculous.

Who cares?

Who cares if, yes, maybe I did still like Ryan? Because he had a girlfriend, who he was gushing over last night. And I had a boyfriend that I loved. One I didn't want to lose.

Who cared if I still had lingering feelings? Ryan lived hours away; I doubted we'd see each other that much. This weekend was just a trip down memory lane.

A trip that would end today.

CHAPTER TWELVE

Ryan's train was booked for three that afternoon. On the way to the station, I tried not to think of the proximity of my knee to his, suddenly regretting the decision to sit in the back with him.

Dad and Mel maintained a steady stream of conversation, and I kept my eyes low, or out the window, watching the afternoon traffic get thicker the closer we got to the station. Although we'd texted a lot recently, it was different having him right next to me; the heat of his body, the aroma of his cologne, noticing the texture of the skin on his hands, nails cut short with white, pronounced cuticles, hair curling just above the neck of his T-shirt.

I spent so long pining after him when I was younger, it was a relief when I thought I was over him, but apparently, my hormones had a different plan.

Because that's all it was. Hormones. Reacting to the familiarity of him.

That was it.

At the station, his hug was warm and tight, and for one strange second, there was a moment—a split second—when his arms were around my shoulders, my hands spread over the warmth of his back, head tilted over his shoulder, that something strange tugged inside of me. It was gone within a flash, like an electric shock deep within my chest. When he pulled away, there was a nagging feeling as when a thorn is stuck in your foot, or a splinter in your finger.

Backpack over his shoulder, Ryan disappeared through the automatic glass doors, and dad wrapped an arm around both Mel and me, pulling us close. "Ah," he sighed.

Mel and I shared a look.

"Are you all right dad?" I asked.

"I think dads in love," Mel poked his belly pushing against the buttons of his shirt.

He puffed like a chicken in the rain. "Now, now. He's a nice guy, that's all. And grown up so well. Glad he hasn't turned into some of the riff-raff we see these days."

At home, Adam was waiting out front, cigarette in hand, leaning on the bars of his motorbike.

"Speaking of riff-raff," dad said under his breath. Mel swatted his shoulder; he winked at me in the rear-view mirror.

Adam greeted dad and Mel with a bob of his head before pulling me to his side for a long kiss.

"Adam," I pulled away, wiping my mouth.

"What?" he smiled mischievously.

"My parents."

He chuckled. "So how did it go?"

"Fine. Just dropped Ryan off."

"How come you went with?" smoke escaped his nose.

"Why not," I shrugged, pushing a pebble around with the toe of my boot.

With the hurdle of Ryan's visit over, things went on as usual after that; days spent at college and evenings with Adam.

Spring was ripe in the air, young leaves sprouting on bare branches, grass gleaming with a renewed acidic green, days longer and warmer as the sun rose earlier and set later. Icy cold mornings were replaced with fresh dew, and clouds cleared more often to show off a gleaming blue sky, as if it had just broken out of a hibernating cocoon.

Ryan and I kept in touch regularly after his visit, although I still had to hide the conversations from Adam, no matter how innocent they were.

We're just friends, I reasoned with myself.

That was all.

We weren't flirting. We were just talking. Ryan certainly didn't know I still had feelings for him, and I intended to keep it that way—because it didn't make any difference. I was committed to Adam, and he to Sarah.

On the couch one evening, watching a film, I dashed to the loo during the adverts, and when I returned, there was a look on Adam's face that sent goosebumps over my skin, hair standing to attention. His eyes were wide and dilated so that every pristine gleam of those piercing steel irises were visible, muscles shifting in his cleaned jaw, free hand moving as if squeezing a ball between his fingers.

Pausing at the door, I finally noticed my phone in his hands.

"Adam…"

"What the fuck is this?" his tone was deadly. My heartbeat fluttered like a trapped butterfly. "Have you been talking to Ryan?" He spat Ryan's name as if it tasted foul in his mouth.

"Adam," tears pricked my eyes. I wanted to lie to stop the fury steaming off his body. But there was no way out of it. "Just sometimes, Adam. Honestly, it's nothing," I pleaded with a few cautious steps into the room.

He stood, flinging my phone across the room, where it crashed loudly against the wall. With two vast strides, he was in front of me, hands grabbing my shoulders, shoving me painfully against the door frame, grooves biting sorely between my blades.

"Why have you been talking to him, Tyler?" his face was only inches from mine.

"We're just friends," I squeaked.

"Fuck that! Don't *fucking lie* to me. What happened? What happened between you two?" The viper was back, storm clouds thundering in his eyes, bolts of lightning ripping across his face.

"Nothing. Nothing!" I yelled. "He just messages me sometimes, and I reply. I don't want to be rude. You must have seen it? There's nothing to our conversation. We're just talking," I pleaded.

Surely, he could, at the very least, see that.

His eyes searched mine, looking for the truth, seeking out the lie, a harsh line between his brows. His breathing was heavy, the pulse at his neck fluttering inside protruding veins. Finally, releasing my shoulders, he paced away.

A ball of crackling energy emanated around him. Pushing a hand through his hair, he made a deep, guttural sound, before flinging the remote against the wall. Pieces flew, landing silently on the soft beige carpet. Sweeping an arm over the coffee table, my teeth were clenched so tightly that my jaw began to ache, fingers digging into the skin on my arms. Like being in the eye of a storm, it was as if the room was shaking, my vision dappled by tears.

"Adam! Adam, stop! Please," I wept.

Pausing, he turned, body trembling with rage. "You won't talk to him again." He pointed a menacing finger.

It wasn't a question

"I won't," I shook my head.

Retrieving my phone, the screen webbed in cracks, he unlocked it before opening the contacts to find Ryan's number—*delete*.

Opening my Facebook, clicking on Ryan's profile—*block*. He removed every trace of him. Instagram. Twitter. Even going so far as to delete any previous messages.

Once finished, sitting on the sofa, his eyes stared without seeing into the distance.

I waited. Like a doe aware of a lion stalking in the grass.

When Adam finally looked at me, my heart was still racing, but the storm clouds had finally cleared, and he could see past the thunderous rain, at last noticing the water trails down my cheeks. His features softened, and he walked quickly towards me, placing an agonisingly gentle hand on my cheek, wiping at the tears with his long thumbs.

"I love you, Tyler. Please don't talk to him," he whispered.

"I won't."

"You are everything to me." His arms wrapped around my body, a protective dome, engulfing me in a bubble, pulling me to his chest.

Relief flooded through me, and I leaned into him, allowing him to be the strength when my knees threatened to buckle.

For a minute, I worried he would end it.

I thought he would tell me to get out and never talk to him again. My phone was cracked, the remote in pieces on the carpet, the contents of the table on the floor, but at least I was still here.

At least he still wanted me.

****

I cut Ryan Andrews out of my life for the second time. Except this time, it was partly by choice.

I understood why Adam asked me to do it. Why he didn't want me talking to Ryan. I had betrayed him by going behind his back. If blocking Ryan out of my life was what my relationship with Adam needed, then I'd do it.

For my eighteenth birthday, Adam wanted to take me to his favourite bar, but Hattie moaned that his choice was too dull for an eighteenth and that we should go to a nightclub instead. In the end, we compromised—Adam's choice first, then Hattie's to end the night.

"I want to give you your present," Adam said delicately to me that morning, long fingers trailing patterns along the bare skin of my back.

"Presents? I love presents," I rolled over hopefully.

Sun shone through the window perfectly to catch all the sharp angles of his face, making him look angelic and terrifying all at once.

Lowering his mouth to the tender spot on my collar bone, metal on his tongue sent shivers down my spine, hand snaking beneath the duvet, he tugged at my thighs.

I playfully squeezed them closed.

"Come on, better get dressed," he pulled away.

"What?" I sat up, frowning, "I thought I was getting my present?" I pouted.

"You are," he pulled on his jeans, "but this isn't it," he winked, throwing me a shirt.

Walking down the High Street, hand in hand, my eyes drifted over every shop, wondering which one he'd pull me into. Eventually, instructing me to close my eyes, we walked a few metres more before stopping, and he turned my shoulders.

"Open," he said quietly.

My lids parted slowly until a store with a big, black sign and purple looping ink was revealed in front of us, 'Skinz'.

I spun to face him. "A *tattoo*?"

Adam smiled proudly. "Yeah. This is where I got most of mine done. Remember I said it was something we could do together?"

My pulse raced. "Adam." I shook my head, but adrenaline coursed through me.

He guided me into the shop with a secure hand at the base of my back before my mind had even stopped reeling.

The inside was dimly lit, walls black with hints of silver and purple shimmering within the wallpaper. The lights had deep mauve shades around them, giving the room a violet glow, windows blacked out so that only once inside you could see the street on the other side.

A chill ran through my body, and I wrapped my arms around my chest as Adam headed to the singular counter, where a burly man with a long beard and bald head with tattoos over almost the entirety of his head sat reading a magazine. If Adam hadn't pulled me in, I don't think I would have had the courage to walk into a place like this on my own.

Heavy, black-bound books lay on tables placed around the room, open to show various assortments of artwork in plastic sleeves. The books were deep, tattoos on each page.

Flicking through the pages, I wondered how I was ever supposed to choose just one. No wonder people had so many. How did you stop with all this beautiful artistry to choose from?

On the walls were bigger, more elaborate pieces in coloured ink, looking more like posters I'd hang on my wall than something that could be put onto skin. Black and silver sofas were in the centre of the room, Adam and I were the only customers, and I sat in an armchair, pulling the closest book on my lap.

What would hold the most meaning to me?

A tree of life—a symbol my mum and grandmother had always treasured. A minimalist kangaroo to define my background. A butterfly—because I always described the feelings Adam gave me as butterflies in my stomach. Or did I go for something more symbolic; a compass to represent all the places I'd lived, each a place I'd call home in their own way.

Spotting an image, suddenly I remembered something I'd found weeks ago. How had I forgotten? I'd shown Adam, saying it would make a perfect tattoo.

Wrapping his arms around my shoulders, Adam placed a gentle kiss on the crown of my head, "Why the frown? I thought you'd be excited?"

"I am, I just..." I sighed. "You remember that design I found a few weeks ago? The one I said would..."

"Make the perfect tattoo?" he finished, pulling a folded paper from his pocket.

"You didn't?" I breathed.

His smile wasn't wide and broad like a Cheshire cat, it wasn't small and bleak, but understated and beautiful, gentle in a way that was as rare as a solar eclipse—and all for me.

"This isn't your only present though," Adam said, handing the design over to the man at the desk, who disappeared to trace it out.

"It's not?"

"I'm getting one too."

"What are you getting?"

"The same as you, but with a few 'manly' changes."

Matching tattoos? My smile faltered. That was... huge. I pushed the thought away; it was just a tattoo, right?

A few hours later, the crook of my right arm burned from the inking, clear plastic wrapped around my elbow where a delicate diamond shape flanked the crease of my inner arm, a small, perfectly gentle flower blooming between it. Hattie was waiting outside the tattoo parlour with a bright yellow balloon floating above her head, the words 'Birthday Princess' printed on it.

Squealing when we exited, she shoved a tiny tiara on my head and the balloon into my hands. Adam shook his head, pulling me in for a deep kiss, which turned Hattie's cheeks pink, before leaving us to shop.

First on the agenda; find the perfect party dress.

In River Island around twenty minutes later—after stopping for a celebratory hot chocolate and brownies—in the changing room, Hattie lounged on a plush mustard sofa, sitting upright when I pushed the curtain of my small cubicle aside.

"W-o-w," Hattie breathed.

"Really?"

"You have to get it."

"It's not too short?"

"It's perfect!"

Tugging consciously at the hem of a strapless white dress that barely reached my thighs, I twirled in front of the mirror. "You sure?"

"Absolutely! It's your eighteenth, you're supposed to be a little slutty," Hattie winked mischievously. "Go on, let's see if you can dance in it."

"What do you mean?"

Hattie pointed a finger to the roof as if shushing me, or trying to point to something, so I looked up. When I looked back, she was bobbing her head, swaying this way and that with the top half of her body. Then I noticed the David Guetta song coming from the speakers, and swayed my hips, twirling.

Hattie clapped, whooping.

"You look H-O-T," she spelt the word, writing it invisibly into the air with her fingers. "That dress is meant for you."

Back in the cubicle and pulling on my jeans, Hattie said from the other side of the curtain, "So how do you like Adam's present?"

My eyes went to the tender tattoo. "I love it. Don't you like it?"

"No, no. I *love* the tat you chose. I just meant, you know, the matching one Adam got?"

Pushing the heavy curtain to the side again, dress draped over my arm, I joined Hattie on the sofa to lace up my boots. "I don't know, I haven't thought about it."

"Did you say you wanted matching ones?"

"No. It was a surprise."

"All good in here ladies?" A chubby, bored-looking store assistant appeared, looking as if she'd been sent in by her manager.

"Fine thanks. I'll take this," I lifted the dress.

"Bring it to the till, I'll ring it up for you."

Later that evening, we met Matt and his new boyfriend Noel, Nicky, Hannah and Gareth from the first party I'd ever gone to, at the club of Adams choice.

The place was more of a bar with low wooden, beam ceilings, red carpet and upcycled wooden chairs and tables. The lights were low, and it was crowded, which was always a good sign.

I'd spent over an hour straightening my hair, and for the first time, wore false eyelashes that sat heavily on my lids, making me feel like I was half asleep. Hattie, Hannah, and I pushed our way through bodies to the bar already sticky with alcohol and peppered with circular stains.

Proudly handing my ID to the bartender, nine shots were lined along the surface, black liquid poured to the brim. Hannah, Hattie, and I knocked one back before the bartender filled three more.

"Happy birthday, Ty! We love you!" Hattie shouted, back at the table, everyone lifting their shots in the air, calling my name, the delicious tang of liquorice and honey sliding down my throat.

A band played noisily in the corner, and already my head felt light. Adam had a protective arm wrapped around my waist the whole night, always tugging at the hem or top of my dress, eyes dipping regularly to the tattoo on my arm with a sensual smile. He whispered loving things in my ear all evening, saying I was beautiful, kissing my cheek, my temple, my hand.

A few hours later, we spilled out of the club, the air fresh on my bare skin, feet already aching in the too high, silver strappy heels. Giggling and stumbling along the road, the High Street was vastly different at this time of night; eery blackness filled the shop windows, doors padlocked shut. Lamp posts glowed brightly, so that if

197

not for the blanket of black above their glow, it could be day. Hordes of people ambled noisily between bars and clubs, Police, with their eagle eyes, dotted here and there, leaning against buildings. Taxis weaved carefully amongst the crowds, the smell of kebabs and pizza drifting through the air.

There was a line leading to the doors of Hattie's choice of club, but she insisted we wait, promising it'd be worth it. When we eventually made it inside, it was like nothing I'd ever experienced.

Strobe lights danced in the darkness, moving to pounding music. A bar ran around a big, open room, in the centre, a dance floor, packed with bodies. A DJ booth was a step above, disco ball hanging from the roof, sparkling in the dancing lights. There was no way people came here to talk.

This was where you come to dance.

Music resonated through my body, drumming in sync with my heart, whispering *dance, come, play*, like those of fae revels.

With the acidic glow of the strobe lights, it was easy to imagine that we were at a party filled with fantasy creatures; wolves lurking in the shadows, vampires sucking from necks on the dance floor, fairies floating through the air.

Matt grabbed my hand, pulling me straight into the throng of bodies at the centre of the dance floor, and for the first time that night, the warmth of Adam's hand left mine. Over my shoulder, I watched as he disappeared at the edge of the crowd, bodies crashing around me like waves of an ocean.

Adam's eyes twinkled, as if he belonged to the shadows, sucking in around him. Like an angel of darkness, velvety black wings spread behind him. Lifting my gaze away from his, I laughed into the air, Hattie and Matt either side of me. I began to move, swaying with the crowd.

We danced and danced until our skin was slick with sweat and my feet couldn't take the aching any longer. When we finally stumbled off the dance floor, the ground tilted under me, and I was about to fall, when there was the familiar warmth of Adam.

The rest of the night and journey home was a blur— there was a taxi, and I remembered resting my head on Adam's shoulder, but how I found my way home and into bed, was a mystery.

The next morning, I woke in Adam's bed, wearing his T-shirt, a low laugh coming from beside me.

"She's alive," Adam snickered.

I tried to hit him, but my head throbbed. "Ow," I croaked, voice barely there.

"Well, we know someone had a good night," Adam chuckled again.

Rubbing a hand over my face, the false lashes pulled painfully at my skin. With a tug, they came free, I sighed in sweet relief.

Adam and I spent the day in pyjamas watching trashy TV. That evening, we ordered from my favourite Chinese restaurant.

Turning eighteen meant the end of college, and on the horizon, the big decision of university. In the months prior, I had sat with my college tutor, filled in all sorts of paperwork, written at least five personal statements, and applied to countless Universities.

A few days after my eighteenth celebration—when the alcohol had finally worn off—mum and I sat at the dining room table, Googling University website after website.

The thought of university was daunting, especially when half of those I had applied to were over two to three hours away. Adam was the little devil on my shoulder, whispering that I didn't need to go. He'd never gone so, of course, that's what he thought. But truth be told, I didn't want to go too far away from him. I didn't want to have a long-distance relationship, and I didn't want this to be yet another relationship forced to end because life said it was time to move on. Though I also wanted to honour my parent's wishes and going to Uni would mean a lot to them.

When Plymouth University cropped up during our search, mum tried to convince me it was a good option. I was sure she was partly only pushing for it because Plymouth was where Ryan was. Immediately, I struck that one off my list. Not only was it too far, but Adam wouldn't allow it.

"Have you heard from him?" Mum asked.

"Who?"

"Ryan."

"No."

"Why not? I thought you two were keeping in touch?"

I shrugged. "Just because. It happens."

Thankfully, she dropped it after that.

****

On our first anniversary, I'd already started Uni at Hereford University of Arts, studying Graphics and Illustration, which was a sweet forty-five-minute drive from home. That evening, Adam picked me up from my house in dress pants and a button-up shirt, whisking me away for a romantic meal.

One year rolled into two, and for our second anniversary, we paid for a night in an extravagant hotel.

I slipped easily into university life, enjoying my classes, the teachers even more eccentric than the college ones. But, unlike the rest of the students who lived in halls or digs, I still lived at home, meaning I still got to see Adam all the time.

Mel gave me updates on Ryan—that he was still with his girlfriend, and in his last year at Uni, as was she. I tried to put him out of my thoughts, but just as I had always known, Ryan was destined to be in my life one way or another—it was just a shame that this fact

201

had such a negative impact on my relationship with Adam.

Mel and Ryan intended to meet up to go to a festival in a few weeks, and during our weekly catchup, she asked if I wanted to join. I hadn't thought of Ryan in almost a year—that was a lie—I *had* thought of him, but always pushed the thoughts quickly away, an ache in my chest for the friend I'd lost.

I didn't dare bring Ryan up with Adam since that incident all those months ago, but as Mel enticed me into seeing him again, there was a yearning that I want to give in to. But I knew better, politely declining her offer with the excuse of a deadline that week that would require all my attention.

At the stove in Adam's kitchen a few weeks later, pasta boiled sticky heat into the air, the radio played some generic, overplayed song, soap suds up to my elbows whilst doing the dishes. Through the window above the sink, trees swayed in an icy wind, light patter of rain dappling the glass.

Adam and I didn't officially live together, though I spent more time at his than at home these days, only returning to pick up new clothes or for a dinner here and there with mum and dad. Adam had asked me to move in multiple times, and as much as I wanted to, something kept me from saying yes.

Maybe it was the need for that other option, the escape, the excuse I could make when I needed a bit of my own space. Maybe it was simply knowing I wasn't ready for the commitment of my own home. Although, it wouldn't be *my* home. Adam would still have to take care of all the expenses, and that didn't sit right with me. I didn't want to have to depend on him entirely, and that thought scared me. Where would I be if he left me? Everything in this house was his, I would have no say to any of it.

"Tyler?" Adam's voice drifted from the other room, the clink of ice, a glass being put heavily down.

There was an odd note to the intonation of the question that I'd come to recognise. Straight away, my stomach somersaulted, mind scrabbling for what might have upset him.

I hadn't messaged Ryan, so it couldn't be that. I hadn't messaged, called, or spoken with any other guy...

"What is this?" he entered the kitchen, my phone facing outwards.

He was shirtless, long, lean, tattooed torso on display, a pair of Calvin Klein boxers peeking above Superdry joggers hanging low on his hips. My heart was already hammering. I wiped my hands on a dish towel, squinting at the screen. There was a message from a guy at Uni who was on the blacksmithing course. Just a single message, with no reply.

"What about it?" I asked, although I knew I was playing nonchalance, hoping it resonated on my face— just stalling the fight I knew we were about to have.

"Why is he messaging you?" Adam's tone was clipped.

"I don't know. You can see," I pointed to the obvious, one questioned message, drying my hands on a dish towel. "He was asking about my weekend. It was the weekend we went to Bath. He's from there, I guess he was just curious how it went."

"I can see that. But why does he care?"

"I don't know, Adam," I sighed in annoyance, throwing the towel onto the counter. "I didn't bother replying."

"Why does he feel like he can message you in the first place, is what I'd like to know." He slammed the phone down. I closed my eyes with a deep breath, the screen better not be cracked, *again*.

The guy in question, though on the blacksmithing course, was part of my friendship group, so I saw him often at lunches or even free periods when we walked into town. I got the feeling he purposefully tried to sit next to me, which was flattering—but I would never admit that to Adam, because I had no interest in him like that, and it wasn't worth the fight.

"What do you want me to say?" I asked.

Adam went icy still. "You know he fancies you?"

"So?" Probably not the best answer. I should have gone with deny, deny, deny, but it was too late.

His eyes widened as soon as the syllable left my lips. "So why are you leading him on enough that he thinks it's appropriate to fucking message you?"

"I didn't reply, Adam!" My own anger rose.

The pasta water boiled over with a hiss, and I pulled it off the hot plate, turning down the heat.

"You know I don't think of him like that, so why is it such an issue?"

"Because you must be acting like a slag at Uni when I'm not around."

I baulked. It wasn't the first time he'd accused me of such nasty things, but nevertheless, it hurt every time he did. Maybe he didn't see it as big of a deal as I did when he called me a slag, a slut, even though I recoiled every time.

"I'm not doing anything to lead him on," I snapped. "Why are *so* insecure that you have to keep asking me every time anyone messages me?" I specifically didn't add the part about looking through my phone, *again*. I suspected he did it often, which was why I was glad Mel had mentioned going to the festival with Ryan over a call.

Adam was quiet, there was a tangible shift in his energy, a change in the air, static zipping across my skin. Before I had a chance to register the change, his hand whipped out, slashing across my cheek. The skin burned hot, and I tasted blood where I bit down, splitting the skin.

Music played disjointly into the silence as we stared at one another. His chest heaved, nostrils flaring. Holding a hand to where he struck, tears pricked my eyes as the moment moved on, and it slowly dawned on me—Adam just *hit* me.

"How could you?" I whispered.

Of all the nasty things Adam said to me, he'd never struck me, instead, he turned fists on the walls or anything around him.

His stance was rigid, hands clenched at his sides and, for the first time, I was afraid that those fists would turn on me. His eyes clouded over, the veil only dropping lower and lower.

I needed to get out of here.

Turning, I lunged for my car keys on the counter, darting for the door leading onto the street where my car was parked. Adam, clearly not expecting it, took a second before chasing.

Sharp rain caught my bare skin, biting into the soles of my feet like shards of glass. I ran for the car, shoving in the key, slamming the door and hitting the lock just as Adam reached me. His shouts were muffled behind the glass, hair already hanging limply around his face, hands pulling at the handle.

Inside, the cab was dark and cold, my breath turning to mist, my hands shaking as I struggled to get the key into the ignition. I tried to ignore the pounding of Adams fists on the roof mixing with the heavy rain drops, the shouting, the swaying of the car as Adam pushed it, as if he could turn it over.

The key slipped in, and the ignition caught just as Adam turned, pulling a loose brick from the paved drive. Stomping on the accelerator, I was only mere meters away when he hauled the brick at the car, catching the boot with a deafening crack.

Wipers swished furiously across the windscreen, my mind and limbs disconnected. I raised my hand in apology to multiple other drives that hooted and shouted as I careened away from the house.

Gripping the steering wheel so tightly, my knuckles turned white, and when my hand moved to turn on the radio, to drown out the frantic swishing of wiper blades and pelting rain, my fingers trembled.

I didn't know where I was going, just that I drove and drove. Car headlights passed as I raced down the motorway, foot heavy on the accelerator, music blaring.

He didn't mean it; I saw the moment Adam wished he could have taken it back.

Why was he so angered over something so *minor*? Over someone who didn't matter to either of us. I always understood his anger towards Ryan—because Ryan wasn't a no one.

A finger absently rubbed over the tattoo on my arm. It had become the embodiment of Adam, something that always made me think of him whenever I looked at it. Typically, I loved that. But now, I scratched at it as if trying to scrape it from my skin.

I had lied to my parents when they'd first seen it; not an outright lie, just a lie by omission. If they knew that Adam had a matching one resting on the tip of his shoulder, a prickly vine where my flower bloomed, they would have been furious.

On autopilot, I drove until I pulled up outside Mel's dorm, surprising even myself when I'd realised the direction I'd been heading.

The rain had finally receded to a soft patter, and I sat in the silence of the car for a few minutes. I couldn't go running into Mel's room shoeless and frantic, or she'd be suspicious. This was just a normal visit… I took a deep breath in. I'd missed her and thought I'd take a spontaneous trip seeing as Adam was… out with friends.

Rummaging around the back where I kept a lot of my clothes these days, I pulled a pair of boots and coat from the back seat. In the mirror, I smoothed down my hair, wiping fingers under my eyes, even though, miraculously, no tears had been shed.

Her dorm was part of a row of tall houses, and I searched the numbers until I found number eighteen, hitting the buzzer.

"Hello?" she answered quickly.

"Mel, hi, it's me," I grinned tightly into the speaker.

"Tyler? What are you doing here?"

"I'll explain in a minute, can you let me in? It's bloody freezing."

The door buzzed, and I pushed it open.

Mel was dressed in pyjamas; laptop open on her desk beside a stack of papers. "Baby sister!" she pulled me into a hug. "What are you doing here?"

"Aren't I allowed to want a spontaneous trip to see you?"

She raised her eyebrows.

"Plus, Adam is out with the guys, so I thought why not use the evening to pop round?"

Mel looked at her watch. "Bit far to 'pop round,' but I'll take it," she grinned, pulling me into the room.

It was dark, only the light from the laptop and a single lamp filling the room. On the desk, beside her work, was an empty plate, Ketchup smeared over it. Two beds sat on either side, Mel's crumpled with use, the other pristine and unused.

"She's away for the weekend," Mel explained, following my gaze.

"Even better timing then," I smiled.

I didn't want to tell her about what happened. I didn't want her to hate Adam—I wasn't even sure I did. All I knew was that I was mad at him.

But I didn't hate him.

I had baited him. I had shouted too, said horrible things that might as well have been a slap in the face. I couldn't talk to Mel about it until I'd sorted it out in my head, because it would only make Mel even warier about him than she already was. And I didn't want that.

I waited on her bed while she finished up what she'd been working on before she handed over some leggings and a hoodie to change into—because I might as well stay the night—and then she made hot chocolates.

209

"Are you sure you don't want to come to the festival?" Mel asked again in the darkness of her room.

The quiet buzz of the hallway light flickered below the door, distant voices of university nightlife that never slept coming from the hall and windows.

"No," I shook my head.

Even though I was angry at Adam, going to see Ryan wasn't the answer. Even if, after all this time, the thought of Ryan's secure arms wrapping around me brought a lump to my throat.

No, I couldn't think like that. I pushed the thought away.

Curled up on Mel's bed, we watched a Disney movie, though I barely made it twenty minutes in before my heavy lids slid closed.

The next morning, I woke pressed up against the cold wall on Mel's small bed, Mel shaking my shoulder, the smell of coffee in the air.

"Wakey, wakey eggs and bakey," she sang.

Rolling over groggily, my hands wrapped around a warm mug. "I should come to stay more often," I smiled sleepily. "Hot chocolate *and* coffee. You're spoiling me."

"You're easy to spoil," she ruffled my hair. "But I do have an actual surprise for you," she sat on her roommate's bed.

The space was small, each with a study desk at the other side of the room and a tea station, fridge and sink in the far corner. Mel's desk was piled with books and papers, post-it's stuck on the wall amongst pictures. Her hair was short cropped around her shoulders, the ends bleached lighter than the rest.

"You have a surprise?" I sipped coffee just as a knock sounded at the door.

Mel squealed, leaping to her feet.

Oh no, dread sunk like a rock in my stomach, what if she'd called Adam? I wasn't ready to see him. Not yet.

But when the door opened, it was worse than I could have imagined.

Because in the doorway, was Ryan.

CHAPTER THIRTEEN

Ryan's smile was as warm as the last time I'd seen him. I tried not to let the shock at his appearance show on my face.

"Ta-da!" Mel said, like a magician who'd just pulled a rabbit out of a hat. But this was no rabbit—this was the inevitable ticket to my downfall.

"Mel," Ryan pulled her into a one-armed hug. "You didn't say Tyler was here." He turned those warm, brown eyes on me, a bag hanging from his hand.

"She surprised me last night. So, I thought I'd surprise you both," Mel clapped her hands like a cheerleader.

Dropping the duffel on the floor, Ryan walked to the side of the bed, pulling me into a gentle hug as if it was the most natural thing in the world. His sunlight and rain scent filled my nose.

No. No, no, no, no. This was not what I needed right now.

"Ryan," I finally managed, trying to shake the dumbstruck look from my face. "What...? How?" I looked between Mel and Ryan, eyes widening, nausea rising in my stomach.

No. Please tell me they weren't sleeping together...

Mel burst into laughter. "Come on, Ty," she said around hysterical giggles. "It's not what you're thinking, I swear."

Relief settled in my veins. *You shouldn't care even if they were sleeping together*, a dark corner of my mind whispered.

"What are you doing here then?" I looked at Ryan.

"Didn't Mel tell you? We're going to Reading Festival?"

"That's this weekend? Now?"

"Yeah, well you seemed upset last night, so I didn't want to talk about it too much," Mel shrugged.

"Upset?" Ryan's russet eyes turned to meet mine. "Is everything OK?"

I didn't know what it was, but with Ryan looking at me the way he was, the evident concern etched all over his familiar face, at the idea that I might be upset about something, *anything*, caused tears to prick my eyes. I looked away before they spilled down my cheeks.

I hadn't cried last night. Not during the two-hour drive to Mel's, or the sickly-sweet Disney film. Not even when we were tucked in bed, Mel's protective arm draped around my body.

But now, as Ryan waited for an answer, I scrambled to get my thoughts together, willing myself to keep it together.

"Nothing," I shook my head. "I'm fine," I forced a smile that felt wrong. A sharp pain pricked across my cheek. I flinched.

Shit.

"What was that?" Mel asked.

"What?" a hand went to my hair, pulling it over my cheek, praying there wasn't a mark.

"Why did you flinch?" Mel pushed.

"I didn't."

"You did. She did, didn't she Ryan?" Mel was like a puffed-up alley cat, hair raised along its back and tail, ready to fight.

Ryan was frowning too, and he nodded.

"I have a toothache," I tried to explain, rolling my eyes for effect.

"Oh, right. Well, you should go to the dentist," Mel conceded, the alley cat in her backing down.

Ryan's frown relaxed too, but didn't entirely disappear, when Mel began flitting around the room. His attentive gaze burned the skin on my cheek, and I became overly invested in drinking my coffee.

I couldn't believe he was here. Couldn't believe I'd spent so long avoiding him, and suddenly, we were in the same—relatively small—room. The air was tight, constricting my lungs, as if even sharing the same oxygen with him was wrong.

I was embarrassed that I hadn't spoken to him because Adam had deleted all traces of him a year ago. I was ashamed, the familiar pang of guilt rising—if Adam found out Ryan was here…

"Be right back," Mel said over her shoulder, disappearing down the hall, wash bag in tow. *Great.*

214

Ryan padded to the bed beside mine, and if not for the creak of bedsprings, I could almost have imagined he wasn't there.

"Tyler," Ryan said gently. "What happened?"

I didn't want to look at him. I couldn't. Scared that if I did, I might break into thousands of tiny pieces. And if that happened, I wasn't sure I'd be able to put myself back together again.

Instead, my finger traced patterns along the wall beside my elbow. "Nothing," I tried for a light-hearted laugh. "I just had a bad night, honestly."

I hadn't realised Mel had noticed, but I should have known I couldn't fool her.

Ryan sat so silently that, eventually, like a curious animal, I couldn't help looking at him.

His strong arms were braced on his knees, hands steepled in front of him. "I don't think that's true," he finally said. "Why is there a mark on your cheek?"

My eyes widened, but I schooled my features back into vague interest. "Oh, that? Nothing, like I said, I have a toothache."

"Toothaches don't cause marks, Ty."

"Well, this one has. I'm not a dentist. I don't know how," I snapped, not needing his questioning or judgement right now.

Dropping his head in his hands, Ryan pushed fingers through his short hair. I couldn't let him find out what happened, or he'd blow it out of proportion.

I could handle it.

215

"Look, I'm fine Ryan," I tried again. "Honestly."

Placing the empty mug on the side table, I climbed out of bed and began gathering my clothes from where I'd left them on the floor.

Don't let him get too close. Don't encourage him. Adam will be furious.

"I better get going anyway."

"You're not coming to the festival?"

I paused, biting the inside of my cheek.

Maybe I could go. I was here anyway, and what difference would a few more hours away make? "No, I have Uni work to catch up with."

Ryan rose, wiping palms down his jeans.

Don't look at him. Don't look at him. I swallowed against the urge, willing my eyes to stay focused on folding my clothes.

"At least, stay for a little? I haven't spoken to you in forever."

My heart raced and ached and stuttered.

A large part of me wanted to do just that. It felt like there was a magnet in my heart, pulling towards him, and it took everything I had to keep the distance between us, afraid that if I stayed, I wouldn't be able to leave. That he'd ask about my sudden radio silence a year ago and I wouldn't know how to answer.

So instead, I pushed past him, things bunched in my arms, out into the hall.

He followed to where I pulled on my boots, keeping my gaze on the floor, on anything but him.

216

"I have to go. Please tell Mel I'll message her," I said over my shoulder before walking quickly to the car.

Throwing my things into the back, I shoved the keys in the ignition and pulled away before Ryan could say anything else. Before I let myself give in to the need to hug him again. Rounding the corner, I allowed myself one secret moment, to flick my eyes to the rear-view mirror, to where Ryan stood at the door, shaking his head, retreating inside.

On the motorway, relief washed through me. I was neither here nor there, and in this place, nothing could hurt me, and I had nothing to feel guilty about.

Cranking the music to fill the silence, I let my favourite Taylor Swift CD fill the cab, drowning out thoughts that threatened to ruin the momentary release, with knowing that every minute, I got closer to Adam.

And with every minute, I got further from Ryan.

Why did I keep feeling like this around him? How had I let myself fall into this yet again?

It doesn't matter. You're with Adam, you still love Adam.

The words sunk across my mind, chest tightening in fear, in love, in concern. In burden. And a tear finally escaped down my cheek, leaking over the brim to obscure my vision.

****

217

I went home first. Running up the stairs before either mum or dad could see me.

I'd left all my things at Adam's, including my makeup bag and phone. Digging out an old foundation stuffed in the back of the dresser, because it was a shade too light, I pulled my hair away from my jaw to look in the mirror.

The mark wasn't big—how had Ryan even spotted it? There was a small blue-purple mark surrounded by red skin, which was thankfully easy to conceal.

Mum opened my bedroom door, head peeking through the gap. "Ty, honey? Oh, your home," her searching eyes found me at the dressing table. "I just wanted to let you know that Adam was here looking for you. I thought you were staying at his?"

"Oh, yeah, I was, but then I decided to drive and see Mel for a bit. So, I stayed the night there."

"OK," she nodded thoughtfully. "He dropped this off for you." She placed my phone on the side table, pulling the door shut behind her.

I had to talk to him. He was probably going crazy wondering where I was.

Sure enough, when I unlocked my phone, there were dozens of messages, missed calls and voicemails, all from Adam.

****

I didn't call Adam straight away. Instead, I lay on my bed, staring out the window for a few hours, watching the leaves on the tree shift against the wind, specks of sunlight filtering through to dance across the windowpane.

Finally, when it felt like the raging storm that Ryan elicited had calmed, I dragged myself up. Pulling on a pair of jeans and a grey jersey, stopping briefly in front of the mirror to check that the foundation hasn't rubbed off my cheek, I headed back for the car.

At Adam's house, it was only a few seconds before he came crashing out the front door. He didn't look angry, instead, his eyes were helpless and worried, hair standing on edge as if he hadn't stopped running his fingers through it since last night, deep bags hanging under his eyes.

In front of the car, he waited. I stared back, willing myself to hold it together.

My heart ached at the sight of him; shirtless, as beautiful as a tattooed angel, yet too dark, too full of angles and shadows. Spotting the tattoo on his shoulder, *our* tattoo, and as if reading my mind, he placed his hand over it.

Slowly opening the door, I stepped out, holding my head high, jaw clenched.

Adam's eyes frantically searched my face. He took a few small steps towards me, then fell to his knees in the grass, long arms wrapping around my waist.

"I'm sorry, Tyler," he wept.

My chest hiccupped at the sound of his broken voice, arms shaking around my body. My hands stayed mechanically at my sides, but as Adam's body shook and shuddered with tears, they found their way into his hair, where my tears mixed with the dark strands.

Seeing Adam on his knees in front of me, this usually strong and intimidating man, broken and asking for my mercy, I lost all resolve. Any thoughts I'd had of leaving him were washed away with both our tears.

****

I didn't tell Adam about seeing Ryan that morning in Mel's room. After our fight, he knew better than to push where I'd gone after I'd forgiven him. So, to my relief, it never came up.

Mel said that Ryan had been asking questions. That day at the festival, he told her that his messages didn't come through to me any more. That he couldn't find me on any social media platform, and what angered me the most, was that Mel didn't even bother asking why that was. Instead, she immediately questioned why I would let Adam do it.

Which was precisely what I didn't want.

I didn't want to feel like I had to defend my relationship to her. I didn't want her to judge it. I didn't want her to look down her nose at Adam, or us. But mostly, I was annoyed at Ryan for saying anything to her.

He's worried about you.

Mel had said in a text when I didn't respond.

And I'm beginning to think I should be too. Maybe Adam is bad news.

Maybe Adam was bad news? I couldn't believe I'd read it right. Sure, he was a bit overprotective, but it was just because he loved me.

Hattie messaged one day after Uni, a month or so after 'the incident', asking if I wanted to meet for a catch up at Costa, and I couldn't think of anything better.

I messaged Adam quickly to tell him I was going straight into town to meet Hattie, before shoving my phone in my bag. Once parked in the double-storey lot in town, a noisy wind whipping through the cement structure, I grabbed my phone to message Hattie, noticing a reply from Adam.

Do you have to go and meet her? I've been waiting all day to see you.

I smiled, feeling bad for blowing him off.

Tyler: *I'll only be about an hour. I haven't seen her in so long. I'll message you when I'm done, and you can meet me at the house if you like?*

Adam: *It might be too late by then. I have an early start tomorrow. Do you have to stay that long?*

Tyler: *I'll see how it goes. Talk to you later xx*

At Costa, Hattie was already in an emerald armchair beside a tall window, two large hot chocolates topped with whipped cream on the small coffee table between the chairs.

"Tyler!" she waved, as if it was possible to miss her flaming red hair that had only gotten brighter with the years.

"Hat!" I walked quickly into her arms.

She smelled familiar, of cinnamon and apples. Pulling apart, there was a shiny new nose ring around one of her nostrils.

"You got your nose pierced!"

"Yeah, finally," she touched a gentle finger to her nose. "Only got it done the other day, so it's still tender."

"Well, it suits you."

"How have you been? I can't believe we haven't met up in so long."

"I'm OK," I nodded. "How're things with you? How's Uni?" Hattie went to the University of Bristol, studying textiles.

"It's good. I got a recommendation from my tutor for one of my designs. He wants to put me up for an internship at a local design company."

"What? That's fantastic!"

She beamed. "Thanks."

"How's Callum?"

Her mouth quirked to the side in a grim little line. "We broke up."

My eyes softened, "Oh Hat, I'm sorry."

"It's OK," her playful smile returned. "It wasn't really working. And Adam? You guys seem to be going the distance." She playfully tapped my arm.

"Yeah, we're good."

"You sure?" Hattie asked. Whether it was the look on my face, or her best friend intuition that made her ask, I wasn't sure.

"It's good. It is. We've just... had a few problems."

"Spill," Hattie knotted her hands in front of her, settling in, ready to hear all my woes.

But where to start?

I didn't want to tell her about when Adam hit me. Even though she was my best friend, I didn't think even she would understand. Instead, I told her about the fighting, about Ryan and how upset Adam got over him. She sat quietly, listening to every word, rolling her eyes every now and again.

"He's just... a bit overprotective," I finished.

"Pfft, overprotective is an understatement! Sorry, but he's more like *controlling*."

Controlling? I'd never thought of it like that.

"No," I shook my head. "He's not controlling. He just..." I sighed. "He just loves me."

"Look, Ty, you might not want to hear this—and I'm not questioning his love for you—I'm just saying that with a guy like Adam, you need to put him in his place a little. Or he'll walk all over you."

I thought of the way Adam watched over my shoulder when I got a message. How he waited for me every day after Uni. How he didn't like it when I made plans, like this, instead of seeing him. But that day he hit me *was* the day I'd attempted to 'put him in his place' and look where that got us.

My phone vibrated, Adam's name flashed on the screen.

"Speak of the devil," Hattie mumbled.

I opened the message with a sigh:

Are you done yet? It's been over half an hour.

Irritation flared in my veins. I wanted to tell him that I'd be here for another few hours.

"How long have you been together now?" Hattie broke through my thoughts.

"Almost three years."

"Wow," Hattie breathed. "That means it must be your birthday soon? Twenty, getting old."

"Shut up," I swatted her across the table.

Hattie giggled, smacking me back. "We should go out for old times' sake."

"That would be nice."

My phone vibrated with another message from Adam.

Hello?

"Sorry Hat, but I better go," I finished the last of the hot chocolate.

"That's OK. This was fun," she smiled. "Ty?" I was gathering my things, pushing back the heavy armchair.

"Yeah?"

"Just remember, I'm here if you ever need anything."

I smiled, "Thanks, Hat," pulling her into a long embrace.

Instead of going home so Adam could meet me there, I went straight to his house, finding him in the garage, oil staining his fingers, fiddling with his bike. There was a definite argument coming on with the heat in my veins, and it wasn't something I wanted my parents to witness.

"There you are," he placed an oblivious kiss on my cheek, wiping hands on a cloth. "That took longer than you said it would."

Sighing heavily, I tried to quell the irritation bubbling inside me.

"I wanted to see Hattie. I hardly ever see her any more."

Adam shrugged lazily. "I don't see why you bother wasting your time anyway. Especially with someone, as you said, you hardly ever see."

"She's my *best friend*, Adam," I snapped. "Of course, I want to put the effort in to see her."

"I just don't see the point."

Anger surged. "Just because you can't be bothered to have a social life doesn't mean I shouldn't either."

"It's not that," he looked at me, clearly startled by my outburst. "It's just that I haven't seen you all day, and now we only have a few hours."

Controlling flashed across my mind.

"Hattie wants to go out for my birthday, and I do too."

There was no point waiting to tell him. I already knew he wasn't going to like it, but Hattie's words kept echoing in my head; *with a guy like Adam, you need to put him in his place a bit. Or he'll walk all over you.*

Sometimes Adam's love felt like more of a burden, and as soon as the thought left my mind, my chest immediately squeezed.

"Go out? Where?" Adam asked, a hint of expected annoyance in his voice.

I shrugged casually. "I don't know, maybe to town. I haven't done that in a while."

"You're just gagging to go out, aren't you?" he barked sharply.

A few weeks ago, my Uni was having a mixer event in Hereford. When I'd mentioned it, he'd said he would prefer it if I didn't go. I fought back, a little—all my friends were going, and I hadn't been out with the Uni lot again since my first fresher's week.

Although now, Adam was forgetting that I didn't go in the end. I didn't go because he said we could go to the movies and get dinner—which never happened.

"No. I am not *gagging*. It's my bloody birthday! I think you should be OK with me at least going to celebrate that."

"Yeah, that's fine. I didn't say don't celebrate it. I just don't see why you need to go out?"

I let out a breath in exasperation.

His hair was long enough now that it easily tucked behind his ears, a greasy strand falling across his eyes.

Putting fingers to my temples, I rubbed in slow, circular motions.

"Adam, I don't want to fight. Hattie and I haven't even decided what we are going to do, just that we should. And I would like it if you could be a part of whatever that might be."

He watched as I spoke, tongue running along his bottom lip. "Fine," he shook his head. "But I'd rather not go out."

A few nights later, Adam insisted on taking me to dinner—an unusual surprise, his way of making up for the fight I assumed. We sat in a restaurant overlooking the river. The lights were dimmed to create a romantic ambience, and Adam pulled a ring from his jeans pocket.

My breath caught in my throat.

No, panic skittered through my body like lightning.

Adam laughed, grabbing my hand. "No, Ty," he shook his head. "No, no, it's not that kind of ring."

I let out a small, controlled sigh.

The ring Adam gave me wasn't an engagement ring. "A promise ring," he said, placing the heavy thing in my hand.

It was the embodiment of Adam: beautiful and dark with heavy metal twisting in the centre around a deep, red stone. Haunting.

Slipping it on the middle finger of my left hand, Adam smiled proudly with a kiss to the stone.

"Do want to get married, Ty? Not to me necessarily, but in general?" he asked once our food arrived. But my stomach was still in knots, the pasta I'd ordered no longer appealing.

Contemplating his question; the answer was yes. Though after my reaction to his almost-proposal, I was afraid to tell him that now. There was no explanation for why I felt the immediate surge of panic. Maybe I just wasn't ready for marriage right now, not that I didn't want it with *him*.

"Um, yeah, I think so. Why?"

Adam shook his head. "I just don't think it's in the cards for me." A sigh of relief escaped my lips. "To me," Adam continued, "that," he pointed at the ring, "and the tattoo, are my kinds of commitment."

A flush warmed my body.

228

I'd somehow accepted two of the things he considered more important than marriage.

****

By the time my birthday rolled around, I was excited beyond words. After a lot of coercion, Adam finally agreed to the night; we'd go to The Regal and have a few drinks, seeing as it was a half bar, half club. A happy compromise.

Adam invited one of his friends so that he didn't feel out of place with Hattie and me, and I was glad he did, so we could do our thing without having to worry about him. I didn't know his friend well; he cropped up every now and again when I made plans to do something. Harley was a slimy guy that, for whatever reason, I always felt uncomfortable around. But for tonight, I'd take whatever I could get.

Digging out the dress from my eighteenth birthday, the white one that I hadn't had a reason to wear again since, I grinned when it slid easily on.

Adam tried to tell me I couldn't wear it, but Hattie and I had already had a few pre-drinks, and I was feeling the liquid courage coursing through me. I marched out the door before he had a chance to force me upstairs to change, which he did too often these days.

As soon as we stepped into the crowded club, a surge of happiness washed through me. I'd missed going out. I used to love the vibration of the music, the way the flashing lights created a kaleidoscope of colours behind my eyelids. Maybe it was Jamaica that had instilled the love of dancing in me. I'd never forgotten that time I'd danced with Luke, the rain falling around us, humid air caressing our bodies.

The Regal was as grand as its name. With tall ceilings and fancy chandeliers, the front more 'bar', with the 'club' section starting with the dance floor at the centre.

We found a table and ordered a round of drinks on the level up from the dance floor near the back. Pulling my phone from my bag, there was a message from Mel:

Happy birthday, baby sis! I hope you have fun tonight and dance your little butt off! By the way, Ryan asked me to wish you a happy birthday too.

Ryan. He kept cropping up.

I used to be the one that tried to stay in contact with him, but now it seemed that the tables had turned.

"Who's that?" Adam's voice drifted across the table.

Thankfully, he sat on the other side, so couldn't read over my shoulder. I quickly deleted the message and smiled.

"Just Mel wishing me a happy birthday."

He sat back in his chair, inquisitive eyes searching my face.

I wasn't going to let him ruin the night, wouldn't let his 'controlling' get under my skin. Smiling sweetly, I sipped my vodka and coke.

We ended up staying most of the evening in The Regal, even though we'd planned on moving on—but the music was too good, and Hattie and I were having too much fun on the dance floor to worry about going anywhere else.

After what felt like hours of nonstop dancing, singing at the top of our lungs, hair sticking to the sweat on my neck, feet aching, Hattie shouted, "Outside!"

Adam was still at the table with Harley, both looking glum and moody when Hattie and I spilled into the beer garden, tripping over our own feet, giggling and hanging on to one another for support.

The world was coated in a haze. I didn't care though; a free kind of happiness that I hadn't felt in a long time filled my veins.

The beer garden was filled with wooden tables and benches, a pergola to one side, creeper winding its way through the rafters, fairy lights twinkling amongst the vines. Tall, burning red heaters towered over tables, plumes of smoke and cold breaths lifted into the air.

Hattie pulled us onto a bench beside a table with a group of people, bargaining with a guy for one of his cigarettes. Bargain-flirting was more like it.

"But what do I get out of it?" the guy said playfully, quirking a blonde eyebrow.

"You'll get the pleasure of our company," Hattie draped an arm around my shoulders.

"Oh, well then, that sounds like a decent bargain," he laughed, light and easy.

Handing Hattie a cigarette, he lit it for her before offering one to me. I began to say no, but then Hattie bumped my elbow. "Go on."

"Oh, why not," I laughed, taking it from his hand, inhaling as fire met the end.

The smoke burned its way into my lungs, and I choked, feeling as if I'd swallowed acid.

Hattie and the guy laughed.

"She's a rookie," Hattie said.

"Urgh," I held a hand over my mouth.

"Try again, it'll be easier this time." Hattie took a long drag, thick smoke billowing into the air—she made it look so cool.

On the second go, Hattie was right, it was easier, and as the smoke circled through my lungs, my head felt light, amplifying the alcohol already flooding my body.

"Wow," I swayed. "You're sure this is just a normal cigarette?"

Hattie and the guy laughed.

"So what's your name?" Hattie asked, moving closer, huddling together for warmth.

"Hmm, the power of a name," he contemplated.

"Hey, no fair, you know ours," I raised my eyebrows.

"Fine, fine," he chuckled playfully. "It's Ozzy."

"As in Ozzy Osbourne?" Hattie exhaled.

He laughed, nodding. "As in Ozzy Osbourne."

When Ozzy's group retreated inside, he joined us at our table. He was sweet, easy to get along with, and Hattie was definitely flirting with him. We'd been outside long enough that the sweat dried on my skin, a cold chill running down my body.

"You're cold?" Ozzy asked.

"Just a smidge."

"Here," he shrugged off his jacket.

"How chivalrous," Hattie cooed.

It smelled of beer and smoke, making my mind turn to Adam, wondering where he and his surly friend had got to. A part of me hoped that someone had joined *his* table, eliciting a laugh out of them both.

"Have you ever seen one of these?" Ozzy presented a small, rectangular item with an engraving on the front.

"Yeah, it's a lighter?" Hattie said, unimpressed.

"Not just any lighter. It's a limited-edition Zippo."

"Let me see," I grabbed his hand, pulling Ozzy and the lighter closer.

"What the *fuck*," Adam's snarl cut through the noise.

Ozzy was yanked backwards, flying off the bench, arms sailing into the air.

"Who the fuck do you think you are? Get your hands off her!"

Falling to the ground, Adam towered over Ozzy, fist held just above his face, shirt balled in Adam's other hand.

"Adam, no!" I shouted, but it was too late.

Adam's fist collided with Ozzy's jaw, his head snapping painfully back. Blood streamed from Ozzy's nose, and he held his hands out desperately in front of him. "I'm sorry man," Ozzy pleaded. "Nothing was happening, I swear!"

Adam looked like the angel of death towering over poor Ozzy. His eyes flared red. He didn't stop. The sickening sound of flesh crunching together, the metallic stench of blood filling the air.

Hattie's hands were around her gaping mouth, and I ran to Adam.

"Adam! Adam! Stop it!" I grabbed his arm, but then the fist that was meant for Ozzy suddenly turned on me.

The force of the punch knocked me back, a stranger's hands catching my shoulders before I hit the ground. Small bursts of light crackled behind my lids, and my brain turned fuzzy.

"Tyler? Tyler, are you OK?" Hattie's voice filtered through the fog. She stood just above me, one hand shaking my shoulder, the other resting on my cheek.

Tears ran down her face, mascara streaking under her eyes. I wanted to tell her not to cry, that she was ruining her makeup, but the words wouldn't come.

"Get out my fucking way! Move you fucking idiot! *Move*!" Adam's voice echoed around us.

"No mate, you stay where you are" came a voice I didn't recognise, then there were the sounds of flesh meeting flesh again.

I needed to get up. I needed to stop Adam, but my body wouldn't respond. Then Hattie's soft hand was ripped away, and hands grabbed my arms, yanking me off the ground.

I knew it was Adam, and suddenly I was scared. Scared like I'd never been before.

My head hurt as he jerked me up. I tried telling him to stop, but he shook my body like a ragdoll. Through fuzzy eyes, I saw a man—a man that was once my loving Adam—but the man in front of me, digging his fingers into my arms, shaking me so painfully that a searing pain ripped through my head, was not that Adam.

This Adam, the one that turned my veins to ice, whose too dark eyes became endless black wells, was out of control, anger rippling through his body as if he had finally let the transformation take him. Let the viper out.

"You're wearing his jacket?" Malice seethed from Adam. The jacket was yanked from my body, cold air meeting my skin again, an involuntary shiver quaking through me. "You bitch! What were you doing with him?" Adam barked.

Two men with bulging muscles pushing against black T-shirts grabbed Adam by the arms, but he wouldn't let go, his fingers digging into my arms.

"Let her go, mate," one of the bouncers warned, the other attempting to pry him away.

A crowd had gathered around us, angry shouts coming from onlookers, and on the floor, Ozzy's friends had gathered around him.

"Adam," I pleaded in a weak voice.

Fairy lights turned to hazy halos, Adam's form split and multiplied in front of me.

"Let her go, Adam!" Hattie cried, hysteria and panic in her voice.

Finally, Adam released his grip, quickly pulled away by the bouncers. Without his support, my legs buckled underneath me, but Hattie and another girl were quick to wrap their arms protectively around my body.

Holding my head in one of my hands, I squeezed my eyes shut against the thundering pain ripping through my brain. Hattie cried beside me, nuzzling into my hair. Placing a hand on her head, I wanted to tell her I was fine, that she shouldn't cry.

The darkness was sucking me in, but I forced my eyes open to where Adam still fought against the bouncers, herding him out like a wild animal, arms wide, levelled voices forcing him to retreat.

Our eyes met, and I truly had no idea who he was.

His eyes were no longer comforting steel, instead, they were slit like a snake, black, with anger and hatred pouring from them. He was shouting, yelling something at me, but I couldn't hear past the buzzing in my head, and then, the world turned dark.

CHAPTER FOURTEEN

The bright lights of the hospital bed made my head ache even more than it already did, stench of bleach heavy in the air. I woke a few hours after passing out, with Hattie's hand tucked in mine, to a doctor shining a light in my eyes, telling me I had a concussion.

The doctor said I had been lucky—though I didn't think that was quite how I would have put it—that it could have been worse if Adam had managed to get my jaw. I should be glad it was only my forehead…

The statement didn't sit quite right with me as the gruff doctor left the room. *I should be glad it was only my forehead*…I guessed that at least was true. It could have been worse.

The idea scared me so much that it was an effort to keep my body from trembling, remembering poor Ozzy. Was he here too? Was he OK? The doctor said he was fine, a lot more banged up, but he'd heal.

An angry purple bruise blossomed over my right eyebrow, small bruises from Adam's fingers dotted down my arms.

"I'm sorry," I whispered once the doctor was gone, but Hattie shook her head.

"It's not your fault." Her eyes were red, mascara smudged down her cheeks. It was strange to see her this way, as if the ever-present glimmer inside of her had dimmed. It wasn't long before my parents came rushing to my side too—there was no hiding what happened this time. No hiding it from anyone.

Adam had been karted off to who knows where, and honestly, I didn't want to know. Harley was strategically absent from the whole thing—taken off when Adam had started punching, probably. The details of the end of the evening were hazy and unclear, but what I could remember as clear as day, was the fear that had gripped me at that moment. When Adam's fingers dug into the skin on my arms. The feral look in his eyes.

The stranger.

I'd never been so afraid of him, even when we fought, even when we argued. But there was something in his eyes that night, as he shook me. The rage had finally consumed him.

When the hustle and bustle of doctors, nurses, mum, dad and Hattie cleared, and I was left alone at last, my heart shattered for Adam. For us. Because we couldn't be an *us* any more.

Not this time.

I couldn't understand why he acted the way he did. If only he could see into my heart, know that he was who I wanted, who I chose, every day. That was impossible though, no matter how much I tried to explain it to him, and that was why this had to end.

A bruise along my forehead this time... but what about the next?

We'd been plastering over a wound that needed surgery, trying to pull together the edges of an injury that only festered and gnawed and worsened with every attempt to conceal it.

I missed the next week of Uni, not wanting to explain the bruise that was taking its sweet time to heal. I was ashamed that I'd let someone do that to me. Even more ashamed that it wasn't just anyone, but someone I thought loved me. Though even now, I didn't doubt Adam's love, but I was coming to understand it was too all-consuming. Unhealthy.

With every step I took back from our relationship, I saw clearer and clearer how every moment lead up to the inevitable of that evening. If it weren't that evening, it would have been another. Perhaps I should be grateful that it happened as it did... What if it had been just the two of us? I shuddered, always pushing *that* thought away.

I was stupid for always going back to him. For pushing away the warning signs, ignoring the cautions of others. After all, it was harder to see things for what they were when in the middle of it. I knew that now—especially when I didn't want it to be true.

One evening, the bruise had finally faded enough to allow foundation to cover it and sitting on my bed watching a movie on my laptop, my phone pinged.

Then again, and again, and again.

Frowning, I paused the film, grabbing it from where it lay on the duvet, stomach sinking at the name continuously flashing across the screen: Adam.

Tyler, I need to talk to you.
I'm so sorry, you know I didn't mean it. I was angry.
I know nothing was going on with that guy. I can't make excuses for what I did, but I know it was wrong.
Please talk to me.
I need to hear your voice.
I need to know you're OK.

The pinging stopped for a moment. I bit my thumb.

Tyler, talk to me. Please. I need you.

Wind howled outside my window, tree branches scarping eerily against the glass, silhouettes of leaves shifting against the curtain. An undeniable longing made me want to press reply, when I thought of Adam, torn apart and miserable. A piece of me wanted to stop him from hurting, to comfort him.

My finger hovered over 'reply'.

Was I overreacting? He was clearly sorry for what happened, and he wouldn't do it again. This could be a lesson for him. If I left him now, was I throwing away the progress he'd made?

My chest shuddered.

The image of Adam when we'd first met flashed through my thoughts; the beautiful shadows that curled around him, the way the flames of the fire in the park that day flickered across his perfect face, the pull I felt even then.

Heavy rain began to fall outside, pelting the house like bullets, drumming against the window. Pulling the curtain open to watch the drops smacking against the glass, I closed my eyes, listening to the rhythmic beat of their onslaught. Maybe I'd message him back…

"Tyler?" Mel paused at my door. "Are you OK?"

She'd been home more often these days, on my account.

Turning, I knew my eyes were brimming with tears. Her frown softened, and she walked quickly across the room, in time to catch the buckle of my knees. "Shh," she cooed, guiding us back to the bed, hand stroking soothing circles down my back. Holding me silently for a minute, she finally asked, "What happened?"

As if in answer, my phone vibrated in my hands. Mel's eyes pulled towards the screen, but she didn't need to read it to know it was Adam. To know what was going through my mind as she pulled away, wiping a stray tear from the tip of my cheek.

"Ty," she breathed. "I know what he meant to you; I do. But please, *please* try to understand what he did wrong. Not just the hit, but the other stuff too."

The other stuff. The stuff that I hadn't realised—the manipulation, the gaslighting, the *controlling*.

"I know," I croaked. "But he won't do it again. I know he won't. He was just as scared as I was—"

"Tyler," Mel cut me off, voice stern. "It wasn't just that he hit you. That was fucked up, but there's more to it than that. Surely you can see that now?"

All the times he tried to control me. All the times I thought he was cute when he would tell me I shouldn't wear this or that, or my skirt was too short, my top was too low.

I saw it now.

But most of all, I was coming to understand how the guilt I always felt was a product of his creation— because he was the one that made me feel like it was wrong to see my friends. Wrong to want to go out. Wrong to even talk to another guy that wasn't him— even if it was just out of friendship.

Mel watched while I processed through the thoughts, reminding myself why it wasn't just the punch that was the problem.

Tears dried on my cheeks, my breathing became easier. In the quiet, the rain continued to fight against the wind, ripping through the night air.

"You see, don't you?" Mel's hand held tightly to mine.

I nodded. It was only small, but all the recognition she needed.

I read the new message he'd sent:

Baby, please come back. Maybe our relationship just needs some work. We can work on it. I promise.

He did this. He did this to me, to *us*.

Sitting straighter, Mel nodded curtly. With a firm kiss to my head—the side without the bruise—she left. I hit reply:

> *Adam, we can't do this. Not after what happened. I believe that you are sorry, I truly do, but it has to stop. I can't let myself be sucked in by you again.*

I read the message over, deleted the end and retyped:

> *Adam, we can't do this. Not after what happened. I believe that you are sorry, I truly do, but it has to stop. Please stop messaging me. It's over.*

I hit send. A moment later, he was replying.

> *No, it's not over Tyler. I don't want it to be over. I can change. I can be better. I can take you out every night. We can spend as much time with your friends as you want. We don't even have to see each other every day any more if you need some space. Please.*

My heart hiccupped with all the new promises. All the things that inevitably led to our demise. All the things I wanted from him over the last few years.

Heart pounding; my cheeks were on fire, I decided to send one last message:

You hurt me, Adam. We can never be together again. I just hope that you learn from this, and the next girl you're with, you treat her better. Learn to compromise on the things she wants as well as what you want. But mostly, please know that violence is never the answer. I pray that the anger I saw in your eyes the other night never returns.

Then I did the thing I'd witnessed him do those years ago; I blocked his number from my contacts, and everywhere else.

****

The next few months were excruciatingly hard. Although Adam was blocked from contacting me, he knew where I lived and went to Uni.

The first day he turned up outside the house, it took everything I had not to break. Seeing him made it so much harder to turn him away; his dark, bruised and bloodshot eyes, the way his skin seemed to sag, the sadness pulling down his mouth. Honestly, I wanted to give in to Adam that day. I knew what he did was wrong. Knew I shouldn't want to go back to him, but there was something, as I looked into his red-rimmed eyes, that pulled me to him. I wanted to comfort him. Make his pain stop. Maybe I could help him…

But I stood silently; his arms wrapped around my waist. It was Mel that finally helped me escape. Striding from the house, exuding the air of a goddess of war, with gentle hands at my shoulders, she guided me from Adam's destructive gravitational pull.

Adam tried sending flowers too, but mum always turned them away, hoping I wouldn't notice, but how could I not? The deliveries came so often.

It was a slow and agonising process, like pulling ivy from the gaps of a building, leaving gaping cracks in its wake. I was the house, Adam the ivy that grew in between everything I was, weaving his way through me, until every brick was so twisted with vines that there was no way to tell where the house began, and the ivy ended.

I gave everything to Adam—every piece of me and removing him would take time. Although the vine was finally gone, between those cracks, I still found pieces of him. It was as if he'd died. Even though it was my choice in the end, the option of staying together had been ripped away when Adam made that final blow.

During the last few months of Uni, I was determined to make up for lost time, for the experiences I'd lost. Adam never liked me going out, so I went out every weekend, taking full advantage of my newfound freedom, drowning my sorrows in alcohol and late nights, strangers, and strange places.

I watched the sun rise on my many walks home, the ghosts of unfamiliar hands plaguing my skin, until I got home and scrubbed my body raw—then did it all over again.

I woke in the dark of nights to dreams of steel blue eyes, tattoos blurring into collages of colour that drowned and choked me, the only way to banish the nightmares with alcohol. I looked through the window of our love, pulling away the boards, scratching at the nails until my fingers bled, just for a glimpse of what was.

I'd finally got my great love, but had I made the right decision in leaving it behind…

Graduation was now just around the corner, and I stared at the reflection of a girl in a short, lacey, peach dress with a round neck and capped sleeves, the waist coming in at the middle with a black belt, paired with low, pale pink kitten heels. I looked feminine, grown-up, and I was proud of the girl in the mirror. She'd come a long way since her idea of dressing up was a 'nice khaki T-shirt and jeans'.

But below my eyes was still the unmissable sag of exhaustion and sleepless nights, the droop of my skin, too sharp collar bones.

The red ruby on the ring I still wore glinted on my finger, and I stared longingly at the beautiful stone, guilt twisting in my stomach at how I had reacted the day Adam gave it to me.

Pulling it from my finger, I squeezed it in my hand for a moment, feeling the bite of sharp metal against my skin, before opening the small wooden box mum had given me for my birthday. There, at the bottom of the box, was the graduation ring from Luke.

My chest ached as I added Adam's beside it, at the rather pathetic collection of gut-wrenching memories tucked away in a box.

Mum gasped at the door. "Oh, Ty, honey. You look *gorgeous*. So grown-up," she came to stand behind me, I pushed the lid of the box shut, turning to face her.

"Don't cry, mum," I chuckled. "It's not graduation yet."

"I know, I know," she dabbed at her eyes. "I'm just so proud of you sweetheart, and it will be sad to see you go after graduation."

She pulled at the back of the dress, at the extra material that had once fit snugly, before letting it drop with a wave of her hand and a shake of her head. "What made you pick Peru, anyway?" she asked, sitting on the edge of my bed.

A spark ignited in my chest at the mention of my new adventure. An adventure that promised to take me far away from everything.

"Well, you know Natalia, the lady I told you about that runs the animal sanctuary there?" Mum nodded. "I've followed her for ages on Facebook, and I've

248

always thought how awesome it would be to go and volunteer there," I leaned against the desk. "And you know, after graduation, there'll be nothing holding me back. I don't have a job yet, and I know I'll have to get one eventually. And no… boyfriend around, so why *not* Peru."

Mum nodded again. "Yes, I see. It all makes sense, of course," she fiddled with the childhood rabbit I kept on the bedside table. "It's just so far."

"Well, I've moved around enough, I think I can handle it," I winked.

"That is very true," she sighed, placing the rabbit tenderly back on the side table.

The one-way ticket to Peru was in my inbox, ready to be printed the day after graduation. I needed to go somewhere I could have a clean slate. Somewhere where every corner didn't hold painful memories. To put some distance between Adam and me, so that not only I, but he could heal too.

The animal sanctuary run by Natalia was on the coast of northern Peru, in a small town called Colán. Natalia was always taking on volunteers and, during their stay, gave them free bed and board in exchange for much-needed help around the sanctuary. Now was the time to do it, I'd realised a few weeks ago. Probably the only time in my life that I'd have as much freedom as I did. Before I stepped fully into adulthood.

Peru was far enough away that I could escape it all, get away from the memories, get far enough away from the pull of Adam.

****

The night before graduation, a large suitcase sat at the base of my bed, already half full—I'd spent my days thinking more about the upcoming trip than graduation. On my bed with my laptop, even now, I scrolled through pictures of Machu Picchu, eyes filled with wonder, heart racing at the thought that I'd be there, standing amongst the ruins, soon.

A soft knock came at the door, the handle pushed down, Mel appeared.

"You should be getting your beauty sleep, you know?" she raised her eyebrows. "You want to look your best for those graduation pictures tomorrow. Trust me, I know about a bad graduation picture haunting you. You don't want that."

I laughed, pushing the lid of the laptop closed. "Yours isn't that bad. You can hardly see the seed stuck in your teeth."

Mel dropped her face between her hands shamefully. "It's going to take a lot of work to get mum and dad to take that picture down. I might have to get married just so they use the wedding photos instead." Coming to sit on the side of my bed, she eyed the suitcase. "I can't believe you're leaving."

"It's not for good."

"No, but it *is* a one-way ticket. Do you have any idea of when you'll come back?"

I shrugged. "A couple of months?"

"You don't have to go, you know?"

"I know. I want to. I need this. A fresh start."

Mel nodded.

"You could come with?" I tried, but we'd had this conversation before.

"I have a job now. I'm doing the grown-up thing, remember?"

A smile tugged at my lips. "I know, but it's worth one last try."

"Well, I'm going to go get *my* beauty sleep. Maybe I can sweet talk your photographer into retaking my picture," she wagged her eyebrows, now standing back at the door, pausing her retreat. "Oh, I almost forgot to mention. Ryan said good luck tomorrow."

My smile faltered. Mel's eyes gleamed before closing the door with a soft click.

The absurd thing about the whole situation with him, was that nothing *actually* ever went on between us. We were just old friends, trying to be friends again. To keep the friendship alive. But the way Adam perceived it all put an air of something else over it. Something more than friendship. Embedded an idea that was never actually explored by either of us.

Of course, Ryan had said something a little confusing that time in the pub, and I had

had *those* dreams, but in reality, there was nothing between us—I laughed at the absurdity of it.

Grabbing my phone to open Facebook, I searched for the list of blocked contacts. When I finally found it, my eyes widened—there was more than just Ryan on it. When had Adam added all these people to the list?

I began the task of unblocking everyone, getting to Ryan, clicking unblock, then onto his profile to open a new message.

Thinking for a moment, I considered what to say. The fact that he had asked Mel to tell me good luck meant he was still willing to try at this friendship thing, even after what I dragged him into.

Hey stranger.

I wrote, pressing send—happy with the simplicity of the statement. I was about to place the phone back on the bed when the screen lit up with his reply.

Well, well, well. Look who it is. Nice to finally hear from you.

I laughed.

Tyler: *Yeah, yeah. Mel passed on your message. So, thanks xx*
Ryan: *What message?*

My cheeks turned hot.

Tyler: *To wish me luck at my graduation tomorrow?*
Ryan: *That's tomorrow? I'll have to thank her for thinking of things for me before I do.*

My face flamed with embarrassment. *Mel.* She knew exactly what she was doing by passing on that fake message, knowing I wouldn't message Ryan if she had been the one to suggest it.

Ryan: *I heard about you and Adam.*

My heart hammered.

Tyler: *Yeah. I'm sorry about everything.*
Ryan: *Don't be sorry. I'm just sorry I couldn't do more when I saw the signs.*
Tyler: *I think if you had tried, we wouldn't be having this conversation now.*
Ryan: *Probably, I guess everything happens for a reason, hey?*
Tyler: *I'd like to think so.*
Ryan: *Are you OK?*

There was so much weight to the question, so much behind it.

Tyler: *I will be.*
Ryan: *That's the Tyler I know. So, am I allowed to come and visit? What's your plan for graduation night?*

My heart fluttered weirdly at the thought of seeing him again. Maybe we did have a real shot at this friendship thing. After all, I'd probably only be in Peru for a few months. We could keep in contact while I was away, and honestly, I wasn't worried about the whole last-time-I'd-seen-him-I-still-liked-him thing. Because one, he still had a girlfriend even if I was single. And two, I wanted to be on my own for once. I didn't want to jump straight into another relationship. I needed time to myself, to figure out who I was on my own. I just hoped my stupid hormones respected that.

Tyler: *Want to come visit tomorrow? You can help me celebrate.*

****

Graduation went off without a hitch; I walked on stage to accept my degree, smiling for the picture, shaking hands with the heads of the University. Outside, I posed with my classmates while parents surrounded us, snapping proudly away, before gathering in a group to throw our hats in the air.

The day was beautiful; sky blue, air warm and, even better, my hair had somehow turned out perfect. I felt light, carefree, and looking forward to the future.

Standing beside Mel while dad took our picture, she'd worn a figure-hugging, royal blue bandage dress hugging her curves, an arm draped over my shoulder, we pulled silly faces. Over dad's shoulder, a movement caught my eye, goosebumps ran along my skin, and I spotted a familiar shadow under the tree.

"That's enough, dad," I laughed tightly, hand in front of my face like a celebrity, "How about some with mum and Mel?"

"All right. Go on, your turn." Dad tapped mum on the bum, and she ran to join Mel, just as Mel said, "These pictures are *so* nice, we should definitely replace the ones on the wall at home with these."

I stared across the grass, unmoving, watching the man under the trees run his hands nervously through his hair, as I built a wall of adamant around my heart, pieces clicking and locking into place, slotting together like a puzzle. With a breath, I walked across the green, heels catching in the ground, graduation hat twisting in my hand.

The dark shades surrounding him melted away the closer I got, until his true form appeared—my angel of shadows.

Adam's hair was cut shorter than I'd ever seen it, and he looked hauntingly handsome in his black suit and matching dress shirt. The bags under his eyes were only slightly visible, a shiny new ring in his eyebrow catching in the light. A smile tugged his mouth to the side, and I remembered why I found him so irresistible.

"You look nice," Adam said in a gravelly voice when I stopped a few feet in front of him.

I tugged consciously at the girly lace dress—I must look ridiculous beside him.

"Thanks," I smiled back. "How are you?"

The chatter of voices at the cathedral behind was full of glee. Hopeful tones for the future as students and parents said their collective hellos and goodbyes to tutors. Well-wishes, pats on the back and hugs full of tears between friends. Amongst the commotion, gentle music spilled from the cathedral.

Adam nodded, bringing a hand to his hair, too low, and laughed. "Still getting used to this length."

I giggled too. "It looks perfect. Suits you."

"Thanks."

We lapsed into silence. I waited for him to speak.

"Look, Ty; I just wanted to come and see you. I know how important today is for you, and I couldn't bear not being here. I hope you don't mind?"

I thought for a moment, then gently shook my head.

We were meant to come together; he was going to drive, then he would join us at the restaurant afterwards, where his arm would drape around my shoulders. I would lean on his chest and we'd clink our glasses together, kissing fizzy bubbles from each other's lips.

Adam's grey eyes watched my face, as if taking everything in, drinking up the sight, just as I was.

"I wish everything and more for you Ty," he said so quietly it was almost a whisper. I bit the inside of my cheek to stop the tears that clogged in my chest.

"You too Adam," my voice broke on his name.

"May I?" He lifted his arm questioningly.

I froze for a moment, flinching ever so slightly. But I wasn't afraid of him. Not when he was like this. I knew he would never hurt me when he wasn't blinded by rage. Not when his gaze was crystal and clear, eyes sparkling with love, warmth radiating around him in waves.

Slowly, I nodded, and he stepped carefully forward, arms tucking under mine, lifting me into the hug. His arms were so tight I could barely breathe, but I didn't mind. I let him crush my chest to his, pulling myself closer too as if we could absorb into one another…

I pushed him back, though it felt like pulling apart Velcro. His eyes were glassy, and he blinked the tears quickly away, shoving his hands into his pockets.

"Well, see you around," Adam smiled.

I smiled back, not trusting my voice, watching him disappear down the alley beside the Cathedral.

Not long after we got to the restaurant, Ryan arrived, striding straight to pull me into a congratulatory hug, and I was suddenly glad he hadn't come any earlier. It wouldn't have been right saying goodbye to Adam with Ryan there.

257

Unexpected joy filled my heart at the sight of Ryan. Like breathing in fresh air after my lungs had been clogged with smoke. A soothing cream over hot burns. A blanket around shivering shoulders.

Sitting beside Mel, she and Ryan fell into easy conversation, and I was jealous of the friendship they had managed to preserve. As we ordered our meals and toasted our drinks, I couldn't help watching Ryan from the corner of my eye; his hair was longer than the last time I'd seen him, long enough that it curled ever so slightly at the ends around his ears and face. He wore a blue polo shirt, buttons open at the top, warmth and laughter filling the air.

After everything that had happened, I couldn't imagine a more perfect graduation.

A new chapter in my life.

CHAPTER FIFTEEN

The warmth of the day receded with the arrival of a romantic pink dusk. Like the work of an artist, the sky had strokes of dreamy blues and purples, vibrant orange where the sun kissed the horizon. Back at the house, and in the garden, a blanket draped over my shoulders and a warm cup of tea tucked into my hands, the contemplative aesthetic of the sunset had my mind turning to how perfect the day had been.

A yellow rose bush at the back of the garden was blooming against the fence, bright petals looking eerily like watching eyes beside a fuchsia with pink and purple hanging flowers. A group of baby starlings chattered loudly at the feeder a few feet away, a pair of doves perched patiently on the rafters waiting their turn. A slight chill ran over my exposed legs, still in my peach graduation dress, when the sliding door to the dining room behind whined open.

"Can I join?" Ryan asked.

"Of course."

Dusk was my favourite time of day; the golden hour when everything turned beautifully idyllic. The way the final rays cast through tree leaves. The air, as it cooled.

The sounds of the birds and crickets as they began their nightly routines.

"I brought these for you," Ryan smiled proudly as if he was presenting me with gold, a packet of half-eaten biscuits in his outstretched hand.

"Thanks," I grabbed one as he sat in the chair opposite mine, snorting a laugh when the chair almost toppled over, Ryan's tea sloshing onto the paved stones.

"So," he said, once the chair was adjusted away from the pebble under its leg, biscuit in his mouth. "Time to join the big wide world, hey? Where will you start?"

In the garden, a robin with a big red chest danced along the fence, singing happily. "Time to do the adult thing?"

He laughed. "Yeah, *adulting*, it's loads of fun."

"How's your girlfriend?"

"She… ah, well, we broke up."

"I'm sorry. When?"

"A few months ago. It's OK, though."

A few months?

"Look, Ryan," I took a deep breath, turning my body to face his. "I'm really sorry about everything. I'm so embarrassed."

"Embarrassed?" He frowned. "Tyler, you don't have anything to be sorry for, and certainly nothing to be *embarrassed* about. It's life. Shit happens."

I smiled.

"But please, stop apologising now. I'll accept this one, *again*. But I don't want to hear it again. OK?"

I rolled my eyes. "All right."

Steam billowed from the top of our mugs. Ryan's gaze trained on the sunset. "It's so different from Aus, isn't it?" he said quietly, as if speaking any louder would ruin the moment.'

There was a time when Australia was all I thought about—yearning for the past and all the things left behind. Ryan being the biggest one.

"Have you been back?" I asked.

"No. Not since I left. I'd like to one day, though."

Thinking of the farmhouse, of the little shack by the pond, about the day he kissed me, and I cried because I thought he was messing with me. I knew him better now, at least, if not him, I'd learned more about the world and kisses, and knew now that he could never have meant that kiss maliciously. I chuckled.

"What?" Ryan asked.

"I was just thinking of that time you kissed me."

"Oh yeah, then you accused me of doing it just to be mean." His grin was wide and true.

"Could you blame me? I had no idea."

"Really? I thought it was obvious."

"No way was it obvious."

"Hey," Ryan defended. "I was a teenage boy; I thought the fact that I was *hanging out* with you made it obvious?"

"You mean, teasing, and even ignoring me sometimes? How did I not know?" I rolled my eyes sarcastically.

He laughed. "Doesn't matter. I like to think I'm much better with the ladies these days, anyway."

I scrunched up my nose, *"The ladies?"*

"What?" he said. I fell into a fit of laughter.

When my laughter died down, and I was wiping at wet eyes, Ryan rose from his chair, eyes looking in the distance.

"Ty?" he said, as if addressing the air.

"Mhm?" I spluttered, still giggling.

He came to stand in front of me, bending so he sat on his hind legs, brown eyes searching mine. Resting a warm hand over mine in my lap, smile lines crinkled around his eyes.

"What?" My heart raced.

"I just…" he looked at the floor with a hesitant sigh. "I don't want to miss my chance again."

And then his other hand snaked to my cheek, pulling gently until our lips met.

His kiss was everything I remembered and more, a fire igniting inside of me that spread warmth through my body. Explosions of fireworks, flowers opening, sun shining. My chest swelled and hiccupped with tears.

Tears for the familiarity of him. From the memories of the boy in the farmhouse next door. For the boy who had haunted my dreams since I was just a little girl. The man who was always so gentle and kind, patient and understanding.

I wanted to fold myself into his body, to let him wrap me in his protective embrace. Hold me until all the pain from the last year disappeared, and a bridge was built over all the space between us.

Pulling away, his eyes searched mine in a panic. "Oh, Ty," he breathed. "You have to stop crying every time I kiss you."

I laughed around tears pooling in my eyes. When one slipped down my cheek, Ryan caught it with his thumb, before wiping both under my eyes tenderly.

"Are they bad tears?" he asked quietly.

He smelled of musk, and something I couldn't quite put my finger on. Something that tugged at the deepest parts of my soul. Something that bound invisible strings from my heart to his, that connected us in an intricately woven web.

Shaking my head, I tried to smile reassuringly. "No."

He dipped his head to plant another kiss on my lips, before pulling me into his chest, where it was warm and soothing and felt like home. I squeezed my eyes shut at the absurdity of the situation; at the weight of the thing, I had to tell him. How was it possible that this could happen to us twice in a lifetime?

"Ryan," I pulled back, looking into his chocolate and gold-flecked eyes. "There's something I need to tell you."

Placing my hands on his shoulders, I motioned for him to sit, catching his hand across the table.

"You're worrying me, Tyler," he frowned.

I swallowed. "I, um, I'm leaving."

"Leaving?"

I nodded. "I'm going to Peru."

He laughed, throwing back his head. "Ha, ha, very funny." My pleading eyes searched his face—silently begging the fates above that this was the right thing to do. "You're serious?"

My heart broke at the look in his eyes. I nodded.

"But you're coming back?"

"Yes, but I'm not sure when. I bought a one-way ticket."

Pulling his hand from mine, eyes turning towards the sky, he laughed again, but this time there was no humour in it.

"I can't believe this."

"Ryan? Ryan, look at me, please."

He shook his head. "Tyler… I—I don't even know. How is this happening again?"

"Ryan, let me explain," I tugged at the hem of his shirt, pulling him back until he sat. "I need to get away. Get away from all this. These last few years, they… I have so many memories here. I need time to let them go."

"So, you're leaving because of him?" For the first time, there was anger in his eyes.

"No. Yes. Sort of," I stammered. "I need to do it for *me*. I need to prove that I can be someone, without being *with* someone. If that makes sense?"

"And you don't want to be with me?" He was calm and collected now.

"That's not it. I didn't think this would happen," I motioned between the two of us. "I genuinely thought... I thought that all we would ever be was friends. I thought that everything that Adam was afraid of between you and me was a figment of his imagination. I thought you'd come today, we'd catch up and hopefully mend our friendship, and that you'd still be with your girlfriend." I stopped, taking a breath. "Maybe I never let myself consider the other possibility. *This* possibility. The possibility that you somehow had feelings for me too. Because, well firstly, I didn't think it was possible. But also, because I was afraid if you did, I wouldn't want to go," I spoke fast, trying to grasp and explain it all like catching smoke.

"Then don't go," he pleaded.

"I have to Ryan." *Was I really doing this?* "I have to do this for me. And if I don't, I'll be betraying all the things I've worked so hard for over the last few months."

There was no anger left in his eyes. "OK," he said quietly. "But what does that mean for us?"

I shook my head. "I... I don't know. I just know that I need to be on my own."

The timing was all wrong, how could this be happening again? Every fibre of me wanted to change my plans. To stay—for him, but deep in my soul, I knew, it was the right thing to do.

How could I give myself to him as I was—shattered and asking him to put the pieces back together again? He didn't deserve that.

I prayed we'd get a second—no wait, a third chance, at this. Prayed I wasn't ruining it forever. Hoped we hadn't run out of chances.

CHAPTER SIXTEEN
Peru

The bedsprings of my bunk creaked and whined every time I turned restlessly. Insects buzzed around the gauze of the window. From outside came the songs of owls and crickets.

The air was hot and muggy, and tonight I tossed more than usual, insomnia refusing to let me sleep—or maybe it wasn't insomnia at all, but because it was my twenty-first birthday in the morning. It had been eight months since I landed in Peru. For the first four weeks after my arrival, I did the tourist thing—first stop: Lima.

Mum and dad had given me an advance on my twenty-first birthday money so that I could afford it. I toured the streets, combing the Inca and Indian Markets, gazing at all the beautiful and colourful alpaca wool jumpers. After that, I caught a small plane into the mountains to a place called Cusco, where I drank a special tea made of cocoa leaves that grew wild to prevent altitude sickness. I spent days wandering the ruins built by the Incas, nights listening to live music in the plaza, and eating at the local restaurants.

From there, I set off to destination number two: Machu Picchu.

A train with a glass roof weaved through the mountains, taking me to the village sitting below Machu Picchu—Agua Calientes—in a valley surrounded by mountains. The town was split in two by the Urubamba River running through the middle, both sides of the village connected by a network of wooden bridges.

I stayed in a backpackers' café called Los Viajeros, ate the local food from a canteen down the road, and wondered the endless markets. There, I found myself mesmerised by a swirling necklace made of moonstone white. The seller at the stall explained that the pattern represented the journey and change of life as it unfolds—it was meant for me, and I was meant to find it. I snapped it up at a bargain price.

Joining a group of backpackers, we began the three-day Inca Trail up to Machu Picchu, hiking by day, spending the nights in pitched tents huddled around a fire. I'd never forget the sounds of the jungle, lying in my tent, the wonderful ache in my legs from a full day of hiking, and the absolute exhaustion that had me effortlessly passing out every night.

On the third day, we crested the mountain, giving way to a bird's eye view of the ruins below. It looked exactly like all the pictures.

Standing on the edge, arms triumphantly in the air, one of my fellow hikers took a picture, ruins sprawled out behind, my face red and tired, hair matted and wrapped in a bandana. I spent the day roaming the ruins and listening to talks from the guides. At the end of it, before catching the bus back down to Agua Calientes, I found the perfect spot overlooking the tops of the trees.

Breathing in the fresh air, allowing myself to soak up the culture, the moment, the freedom, I still felt that nagging pain. Like a rain cloud over every moment, a shadow come rain or shine.

Whenever I stopped, breathed in the moment, it was there.

I pushed it away, heaving my aching body up, looking forward to a good night's sleep in the single bed of the backpackers' café.

Before the day was over, and after a hot shower, I met my fellow travellers in a local bar where we drank an enormous amount of pisco sours, and our local guide attempted to teach us traditional songs.

After the Machu Picchu adventure, I made my way to Natalia's sanctuary on the coast of Colán. She was expecting me, and already had a bed made up with a list of duties.

Colán was hot and muggy, the desert surrounding it dry and brittle. The town sat on the coast, beautiful beaches running its length with tall palms and big, shabby houses.

Tonight was the first night I'd let my mind wander back home. I had no phone, the only way to contact anyone was using Natalia's old computer that resided in her bedroom. It wasn't that Peru didn't have any cell phones, simply that I wanted to cut myself off. Give myself space. The downside, being I couldn't speak to anyone as often as I would like, so I made do with emails and Skype calls every so often.

Now, lying in bed and thinking of my impending birthday, I wondered if it was time to get back to reality—to treat myself to a cell phone.

Eventually, I fell asleep, and when I woke, my eyes were puffy from a restless night—but my duties needed to be fulfilled, even if it *was* my birthday.

Rolling out of bed, five a.m. showed on the clock hanging on the wall. It was already light outside, and I made my way to the shared bathroom. Brushing my teeth and pulling a brush through unruly long hair, I searched my reflection for any new wrinkles or greying hairs.

Pulling on a multicoloured alpaca hair jumper I picked up from the Inca market in Lima, I started my morning by preparing the cats' breakfast. Milo, a Portuguese volunteer, was already doing the dogs', and he wished me happy birthday in broken English.

We worked quietly; it was one of the things I liked about this new arrangement—no one felt inclined to fill the silence with idle chit-chat. There was only one other volunteer, Nadine, a girl from Germany, who wasn't particularly fond of the early starts and feeding times.

From outside the kitchen came the tell-tale signs of cats congregating. Meows filtered under the door, gentle scratches on the wood. Stepping out with a large container holding the mixture I'd just concocted; a sea of cats greeted me.

All colours and sizes of canines sat on the lawn outside, beady eyes waiting for their breakfast. Scrambling chaotically around my feet, I picked a path carefully, although a yelp every now and again as a tail or paw got caught under my foot was unavoidable.

Filling bowls lined along the wall; they fought to get to one until finally settling. Next, I made my way to the cattery, where the temperamental cats stayed in pens surrounded by chicken wire.

All the animals in the sanctuary were rescued from the streets. Some had missing eyes, half ears, shaved or mangy fur, tails cut in half or even hobbling on three legs. My favourite was a boy called Garfield—named because he looked like the cartoon, his big body striped with orange fur.

"Morning boy," I said when he ran at my feet, jumping on his hind legs, claws digging into the bare skin of my thighs.

Placing the drum on the floor, I picked him up like a toddler—he was easily bigger than some of the dogs in the sanctuary. Back legs resting on my forearm, the other two wrapped around my neck, he nuzzled into my hair.

"Aw good morning to you too," I rubbed the fur on his back.

Reluctant to be put down, I peeled his claws out of my jersey before filling his bowl, and on my way back to the kitchen, I ran into Natalia.

"There's my favourite volunteer," she said. "Happy birthday, sweetheart." Smiling warmly, she opened her arms. I walked into her embrace. "Don't tell the others I said that," she whispered. "We'll be having drinks for you this evening, so don't stay away for too long," she pulled back, wagging a matronly finger.

"I won't," I smiled.

Natalia was from the UK, had short salt and pepper brown hair with curls, and a pair of pale blue, transparent rimmed glasses. This morning she wore a purple shawl around her shoulders, five cats trailing adoringly behind her.

One of the other jobs I'd adopted was taking a group of dogs for their morning run. There were so many in the sanctuary that we had to take shifts. When I returned, Milo or Nadine would take out the next lot. I'd never been a big runner, but it was a new, habit that Peru had taught me, and I was glad to have found a passion for it.

Lacing up my trainers, pulling on a sports bra, I retrieved five leashes from the cupboard and clipped them to the usual five dogs' collars. The dirt road in front of the sanctuary was already sun-warmed, and we started up a jog along the road leading to the beach.

Dilapidated bungalows lined the streets, paint peeling and fading from their walls. We ran vertically between houses with small gardens, until gleaming white beach sand crested the horizon.

Spanning the shore were the homes of the wealthier residents, houses larger and grander, compared to that inland, with their tall glass windows and unlimited views of the ocean.

The sand was hard and wet beneath my shoes, the tide retreating, and I raced behind the dogs as they tore across the beach, ears flapping in the wind, tongues hanging from their mouths. After a few minutes, I pulled them to a stop, still unable to keep up with their insatiable appetites to run. Finding a spot under a palm, I unclipped their leashes, and they immediately tore towards the gentle surf, a flock of gulls taking to the air.

Removing my trainers and socks, sand spread around my toes, sweat beading on my forehead, salty air rolling off the sea to caress my neck. Further along the beach, a fisherman unspooled his net from a dugout canoe bobbing in the waves. Locals headed into town, wares packed into reed baskets or balanced on their heads, heading for the local market.

The palm above threw striped shadows over my skin, shifting in the breeze so the patterns moved like tiger's fur. My mind relaxed into nothing, and I noticed—perhaps for the first time—that the ever-present darkness I'd carried around with me finally felt as if it was fading.

Could it be that I'd finally reached the goal I had set out to achieve? That the distance, and new experiences, had allowed my heart and soul to heal?

Conjuring up Adam in my mind, I didn't feel the thunderstorm of emotions. The aching chasm in my heart no longer mourned the loss of him, as if the beasts within the chasm's darkness had finally retreated. Sun bathed the shadows, where renewal and growth turned their faces to the light. The shackles that bound me to Adam were unlocked, my soul stretching in freedom, no longer restricted by the boundaries of that cage.

A phoenix rising into the Peruvian sky.

The dogs played in the surf, bouncing gleefully among the gentle morning waves, a hazy ship on the horizon, a speck in the sprawling cobalt where sky met sea. Tiny crab trails patterned the dune I sat on, sun-dried seaweed already parched and crisping.

I'd thought about when to head home a few times recently, each time brushing the thought away with the notion that I'd think about it later. It wasn't that I didn't want to go home. In fact, I missed everyone terribly—especially Ryan and what could be.

I'd sent him a few emails, curious whether he'd moved on, but couldn't bring myself to ask outright. He'd never indicated any sort of suggestion.

How could I expect him to wait? Why *would* he wait? I'd never said when I would be back, and eight months was a long time. I doubted he was still single. A guy like him. There would be girls just waiting to snap him up.

A part of my reluctance to return, was the possibility of what I'd be returning to. To be reminded of what I pushed aside, and the fear that I'd lost my chance. Ignorance *was* sometimes bliss. Otherwise, I would much rather stay here, in Peru, where I'd begun to forge a new life.

It was selfish and I knew it.

Dropping the dogs back at the sanctuary, I changed out of my sweaty running clothes, pulling on a skirt that billowed down to my ankles in a beautiful pastel yellow, pairing it with a white T-shirt that I tied at the waist. It had been a long time since my skin was so tanned—since Jamaica—and the freckles on my nose and shoulders stood out prominently. Natalia had a set of bicycles for us to use, and I pulled a well-used bottle green one from the rack, beginning the short ride into town.

My first stop was the vegetable market; Nadine asked me to grab some things for dinner, so I piled tomatoes and potatoes into my backpack, before heading to the clothes market. I sifted through the soft materials piled on tables or large tarpaulins in the sand—so different to the shops in England—bobbing my head to the friendly locals with kind faces. The Peruvians were generally short, with sun-weathered brown skin, dark hair framing even darker eyes.

"Tyler!" Mary and Ricardo waved from their fish stall. "Feliz compleaños!"

Ricardo and Mary were twins and ran the family fish stall. My Spanish was rusty, but Ricardo and Mary were very forgiving.

"Gracias, gracias," I pushed my bike to their stall.

"Are we going for a drink later, Tyler?" Ricardo said with a flirtatious wink.

I smiled. "I think Natalia is doing drinks at the sanctuary, would you like to come?" I asked them both.

"Si, of course!" Mary beamed. "She already told us. He's being a stupid." She swatted her brother's shoulder. "Have you spoke to your family yet?"

"Not yet, I was going to when I get back."

"Well tell them we say holá, and that they must come try our fish," Ricardo waved a piece of whitebait in the air.

I shouted over my shoulder. "I will!"

Instead of returning to the sanctuary, I cycled a while longer in the knowledge that I wasn't needed again until later that afternoon, enjoying the feeling of the sun on my shoulders. By the time I returned, it was one in the afternoon, and I rushed to Natalia's room to log onto the computer, opening Skype.

Within minutes, the familiar call sound was playing.

"Happy birthday to you! Happy birthday to you!" A grainy image on screen showed mum and dad, side by side, drinks held in their hands, swaying in song.

276

I waited for them to finish with a grin, then applauded. "Beautiful. Bonita!"

"Thank you," dad bowed, mum giggled. "How is our birthday girl?" Dad asked. "Can't believe our baby is twenty-one!"

"Not such a baby any more, hey?"

"You'll always be our baby," mum said, pretending to pinch my cheeks through the camera. "So how has your day been? Are you doing anything special tonight? We're having a drink for you," she raised her wine glass to the camera, cheeks already rosy.

"I can see that," I teased. "I haven't done anything special. I mean, it's only one here, but Natalia said we'll have a drink tonight."

"I hope you do," dad nodded. "Twenty-one is a big one. I'm just sad you're not here so we can throw you a party."

I rolled my eyes at his idea of a party. "It's the thought that counts, hey dad?"

"Well, it'll have to do this time."

"But," mum cut in, "we *have* sent you a little something."

"No! You guys, you already gave me my birthday money!" I protested.

Dad waved his hand. "No, no. We couldn't not give you something."

"Plus," mum raised her eyebrows, "we were hoping maybe you could use the money as a gift to us and come home?"

"Maybe," I teased.

"I'll take it!" Mum laughed merrily.

"How's Mel?"

"She's… good." Dad's tone was oddly hesitant.

"What?" My pulse quickened.

"No! No, silly," mum slapped his shoulder. "Nothing to worry about, honey. Just something I think she wants to tell you herself."

"OK." What could she possibly want to tell me? "Is she there?"

"Not tonight. But I'm sure she'll call soon," dad said around a sip of beer. "Oh yeah and Ryan—Ow!" Dad began, but mum knocked him quickly on the shoulder, whispering hurriedly.

All I managed to catch was "Shhh," and "You're not supposed to say" before they looked back at the camera, composed.

"What's going on?"

"Nothing sweetheart, nothing. Honestly, don't worry. Anyway, how's that little kitty you love so much? Garfield, is it?"

Garfield was a smart distraction.

I quickly lapsed into the story of how poor Garfield had an operation last week to take out a tumour growing in his tummy. I told them about the bake sale we had over the weekend to raise money, and that everyone loved my lemon drizzle cake. They said that they received the cushion covers I made for them, the ones that Natalia had taught me how to make using different coloured satin ribbons, and they told me all about the new neighbours, who had a son around my age that they just knew I'd get on with—I rolled my eyes. When my allotted hour of internet usage was up, we said goodbye with an airborne kiss, ending the connection.

The room was quiet, a fan whizzed quietly in the corner, soft licks come from the bed where a white and black cat was curled on the duvet.

What could it be that Mel wanted to tell me? That she wanted to tell me herself? Why had dad followed with something about Ryan?

Mel... Ryan...

It couldn't be, *could it*? Nausea sent my stomach roiling.

This was what happened when you and your sister were too close to the same boy. We fought over him when we were younger, so why should anything be different now? I saw the way they were together that evening of my graduation. Although it was *me* he had kissed, what if, since I'd been gone, he'd found a better connection with her?

My stomach was in my throat as I pushed back the chair.

CHAPTER SEVENTEEN

I finished the rest of my chores feeling like I'd swallowed a brick, never being so disappointed since my arrival not to have a phone.

It would be better to know, wouldn't it? Certainly, if Mel was the girl Ryan had moved on with—I would want to know. There would be no way—*no way*—I could go back to the UK if it was the case. It was different when we were younger; I didn't love Ryan the way I did now.

I stopped, broom in hand, pausing mid-sweep.

What? Did I just think that? *Love* him?

Horror swelled through me, waves crashing and sucking, pulling and plunging me to painful depths.

No. No, I couldn't love him. Not if he was with Mel. I couldn't…

Lightheaded and queasy, I dropped the broom, dashing for the bathroom, bending over a seat, but nothing came. I rested my forehead against the cold tiles.

Too little too late, Tyler. My mind taunted. *You had your chance, can't be mad that you realised you loved him too late.*

"Anyone but Mel," I whispered aloud, smacking a palm to the wall.

I needed to talk to Mel. *Now.*

Dashing back to Natalia's room, she sat on her bed, knitting needles between her fingers, two cats on her lap.

"Natalia, can I use the internet again for a few minutes, please?"

"Sorry Ty, but you've had your time. You know the rules," Natalia shook her head, peering over the top of her glasses like a stern librarian.

"Please, Natalia. It's important," I tried not to sound too desperate, but this *was* a desperate situation.

Natalia continued to shake her head. "Why don't you finish up for the day. Go have a nice shower and get ready for this evening?"

I squeezed my eyes in frustration.

****

Hair hanging wet around my shoulders, so long now it easily reached my waist, I could hear Hattie cooing about how nice it looked long. She'd always urged me not to cut it.

"I don't think I'm in the mood for tonight," I glumly told Natalia in the kitchen.

"Don't be silly. It's your birthday. We have to have a drink. Here," she handed me a large glass filled with a white drink, topped with a little blue umbrella. "Piña Colada!" Natalia beamed.

Her attitude was infectious, and when we clinked our glasses together, it didn't take long before I was feeling better. Nadine and Milo joined us with their own fruity looking cocktails, and not long after, Ricardo and Mary arrived with presents wrapped in brightly coloured wrapping paper. They also brought with them a pack of paper birthday hats covered in small images of cats that they insisted everyone wore, and a CD of Spanish singers—none of which I knew.

The courtyard at the centre of the sanctuary had no roof, open to the elements. In a half-moon shape around one side were various buildings; the kitchen, Natalia's room, the bathrooms, the clinic, and the volunteer lodgings. On the other side were the animal pens. Trees and bushes grew in the ample sized courtyard, fairy lights with a honey-coloured glow strung between the branches and latched on to the roof. The kitchen lead into a veranda of sorts, where a small cement wall was adorned in different coloured stones and pieces of glass that Natalia had collected over the years and inlaid in the cement. During the day, when the glass caught the sun, the wall sparkled like a cave made of gems.

Above where we sat on the veranda in winding bamboo chairs, a light hung from the roof with a shade made from cans, and in the corner, a plush sofa, three dogs piled on top, watching our little party. Chimes made from shells, bottles and cans hanging from rafters swayed delicately in the warm wind.

Once the cocktail mixture ran out, Natalia brought out the bottle of rum, topping up our glasses with coke and a squeeze of lime—Cuba libre they called it.

Around eleven, Nadine, Mary and I were dancing to a song that Nadine was demonstrating the dance moves to, when a knock came at the large, wooden entrance doors.

"Who's that?" Milo frowned at Natalia.

She shrugged.

Heading for the door, Natalia put a hand up to stop him, "Oh Milo, let Tyler get the door."

He frowned, turning to me with an inquisitive quirk of his dark brow.

Pulling the handle, my eyes almost popped out my head, because it was Ryan standing on the threshold, bag in hand.

"*Ryan*?" both hands went to cover my mouth, jaw dropping.

"Happy birthday, Tyler."

Leaping into his arms, he dropped the case with a *thunk*, arms wrapping around my back, bracing against my weight. His laugh vibrated through my chest, scent filling my nose, tears marbling my eyes.

I didn't want to let go. How could I ever have let go in the first place?

Finally, I managed to peel myself from him, keeping a hand on his shoulder, afraid that if I let go, he'd disappear.

"And who is this, Tyler?" Ricardo raised an eyebrow.

I couldn't wipe the smile from my face. I knew I looked ridiculous. "This, um, this is Ryan. Ryan, that's Ricardo, Nadine, Milo, Mary and Natalia."

Ryan shook each of their hands, but when he got to Natalia, she pulled him into a hug.

"Don't be silly, we're old friends," Natalia winked over his shoulder.

"Did you know he was coming?" I asked.

"I did," she sat smugly back in her chair.

"But how?" I looked between Natalia and Ryan.

"Your mum told me where you were staying," Ryan explained. "And then gave me Natalia's number so I could organise getting here. I wanted to surprise you."

Chills ran down my spine, goosebumps rising along my skin. "I... I just can't believe it," I beamed.

"Why don't you show Ryan to his room? I'm sure he won't mind sharing a bunk with you?" Natalia ushered us to the sleeping quarters.

"OK," I breathed, as if I'd just climbed off a rollercoaster and was still trying to catch my breath from the drop.

I used to have a roommate, a girl from Holland, but she left a few weeks ago, and Milo and Nadine shared bunks in a separate room. Two sets of bunks were in each room, one on either side of the small space, and Ryan put his case on the bottom bunk opposite mine. With his back to me, I quickly whipped off the silly party hat, throwing it into the corner.

The room was dark, light from the courtyard filtering in through the door, and Ryan wiped his hands along his jeans, pulling at his T-shirt. "Phew, it's hot."

I laughed. "It takes some getting used to."

He was quiet, surveying the room. I watched, still waiting for him to disappear, to wake up to my empty room.

His dark eyes roamed over my things on the side table, balancing on the windowsill, and my unmade bed—suddenly I wished I'd taken the time to tidy up this morning.

"Ryan, why are you here? I mean, I'm so happy to see you, but…"

"Was it a bad idea?" Worry clouded his eyes, shadows dancing across his beautiful face.

"No! No, not at all. I'm just… shocked. That's all. It's been so long."

What about Mel? Was she going to appear behind him at any moment?

"It's been too long," Ryan spoke quietly. "It's always too long between the times I see you."

This time, it was all me.

"I'm sorry," I whispered, hands knotting in my shirt.

285

"Tyler, don't you get it?" He closed the gap between us, warm hand going to my cheek, amber eyes dark and velvety, like the midnight sky. "I tried. I let you have your space. But I can't wait any more. I had to come to you if you wouldn't come to me."

Words caught in my throat. I stared at his open face, breathing in the scent of him.

"Was I wrong to come?" His breath fanned over my cheeks.

I shook my head. "B-but, what about Mel?" I stammered.

He frowned. "Mel?"

"I thought... I don't know. My dad said something that made me think maybe...?"

"That I was seeing your sister?"

I nodded shyly.

"Do you think I would be here now? Do you think I would do this if I were?"

Then he kissed me again, soft and tender. All the tension from the day left my body. All the worrying, all the heartache over nothing.

I love you; the words whispered across my mind. *And you're here, and you came.*

The kiss quickly turned hungry, and I pulled him against me. He knotted his hands in my hair, our bodies crushing together, and I pushed until he met the edge of the bed, awkwardly falling together onto the bottom bunk. I wanted him. I'd denied it with every fibre of my body for so many years now. Who was I kidding? I wanted him, all of him, and I was tired of waiting too. And he was here now, in my room, in *Peru*, his lips and hands on me; my head was dizzy.

I pulled my shirt over my head, fingers hungrily scratching at his shirt too, until he bent forward slightly so I could yank it off.

"Tyler," Ryan whispered, my insides squeezing at the sound of my name so delicately on his lips.

This was *Ryan*.

The Ryan who lived next door. The Ryan I'd always wanted. The Ryan I thought I'd only ever be lucky enough to get a friendship out of. Ryan.

My Ryan.

My mind whirled at the idea of what we were about to do, and I wanted to pinch myself. Everything about him; the way his skin felt, the way he smelled, the callouses on his fingers, even the feeling of his skin under my tongue, was so familiar. So right. Pulling up again to take off my skirt, his hands grabbed mine, freezing them in place. His chest heaved.

"Tyler, are you sure?" he asked.

I'd never been so sure of anything in my life. "Yes," I nodded. I'd been so stupid. How could I stay away from *this*? His kisses were like oxygen, his touch pinpricks of electricity. His body, though I hadn't seen it since he was sixteen, was all rippling muscles; his shoulders broad under my hands trailing hungrily over his arms.

I hadn't seen him in so long. The months alone had left me with only my dreams and thoughts of him that always comforted me in those dark, lonely nights. So many times, I'd imagined what it might feel like to have him hold me, touch me. *Really* touch me, like this. So many times—and now finally, he was.

Sitting up from between my legs, one arm wrapped around my back. He held my body tight to his, fingers pulling impatiently at my knickers, tips finding their way through the material. A sigh escaped my lips.

Trailing kisses along my neck, he whispered my name over and over, so quietly, like a breath in the wind. I moved my hips to meet the movement of his hand, never feeling anything like this before—the intimacy, the closeness, pure, raging adrenaline at the sensation of *him*. Then he moved, shifted beneath me, pulled away to look into my eyes. Brushing a fallen strand of hair behind my ear, he lifted gently, before pushing me back down onto him—his eyes never breaking contact with mine.

****

The sound of Milo shouting across the garden woke me the next morning, and I peeled my groggy eyes open to sun filtering into the room, squinting at the clock. As my vision cleared, the time came into focus, and I sat bolt upright, knocking my head on the top bunk.

"Ouch!"

Ryan shifted awake beside me, rubbing a hand over his eyes. "What did you do that for?" he said around a half-yawn, half-laugh.

I shuffled myself over his body and off the side, stumbling towards my bed to pull a shirt on from the floor. "It's already eight! I'm so late for my rounds."

Looking briefly back at the bed—at Ryan sitting on an elbow, sleepy eyes watching in amusement. His hair was ruffled and fell on his forehead, eyes puffed with sleep. He was still shirtless, and a shiver travelled down my spine with longing to climb back in beside him.

"I thought you were rushing somewhere?"

"Oh, shit!" I jumped back into action, racing out the door, leaving Ryan's laugh behind me.

Dashing for the kitchen, not bothering with washing my face or brushing my teeth, I found the cat drum dirty and used, sitting in the washing area. Outside, the bowls looked as if food had been and gone in them. Hand over my eyes to shield from the glaring sun, I spotted Nadine leashing up the dogs.

"Nadine!" I ran to her.

"Good morning. Did you have a nice night?" she asked with a sly smile.

My cheeks warmed. "Yeah, thanks. Uh, has someone done the cats? How come you're taking the dogs? I'm more than happy to do it."

"No, no," Nadine shook her head. "Natalia said that you get the day off. Spend some time with that man of yours." She wagged her eyebrows. "Milo and I can cover your duties."

"Are you sure? Where's Natalia?" I searched the garden.

"She went into town. Now go, back to bed," Nadine shooed.

Walking back to the room with a giddy smile, I made a note to thank everyone later. Maybe I'd buy them the chocolates we all liked from town.

Back in the room, Ryan sat with his back to the wall, phone in his hands in front of him, sheet over his torso, boxers peeking out from under them, chest bare. I could never get used to the sight.

"All finished?" he asked, mesh door squeaking around my return.

"The others took care of everything. Natalia said I should have the day off," I slumped onto the bed across from him.

"That was nice of her," Ryan smiled. "To be honest, I'm glad. I was looking forward to spending the day with you. Maybe you could show me around?"

"Sure," my eyes sparkled with excitement.

In my quest to find inner peace, I'd fallen in love with Peru. With the different landscapes, the food, the people, even the language. Peru had come at a time when my heart was raw. In the past, arriving in different countries was unbearably agonising, but this time, something changed. In a strange twist, coming to a foreign country had been my salvation. Maybe all those years of moving around created that. Now it was something I *needed* to move on. The thought of taking Ryan to all my favourite places, to all the spots I'd found on my own, showing him the food I'd tried, without coercion, and the people I'd openly met, sent my pulse racing with excitement.

After taking turns using the bathroom, we shared a cup of coffee with Milo and Nadine, before heading out—first stop, the little shack on the beach for breakfast.

The morning was beautiful, as if it was putting on its best face to welcome Ryan. Birds sang melodies in the trees flanking the road, the air still cool as the sun rose gently into the pristine blue sky. We walked in silence, which under normal circumstances would have been expected, but after what we'd done last night, I was tight with nerves. I needed to say something, right?

My mind grappled, but Ryan appeared serene, taking in the trees, the surrounding houses, even stopping to pick up an unusually shaped rock. The strange awkwardness that was flooding me seemed to be completely evading him. Why was I panicking? Maybe, it was because the dynamic had changed between us. It had always been easy to toss my feelings for him aside, to bury them deep within, and ignore them when I didn't think he felt the same way. But now, after last night, it was as if I'd forgotten how to act around him.

"You're quiet," he noted.

My hair, plaited in a single braid, hung over my shoulder, and I fingered nervously with the end. "I know," I chuckled. "Sorry, I…" I smiled shyly. "I don't know."

"It's all right," he laughed lightly. "So, have you enjoyed Peru?" he asked, kindly moving past whatever I was struggling to verbalise.

I nodded and grinned. "Loved it. Machu Picchu was beautiful. You have to see it."

"I'll remember that." He smiled at my enthusiasm. "And Colán? Are you happy here?"

I nodded again. "I have been. It's different, you know?"

"Have you considered coming home?"

The beach rose in front of us, glistening sand and sea sparkling in the morning sun. The small shack we headed towards perched on a dune further down the beach.

"Yes and no. It's different when there's nothing really to go back to." He stiffened. "Not like that! I don't mean you, I meant… urgh, I'm sorry," I touched his shoulder. "Let me try again. Yes, of course, I've thought about it, and I've thought of you almost every day."

"But not enough to bring you home?"

My heart squeezed at the hint of sadness in his voice. "It's not that, Ryan. It's something silly, and you'll laugh at me."

"Try me."

Wanting to hide my face, I said quickly, "I was afraid that you might have moved on with someone else. And you were the only thing pulling me back. But, if you had moved on, why go back? And then," I sighed. "Dad said something that made me think you and Mel were together, and that thought was ten times worse."

"Together? Why? What did he say?" Ryan frowned.

"Just that Mel had something she wanted to tell me, and then your name came up."

He was quiet for a moment. "Well, I don't know what he might have meant by bringing my name up, but we have been spending time together. But not like that, we're just friends."

Stepping onto the small veranda of the shack overlooking the ocean, orange plastic tables covered in blue tablecloths filled the room, faint songs of Peruvian music spilled from speakers. It was empty, and I guided Ryan to my usual table at the front, to the right.

"This is nice," he looked around the restaurant. "But that view, wow. I can see why you like it so much."

The building was built to honour the view. The side that we had entered from, on the beach, had a veranda, wide doors opening the whole side of the wall so that there was an undisturbed view of the sand and ocean. The walls were white. The floor left natural concrete with big, open windows. The sound of sea and gulls mixed with music, salty sea breeze flowing freely through the space.

After a breakfast of pancakes and bacon, we strolled along the beach, flip-flops dangling from our fingers, before heading through town to the market where we waved to Ricardo and Mary. I took Ryan to the school we helped paint as part of the community charity group, showed him the boats along the small marina. It was late afternoon, the sun slowly setting, by the time we ended up at Carlito's bar, the sky turning to a striking sunset—*show off*.

The bar was small and understated with Peruvian memorabilia hanging from the walls. We ordered drinks before sitting in chairs out front, overlooking the beach, legs sinking into the sand.

"I have to ask you something," Ryan finally said.

We'd fallen into easy conversation for most of the day, now his voice became serious, fingers nervously scratching at the label around his beer bottle.

"OK?"

"It's more of a statement really," he shrugged, eyes staring into the distance, where the neighbouring restaurant was setting up chairs and tables on the sand too. "When you left, I felt like I'd lost you all over again. That we'd missed our final chance, you know? That I was too late to show you how I felt, and because of that, if only I'd said something sooner, maybe you might not have gone."

"Ryan..." I started, but he cut me off.

"I understand why you left, Tyler. I do. But I was surprised by how I felt after you were gone. I found myself waiting, hoping you'd come back soon. Every day that went by I panicked a bit more," he laughed nervously. "That with every day, you slipped further and further away from me. Every day away was another step closer to someone else. I couldn't bear it."

His eyes flicked nervously between me, the bottle in his hands, and the ocean in front of us.

"I don't know why I didn't realise it sooner," he continued. "I mean, I know why—because we were both in committed relationships, and I sort of knew that if I let myself get close to you, that would be it for me. And I didn't know if you wanted that. But Ty, I need to know... I need to know if you want this too? And I can't wait any longer, because—"

I pulled him across the table, crushing my mouth against his, chairs dipping towards each other in the sand. Ryan was saying everything I'd ever wanted to hear. Everything and more.

How could I be so stupid? How could I have been the one to almost ruin this, by not going back? I was so thankful that he came to Peru. So grateful that he was here now, pouring out his heart. Because I'd catch it. I would hold it, keep it safe, and never let go.

CHAPTER EIGHTEEN

Hand in hand, Ryan and I stood in the Lima airport, waiting for our flight to board. The timing was right. I'd painstakingly put together the shattered pieces of my heart, rebuilding the house so damaged by ivy, brick by brick, and we were heading home.

After arriving in Colán, Ryan had another ten days before he needed to fly back, so we spent the days tangled in sheets, sand in our toes, salty seawater in our hair. I showed him around my favourite spots, giving him the grand Peruvian tour. Ricardo and Mary took us out to try traditional dishes that they ordered and laid on the table to share, and in a spur of the moment, we decided to say goodbye to Natalia and the animal sanctuary. Ryan and I decided to travel to Máncora, a little town on the coast.

We stayed in a hotel called Las Playas, where Ryan treated us to a room with a balcony overlooking the beach. We went paddleboarding and snorkelling, walked the streets and listened to live bands playing in bars. One evening, out for dinner, we ordered Piña Coladas that came in glasses the size of buckets, and put the little umbrellas that they came with, in our hair, giggling uncontrollably. Our skin was sun-kissed and bronzed, hair streaked with patterns of gold.

That evening, wrapped in blankets, cuddled in a wicker chair on the veranda of our room, distant noises of the ocean lapping at the shore, Ryan whispered in my ear, "Will you marry me?"

From under the blanket, cold metal kissed my skin.

Looking down, Ryan held a ring that sparkled in the moonlight. I stared dumbfounded at his hopeful face. He told me again how it felt right, how he didn't want us ever to be apart, and my heart swelled so big it felt as if it might explode out my chest, eyes stinging with tears as I cried "Yes!" nuzzling into his neck, not a single hint of fear or apprehension to be found.

In the airport waiting room, I gazed at the beautiful rock with swirling patterns, white gold twisting around the edges, still overwhelmed by the ring's beauty, and its perfect representation of a place, and a man, I had come to love so much. Ryan had said he'd seen it in the window of a shop in Máncora and felt the pull to it. He went to pick it up that afternoon when I was in the shower, pretending he was going to buy groceries for our room.

"What do you think your parents will say?" he asked with a kiss on the crown of my head.

I rolled my eyes. "They'll be over the moon. They already love you." His cheeks turned pink, I pulled him to me to kiss him gently on the temple.

As predicted, mum and dad were ecstatic at the news. Mum's eyes were so wide I was scared they'd pop out her head when we told them.

"Ryan!" Mum gasped. "If I'd known you were going to do that, I would have given you the details of where she was sooner!"

Ryan only chuckled.

"I had no idea." Dad shook his head and Ryan's hand. "I didn't even know you two were… anything!"

"I know," I laughed. "We weren't. But when you know, you know, right?"

I planned on moving to London to live with Ryan. In the meantime, we commuted between London and Gloucester, while I tried to get a job in the city before moving, but the job market was proving impenetrable. One evening, over a few glasses of wine, Mel jokingly said that I had finally won the great game that was chasing Ryan Andrews. I laughed, remembering the days when we fought over him. How jealous I was when it seemed that he liked her more than me.

She finally told me her 'news'; that she was in a relationship with a girl called Jane.

I wanted to laugh at the absurdity of what I thought her news *actually* was, drunkenly revealing my original paranoia. We laughed so hard tears streamed down our faces.

"Does that mean you're gay now?" I asked bluntly.

"No," she frowned. "I still like guys."

"So, you're just greedy?" I teased, poking her in the stomach.

She laughed, jabbing me back. "Ryan was really helpful throughout the whole thing. He encouraged me to tell mum and dad. To get it out in the open instead of trying to hide it."

I nodded. "I'm glad he was there for you."

"Honestly, Ty," Mel took my hand. "You have no idea how proud I am of you. Of this," she pointed at the ring on my finger. "Of how far you and Ryan have come. And I'm so glad you *finally* found your way to each other. I was beginning to worry that you never would for a while."

I rolled my eyes.

Fate and a little meddling from Mel had a lot to do with it.

****

One afternoon, strolling through the aisles of Tesco—not the one I would typically do my regular shop at, because I was in the area shopping for bedding and curtains for Ryan's London flat—a mountain of groceries were in the trolley, when I spotted a familiar black jacket and shock of dark hair. I froze, debating my next move, watching Adam read the label of something in his hand, a basket hanging from his long fingers.

A strange shiver travelled up my spine, but before I could get my feet to move, in an instant, he looked up, steel eyes settling on me. My stomach squeezed.

He looked the same, but different.

Those long dark lashes, the sparkling, grey eyes, the open smile as he threw the item in his hand back on the shelf and strode toward me.

"Adam," I smiled, letting go of the trolley, left hand instinctively snaking behind my back.

"Tyler," Adam said with genuine surprise. "How are you?"

He pulled me into a quick hug.

"Good, good," I nodded awkwardly.

"Where have you been? It looks like you've been somewhere exotic?" He pointed at my tanned skin.

He was relaxed and perfectly pleasant, the sound of his voice wrenchingly familiar.

"Oh, yeah, well I've been in Peru for the last eight months."

"Eight months, wow. When did you go?"

"Just after graduation."

I probably should have prepared myself for the possibility of running into him. After all, he still lived in the area. But with all the Ryan excitement, Adam hadn't even crossed my mind.

He had to be over us by now, right?

A brick settled in the pit of my stomach at the thought of telling him about Ryan and me. Not because I didn't want him to know, or because I wanted to hide our relationship, but because I was embarrassed to admit that he was right all along. I knew now, just like I knew the inevitability of what led to our break-up, that no matter what, Ryan and I would have found our way to each other. In a way, did that make Adam's paranoia valid? Could he feel our inevitable connection? Was that why he was so adamant about keeping us apart?

Do I have to tell him? Does he really need to know?

"How are you?" I asked, instead.

"Good," he nodded. "Honestly, I'm good. I've been cutting down on drinking. My therapist says it doesn't help with the rage blackouts."

"Therapist?"

"Yeah, shocker, I know. But my parent's sort of forced me after what happened... you know."

I nodded gently.

"And actually, I'm glad they did. I feel better now. More in control."

"That's such good news, Adam," I smiled. Maybe he wouldn't take the news of the engagement too badly after all.

"So, uh, what are you up to these days?" He pulled a hand through his hair.

There was a part of me that would always love Adam. A piece that still cared about him and hoped that he was happy. One that made me miss the curve of his cheekbones and the dimples in his cheeks. But it was a different kind of love, not the type I felt for Ryan—it

301

would be hard for anyone ever to counter my love for Ryan now that I'd let it in full force.

"Well," I swallowed nervously. "I'm moving to London."

"London? That's far. How come?" A strange look passed over his eyes.

"Uh, Ryan and I are getting married." I blurted before I could change my mind.

His stance changed, stepping back as if I'd shoved him in the chest. "Right," he nodded. Eyes flickering, calculating.

I held my breath.

His face went from open and inviting, to clouded in a second. The look had my pulse racing, a shudder travelling along my spine at the change in his eyes.

My hand dropped from the handle of the trolley. I needed to get out of here.

"Adam?"

He'd gone still, nostrils flaring. "You should go, Tyler."

"But—"

"*Go!*" He shouted, with a step toward me, until his face was only inches from mine.

I backed away, leaving the trolley beside him. Adam's hands worked at his sides, clenching and unclenching, over and over. I turned quickly towards the automatic doors at the end of the room. They opened slow, and I squeezed through them. At my car, I fumbled with the keys, hands shaking.

This couldn't be happening. He'd changed, he seemed so different...

The key slipped into the lock, and my head was tugged painfully back, a body slamming into mine.

"It's all right," Adam's breath was at my ear.

"Adam, you're hurting me," I said, hand fumbling with the grip in my hair.

"Come with me," he tugged.

"No," I tried, but the pain that came when he pulled forced my feet to move. Guiding me to his car, he opened the passenger door, pushing my body inside.

He walked around the back, and I watched in the rear-view mirror, pulling my phone quickly from my pocket. I searched for Ryan's name as fast as my shaking hands would allow, but Adam's long legs appeared at the door, and I dropped the phone between my legs, pushing them tightly closed. Adam slammed the door loudly, hitting the lock, it clicked violently into place.

"Adam..." I whispered.

"Shut up, Tyler!" he shouted. "*Just. Shut up. OK?*"

I bit my lips closed.

He was unravelling in front of me. Coming apart all over again, shifting to the monster within. The veil dropped over his vision, black coating the sides, the dormant demon awakening.

I had to stop it. Stay calm. Find a way to help him through it. He didn't know what he was doing.

His hands squeezed tightly around the steering wheel, frantic gaze out the window.

"I'm sorry, Adam," I whispered.

"You're sorry?" he turned.

For a moment, it was as if no time had passed. That we were the same kids, stuck in the constant, vicious cycle that was our relationship.

"I knew it," Adam breathed. "That's why I never liked you hanging out with him. Because *I knew* you had feelings for him, and I was right."

"No, it wasn't like that, Adam. Not when I was with you—"

"Don't lie!" he screamed.

"I'm not! Adam, I'm not…"

"You lied to me," he turned to look at me again. "You said there was nothing between the two of you."

My eyes were glassy, throat working desperately to keep the tears at bay.

"I knew it. I knew it. I knew it." He chanted.

"Adam, you have to let me go. I need to go home." I tried a different approach.

"No," he shook his head, shoving the key into the ignition, engine roaring to life.

"Adam!" I shouted when he reversed. An oncoming car hooted behind us, he stomped on the brake.

"Fuck off!"

Wheels screeched as we tore out of the car park.

CHAPTER NINETEEN
Ryan

Descending dusk set the kitchen alight, a bronze sky burnt fiercely, creating shadows that scattered and grew with slow precision. It has been three months since Tyler disappeared.

Three agonising months.

The last time I'd seen her, she'd dropped me off at the train station, with a kiss and a promise to see me in a week. The final image of her played like a painful, mocking carousel through my mind; perfect pink of her lips, freckles on her make-up free face, hair twisted into a careless bun, wearing my too-big hoodie that she refused to part with.

"Leave it with me?" she'd requested. "It's like a hug from you when I wear it."

Ryan, her voice whispered in the dead of night. I woke in a panic, searching the room.

In the dim light of my small kitchen-diner, London's sprawling city lights below was a kaleidoscope of colours. My top floor apartment of the four-storey building teetered on the edge of a hill, a perfect view of the twinkling city. On a clear day, the silhouette of the London Eye was visible against the sky. The apartment was small, one bedroom with an open-plan kitchen-diner, a landing connecting to the bathroom, lounge, and bedroom.

A stemless wine glass with thick red wine twirled between my fingers, the bottle already three-quarters empty on the table beside me. I'd never been a big drinker, but these days, it helped me sleep. On a good day, the alcohol was strong enough to numb my mind, momentarily banishing dreams of Tyler and the voice that taunted me.

I had no idea where she was. No idea why she had disappeared. Had she run? Or had something more sinister taken her away?

A part of me—a bigger part than I wanted to admit—wondered if she had disappeared on purpose. If it was me, and our engagement, that caused her to up and vanish. Had it suddenly dawned on her, right there in the frozen food section, what she'd agreed to? Free from the romantic haze of our Peruvian hideaway, and suddenly slapped in the face by reality. Had she decided, after all this time, I wasn't what she wanted?

An even crueller part of my already mocking psyche, taunted me in the dark hours of the night— *there's always something that pulls you apart, why did you think it would be any different now? Do you really think you're meant to be, if so, many things keep getting in the way?*

Wasn't the fact that she had gone to a different country—twice—enough evidence that the universe was trying to keep us apart?

I hated every moment the thoughts coursed through me. I didn't believe them. They weren't true.

Were they?

Then there was fact that, if Tyler was running away from me, she would have contacted her parents by now, would have contacted Mel—just as when she *had* run to Peru. But she hadn't contacted either this time. Something was off. So off that her parents reported her as missing to the Police.

There were no leads though. No suspects. Nothing. She hadn't even gone to her local grocery store for some reason. There was no footage of her arriving or leaving, no sign of her car ever entering the car park.

Adam was the first suspect on the list, given their past, though the way Tyler had talked about him those days in Peru, I had no reason to think he had anything to do with her disappearance. She said he had apologised, and they put the whole thing behind them. The Police even spoke to him, learning that he'd been seeing a therapist, who had already documented improvements.

Where are you, Tyler? I rubbed my aching eyes.

I couldn't focus on anything. All I thought about was whether she was OK, watching my phone like a hawk, praying that the next time it rang, or pinged with a message, it would be her. Work was falling apart; I couldn't concentrate on any of the tasks in front of me. In the mirror, a corpse stared back. My boss had been understanding so far, but even he had his limits.

Chest shuddering with tears that had long since run out, I felt useless just sitting here, waiting for news. I wished I knew Gloucester better. Maybe then I would know where to look. Know the places she might have gone, where she might be. If only I'd talked her into moving to London sooner. I should have pushed that it didn't matter if she didn't have a job yet. I was more than capable of covering the bills.

She's so stubborn, I thought with a loving chuckle, so determined to be able to cover her half.

The clock on the wall showed four hours before I was expected at work, but my mind showed no sign of letting me sleep. I needed to go back. To go to Gloucester and do whatever I could to help.

In the bedroom, pulling a bag from the top of the cupboard, I mindlessly shoved in handfuls of clothes, having no plan as to how long I'd be away, stuffing in as much as the bag could hold. Pulling my phone from my pocket, I sent a quick, apologetic email to my boss before opening the train website to reserve a ticket for the next trip out of London.

My bedroom overlooked Cantwell Road and the steep climb to Brent Road. A bus rattled heavily past, wheels creaking under its load, walls of the flat quaking. Along the street were voices; people returning from a long night shift, or heading out for the early shift,

308

mixing with those who had been out all night, swaying under the influence of alcohol. A baby's cry filtered up from the flat below, a dog barked a few doors down, welcoming its owner home.

The air outside when I left the flat was cool but not cold, caressing my face, chasing away the fog in my head. Within a few minutes, another bus was rattling down the hill, and I waved it down with a hand in the air.

****

By the time I reached Tyler's house, it was nine the next day, the sound of the doorbell jarring my already frayed nerves. I'd slept off most of the wine on the train, but my neck ached from where my head had rested against the cold glass.

Brenda answered, her appearance mirroring mine, and all I wanted to do was pull her into a hug. Her face cracked into a strained smile, grabbing my free hand, "Come in, sweetheart." Her fingers were cold despite the heat inside.

I was here only last weekend, but she didn't question my sudden appearance.

"I'm sorry to surprise you like this," I apologised anyway.

"Don't be silly, you're welcome anytime," she rubbed my shoulder tenderly.

"Any news?".

Brenda shook her gently, and finally, I pulled her into a hug. "Is Mel here?"

"She's in her room."

"And Tom?"

Brenda sighed. "At the police station."

I nodded.

"Go on up, you know where you're staying," she motioned to the stairs, turning to the kitchen.

Up the carpeted stairs, pictures hung along the wall in varying heights. At the top, to the right, Mel's door was shut, and I stopped for a moment to admire the picture hanging on the landing.

The print was large, in an elegant, gold embossed frame, showing a wide-angle of the house in Australia. It was taken from the far end of the field, grass green and peppered with yellow, whisps of dandelion seeds floating in the air like faeries. It was dawn, fresh morning sun gleaming on the wooden porch, the roof of our house just visible behind.

Creeping slowly to Tyler's room, the bright yellow walls greeted me gleefully, though didn't do much to help my mood. My heart twisted at the remnants of the young girl who blossomed into the woman Tyler was today. Artwork from her Uni days plastered on the wall beside her desk. A plush toy rabbit with a bean-filled bum on the bed. Pictures of her trip to Peru arranged in a collage above the headrest, the one with her and I standing on the beach in Máncora at the centre.

I was just contemplating where to start, when the floorboards creaked, and Mel appeared. Her hair was pulled into a bun, tendrils snaking scruffily around her face and neck, wearing a set of matching purple pyjamas with small owls on them.

"Mum said you were here," her voice was hoarse. Deep bruises sunk under her eyes.

"I couldn't stay in London. I feel like I need to be here."

Mel nodded, thoughtful eyes scanning the room. "She'll be back," she said, walking to the desk, fingers tracing over papers littering the top.

"How can you be so sure?"

"I can feel it."

Sitting beside me on the bed, Mel rested her head on my shoulder, hands entwined between her legs. "I miss her," she whispered.

"You know her friend from college? Harriet?"

Mel lifted her eyes to mine. "Hattie?"

"Yeah. Do you have her number?"

She nodded. "But we've spoken to her already?"

"I know. I'd just like to talk to her myself."

"OK. Let me get my phone."

She returned, phone in hand, scrolling through the contacts before turning it to me, Hattie's number across the screen.

"How're things going with Jane?" I asked.

311

Mel smiled tightly. "It's good. A little difficult at the moment. I just don't have the energy to give her what she needs right now."

"That's understandable," I squeezed her knee.

Taking my hand, she rubbed it gently before leaving me alone in the room once again.

The house was quiet, too quiet, as if it was holding its breath. I messaged Hattie:

Hi Hattie, my name is Ryan, Tyler's fiancé. We've never met, but I've heard so much about you. I'm aware that you know that Tyler is missing, and I know you've already spoken to Brenda and Tom, but I wondered if you wouldn't mind meeting up with me? I just want to talk.

Hattie replied when I was in the kitchen helping Brenda put the washing away, asking to meet her in town at Costa Coffee at one. I made my way there early, too eager and too restless to sit around the house, and ambled around the town centre, eyes searching every corner.

I spotted a girl with the same light brown hair as Tyler sitting in the doorway of a closed down shop, but when she looked my way, my stomach sunk in disappointment. Maybe Tyler had a sudden bout of memory loss, unable to remember who or where she was—I read that it happened to more people than we knew—and so, I searched every face, hoping to see those sparkling green eyes I missed so much.

Costa was easy to find, and when a girl with flaming red hair in two braids hanging down her back wearing all black and a yellow coat came in, eyes searching the other faces, I waved.

"Ryan?" Hattie reached the table I was at.

"Yeah. Nice to meet you, Hattie." I put out a hand to shake hers, but she swatted it away, pulling me into a tight hug.

"It's so nice to meet you," she said over my shoulder, before taking the chair opposite mine.

"Likewise," I smiled. "I've heard so much about you."

"And I, you," she beamed.

Earrings ran up both sides of her ears, a nose ring shining in one of her nostrils, bracelets jingled on her arms when she pulled off her coat.

"How are you, Ryan?" Hattie's eyes were kind.

"I'm OK," my hands rubbed up and down my jeans. "I hope you don't mind me asking to meet up. I know you've spoken to—"

"Ryan, hey, it's fine," she cut me off.

I nodded, taking a calming breath.

"I just don't know where to look. I don't know the area. I thought, maybe, you could point me to places you guys used to hang out? I know it's a long shot, but… she could have, I don't know, got amnesia, and

313

completely forgotten it all. Or maybe, she's around, just avoiding us. Who knows at this point?"

"Of course," Hattie's head bobbed. "I was so excited to hear about your engagement, by the way," she smiled warmly.

"Thank you."

"She was over the moon. You know that, right?"

I nodded hesitantly.

"Ryan, don't doubt how much she loves you. She's out there somewhere trying to find her way back to you. I know it. She would never leave you. Not now."

I wanted what she was saying to be true so badly.

"We used to hang out in Gloucester Park," Hattie continued. "It's just down the road from here. We also went to the Chinese restaurant by Cineworld all the time. I can take you there after work if you'd like?"

"Yes. Please. Thank you."

Hattie waved a hand. "You don't have to thank me. I want to find her as much as you do. Meet me outside Debenhams at five. It's over there." She pointed to the store across from Costa.

"I will. Thank you, Hattie."

Planting a gentle peck on my cheek, she pulled her mustard coat back on, the door of the café slamming behind her.

Gloucester Park was easy to find, and I wandered around it a few times, looking behind the damaged buildings, at the faces of people sleeping on benches. Eventually, I ended up beside a pond, where ducks and a single swan floated serenely, oblivious to the turmoil writhing inside me. At five, I met Hattie as instructed, outside Debenhams. She lit up a smoke as we began the walk to the cinema.

I could tell she was trying to lighten the dark mood, telling me stories about her and Tyler, pointing to spots along the High Street where something happened that made her fall into a fit of giggles at the memory. It was nice hearing stories about Tyler, even if I was jealous of having missed so much time with her. We lived separate lives for so long, that it hurt in a strange way not to be included in the memories.

Hattie was careful to word her sentences, saying "Tyler is…" instead of "Tyler was…" and I appreciated all the effort, all her optimism.

Down a road lined with buildings, a few trees dotted here and there, Hattie's hand jumped to my arm, pulling me to a stop, lip caught between her teeth.

"What?" I asked, eyes frantically searching the streets. "Is it Tyler?" I looked around, head swinging desperately.

"No, it's just…" Hattie sighed, then pointed to a sign up ahead. "That's where Adam works."

CHAPTER TWENTY

"I'm sorry, I should have taken us a different way." Hattie's gaze was concerned.

"Don't worry. There's no bad blood between us."

We continued to walk, but when we were parallel to the building, I couldn't help my eyes snaking inside. Adam was easy to spot, lying on the ground, long body positioned under a car, grease-stained on the blue overalls he was wearing. My blood unexpectedly boiled at the sight of him.

As if sensing our presence, and pausing for a beat too long, Adam's head swivelled to where we stood, and he froze. I stared into those grey eyes I always found creepy, a shiver climbing up my spine, as if there were thousands of tiny lizard feet crawling over my skin. Did he know that Tyler and I were engaged? Had she seen him since being back from Peru? He must know she was missing, the police had gone to his house.

My feet moved on their own accord across the street. Adam rose lazily, any surprise from when he'd first spotted me gone, replaced with bored indifference. Hattie didn't follow, instead, pulled another cigarette from her bag, leaning against the wall beside the pavement.

"Ryan," Adam said gruffly, as if the sight of me displeased him.

"Hi Adam," I nodded curtly, there was no need to be brash with one another, I just wanted to talk.

"What do I owe the pleasure?" Adam looked around, as if expecting to see someone else with me before those cold eyes met mine again.

"I'm sure you know, but Tyler is missing."

"Yeah. I know," he said casually.

Odd, considering the all-consuming love he had for her. Even if he was over her, I would have expected some level of concern.

"Hattie and I are going to all her favourite spots, to see if she turns up."

"Mhm," Adam looked from my shoes to my hair.

My skin crawled.

"Have you heard from her?"

"Why would I? You worried she's over your little holiday romance and came running back to me?" he sneered.

"This was a mistake," I turned to leave. I should have known we couldn't have a civil conversation.

"It's your fault, you know," Adam shouted to my back.

I paused, turning. "My fault?"

"Tyler wouldn't have gone missing if you'd just known your place."

"Known my place? How does that have anything to do with this?"

Fidgeting uncomfortably, Adam's jaw clenched, a wrench in his hand swinging menacingly back and forth. I knew he never liked me. Tyler told me the lengths he went to, to keep us apart. Perhaps he thought the reason she left him was because of me.

A laugh escaped my lips. "You just couldn't give her the love she deserved."

"And you can? She never wanted you, mate. News flash, she didn't leave me when you came around. She still chose me over you."

I'd never been one for confrontation, but before I knew it, I'd bundled a fist in his shirt, pulling his face close to mine; he stunk of oil and cigarettes. My hand faltered, spotting a strangely familiar tattoo on Adam's shoulder.

Adam laughed easily, head dropping.

I stumbled back.

"You didn't know?" his voice was cruel.

A callous grin stretched across his face, he lifted a hand to rub a finger across the diamond shape on his shoulder. The tattoo wasn't exactly like Tyler's, but hauntingly alike; thorned vines twisting through a diamond where Tyler had a delicate flower.

"Ryan," Hattie's voice came from behind.

Adam stepped close, until the tips of his toes brushed mine. "She never loved you," he seethed quietly. "Get the fuck out of here, dickhead," he threw over his shoulder, turning to head deeper into the garage.

It was only then that I noticed the group of men that had assembled around me. Hattie grabbed my arm, yanking me from the garage.

The world felt as if it was closing in on me. I couldn't get enough air. The stench of oil and grease filled my nose, coating my lungs, dripping down my throat, even as Hattie pulled me back across the road. Nausea roiled in my stomach. Why had she never told me? My vision blurred.

Absently, I heard Hattie's voice, as if I was in the engine room of a boat, white noise filling my head. My legs buckled beneath me, and I stumbled to the pavement, Hattie's hand going to my arm.

"Ryan? Hey, Ryan, are you OK?"

Tears dripped from the bridge of my nose, eyes squeezed closed, I crouched on the pavement.

"Do they... does he have a tattoo that matches Tyler's?" My voice quivered.

Hattie didn't answer, the look on her face all the confirmation I needed.

"Ryan," Hattie placed a tender arm on my shoulder. "Hey, yeah, they do have matching tattoos. But it's not what you think."

"How can it not be what I think? *Matching tattoos?*" It was an intimate thing to share. Maybe I'd been blinded, stupid to think that she loved me more than him.

"Ryan it wasn't like that, OK?" Hattie sighed. "Adam, he sprung the whole thing on her. She thought she was just getting one, and then he copied her. *He copied her.* She had no idea," Hattie pulled the hands away from my face to look into my eyes. "She didn't want it. But it was too late."

****

Back in Tyler's room later that evening, after having no luck at the restaurant, Adams words still haunted me. *She never loved you. She chose me over you.*

My phone vibrated with an incoming message, but I ignored it, heading to the shower—it was probably just my boss anyway.

The warm water worked the knots on my shoulders, noise lulling my senses into a feeling of false calm, drumming against my skin, mixing with tears being sucked down the drain. Back in the room, I grabbed my phone off the side table with a sigh—time for damage control.

When the light of the screen flickered on, my heart skipped a beat: *Tyler*, a small heart sat beside her name that she had put there without my knowing. Pulse skyrocketing, I scrambled to open the message, but the fingerprint recognition frustratingly didn't want to work on my pruned fingers. Swearing, I swiped to type in the code.

Could it be true?

Was I imagining things?

Was it really her?

Sure enough, Tyler's name appeared at the top of the list, a new message indication flashing beside her name.

I clicked it open, heart stuttering as I read.

Ryan, I'm sorry that I just disappeared without telling anyone. I was just a bit overwhelmed with the whole engagement thing. I should have told you sooner, but I don't want to marry you. Please respect my decision. I'm fine, just taking some time away, please stop looking for me. Ty x

Mel, passing by the bedroom, froze with a frown. "Ryan?" She came in.

Swallowing hard against the block in my throat, I held the phone out for her. "Tyler."

"What!" she snatched it from my grip, fierce eyes reading. "What? No, that doesn't make any sense."

"It makes perfect sense, Mel," I dropped my head into my hands.

Adam was right.

"No, Ryan, this can't be right." She knelt in front of me, pulling my hands from my face. There was no hiding the tears leaking down my cheeks again.

"She wouldn't. Something is wrong. She would never leave you," Mel's breaths came in stutters. "Mum!" She shouted, running from the room, noisy footfalls echoing down the stairs. Their desperate voices carried up the hall, but I couldn't get myself to move.

She never wanted you mate.

Then a thought fluttered across my mind, fighting its way through the onslaught of waves breaking over me; why, the day she finally messaged, was the day I'd confronted Adam? It must be a coincidence. I shook it away. After all, if she *had* gone back to him, surely, he would have thrown it in my face? Surely, he would have said something…

Bile rose in my throat. Could she really have left me again? Would she?

Tom rushed up the stairs, followed by Brenda and Mel.

"Ryan?" his voice boomed across the landing, striding into the room. "When did she send this?" he pointed at my phone in his hands.

"About ten minutes ago," I croaked.

"Oh, my goodness," Brenda's hand pressed against a flustered cheek.

"OK. OK," Mel paced back and forth. "This must mean she's OK, right?"

Tom was frowning at the message. "Maybe."

"Why maybe, Tom? This is a good sign," Brenda breathed.

"It could be," he nodded hesitantly. "I need to tell the Police. Ryan, can you send the message to me with the time you received it?"

My hand shook when I took it back. Brenda came to sit beside me. "Oh, sweetheart. It's OK," she rubbed my arm. "We'll get her back. Then she can explain everything. Right now, let's just be happy we've heard from her."

Of course, I was relieved to know that she was OK, but my heart cracked at the memory of her words.

"Are you going to reply?" Mel asked, standing across the room, arms folded.

"Yes, I guess I should," I nodded.

"Ask her where she is. Tell her to call us. Tell her we're not mad, we just want to hear from her," Brenda rattled.

With a deep breath, I hit reply, typing everything Brenda asked, but not what I really wanted to. It would be selfish of me to make this about me; after all, her message came as a relief to everyone, even if it was mostly asking me to stop looking for her.

When an hour passed with no reply, everyone slowly staggered to their rooms, leaving me to read the message over and over.

It was after twelve when Tyler finally replied. The room was dark, my eyes trained on the glimmer of the neighbours outside light through the window, when my phone lit up:

All is fine. I will call my parents soon. Adam is the one for me.

Adam.

Has I been correct earlier? Did he have something to do with this? She hadn't mentioned him before, but now…

I woke Brenda and Tom to tell them Tyler's latest message, and they hugged each other tightly in relief, but I couldn't bring myself to tell them the last bit.

Adam is the one for me… it nagged at me.

Not just for obvious reasons, but because it didn't feel right. Something was off, especially because I'd confronted Adam earlier, and he hadn't said anything about Tyler.

It had been three months; did she go straight to him? If she had, why didn't he tell the cops? But even if she hadn't, why didn't he say anything now?

My head ached, thoughts swarming through it, and though it was late, I dialled Hattie.

"Ryan?" her sleepy voice said on the other side of the line.

"Hattie, I'm sorry to wake you. But I heard from Tyler."

"What? *Ohmygosh*, is she OK? What did she say? Where is she?"

"I think she's with Adam."

Silence settled. "What do you mean? Why would you say that?"

I recounted Tyler's messages, then ended by asking Hattie to give me Adam's address. If she were there, I had to see her. I had to know she was all right.

"Um, I can't quite remember it. But I have it written down in my address book at work. I can get it for you tomorrow." Hattie's voice was unsteady.

"Hattie, please?" I pleaded.

"I'll send it to you, Ryan. I promise."

CHAPTER TWENTY-ONE
Tyler

My fingers were turning numb from the bindings around my wrist, and I flexed my left hand where it was attached to the bed headboard. The clock on the bedside table flashed eight p.m.

Adam was usually home by now, but the house had darkened to shadows since I couldn't reach a light. My stomach grumbled noisily in the silence.

Adam brought breakfast every day, sometimes cooked eggs and bacon, others simply cereal—depending on his mood. He'd leave a sandwich nearby before heading to work, which I munched on halfway through the day.

I had no idea how long I'd been at his house. At first, I tried keeping track of the days, but after two weeks, I'd lost count. The newest bruise on my chin was still healing, a purple, flower-like mark blossoming over my jaw. It looked worse than it was though.

Adam had been gentle for the most part, but there was undeniably something different about him. Something that wasn't there before. Because if this Adam had been there when we were dating, I would have noticed. This Adam flopped between two personalities; one loving and kind and absolutely convinced that I loved him too, the other taut and on edge, anger and rage always simmering just below the surface.

That first day, when he shoved me into his car and drove to his house, it had taken him hours to calm down. He'd trashed the house, and when I tried to run for the door, he grabbed my shoulders and shoved me against the wall a couple of times until dizziness had my legs buckling beneath me. Only then did he realise what he was doing, pulling me into his chest like a child that suddenly noticed they'd almost broken their favourite toy. He'd hauled my shaking body onto his lap, wrapped his arms around me, and rocked back and forth slowly, as if he were caring for a wounded animal.

We sat like that for hours.

"Tyler?" he whispered when the house began to get cold. "I'm sorry. OK? I'm sorry to have to do this. But I know you love me more than him. You just need to be reminded of how we used to be."

He pulled my face from where it was nuzzled against my knees, hair plastered to my cheeks from tears, smoothing it back before bringing his lips to mine. I'd thrashed, but his large hands and legs wrapped easily around me, pinning me in place.

"You'll see," he breathed. "You'll remember."

I tried everything to get him to let me go. Reasoning, saying that keeping me here was wrong. But nothing worked. I learned especially not to bring up

Ryan. The anger that rippled through him at the mere mention of his name sent chills running through me.

Adam ripped the engagement ring off my finger as soon as he'd seen it. I felt naked without it. I begged him not to throw it away. But he took me into the bathroom so I could watch as he flushed it down the toilet, its delicate metal winking goodbye as it went.

How had he spiralled into this... monster? What had snapped inside of him, to make him believe that keeping me here, tied up, was OK? Because I knew, if he were *my* Adam, he wouldn't be doing this. Even *he* would know that this was crossing the line. I just had to figure out the right thing to say, at the right time—to the right Adam.

If I could get all those puzzle pieces figured out, I could find a way out of this.

Headlights danced across the wall of the bedroom, and I craned my neck to look out the window, to where Adam's car was parking on the street beside the house. Under the lamplight, he stumbled out the driver's door, my stomach twisted.

He was drunk.

Attempting to calm my breathing, I schooled my features into still, neutral. The front door banged open, then slapped shut.

"Tyyyy-ler!" Adam sang from downstairs. "Tyyyy-ler," he said again, feet banging against the floor, stumbling up the steps.

The bedroom door swung open, and his gaze fell on me, a smile pulling at his lips. "There you are."

Of course, here I am, where else was I going to be?

"Hi," I managed.

Crawling across the bed, to where I sat, his lips met my forehead, the smell of whiskey wafting up my nose. He was the most unpredictable like this. Sober, I could pretty much manage to keep the peace by saying what I thought he wanted to hear. But like this, there was no telling what he wanted.

"You're drunk?" I asked.

"I had a bad day," he lay on the bed, arm resting over his eyes.

"What happened?" I searched his clothes, hoping to find something he'd forgotten to remove.

"You… will… never guess," he said slowly. "I ran into Ryan."

My spine stiffened. "Wh-what?"

"Yup, little goody-fucking-two-shoes himself."

"What happened?" I tried for an air of indifference. If Adam hurt him in some way, I'd never forgive him. But for now, I had to keep up the façade. I'd worked too hard, and come too far, to let it slip now. If I could convince Adam I didn't love Ryan, maybe he would allow me some freedom. After all, he wasn't thinking straight.

Focusing on my breathing, I waited for him to respond.

"Nothing happened. The dickhead thinks you love him. Poor idiot," Adam laughed harshly. "You'd think he would have got the message by now, wouldn't you?" I bit the inside of my cheek. "You know what?" Adam sat on his elbows. "I have an idea."

Climbing off the bed, he left the room before returning with my phone.

"You know how we're working on us now?" he sat beside me, looking at me with glazed eyes.

I nodded. "Yes, of course. I told you that's what I want."

"Good, then message Ryan and tell him you don't want him any more. Tell him to stop looking for you."

Stop looking for me? Tears pricked my eyes. "OK."

He snapped his hand back. "No funny business, OK?" He paused.

"Of course not," I sighed with a forced smile. "Would you mind undoing my hand? It's going numb."

Pulling keys from his pocket, Adam leaned over to unlock the cuffs. Rubbing my wrist, flexing my fingers, I picked up the phone.

That first day, I managed to slip the phone into my jeans before he pulled me out of the car, but when he insisted I change into something 'more comfortable', later that evening, and while dutifully helping me out of my jeans, it had fallen to the floor. The sound of it constantly ringing in some far corner of the house, and the never-ending flood of messages, finally drove Adam to power it off. I hadn't seen it since.

330

Adam wasn't thinking in the mind of a kidnapper. No. He hadn't planned to *kidnap* me. He barely even saw it like that now. He never worried if anyone had seen us. Not worried if there were any witnesses to give up my possible location, or even thought of powering off my phone until the ringing got too annoying.

No, he wasn't thinking like a kidnapper, he was thinking like a guy who truly believed there was no wrong in his actions.

I opened a message to Ryan.

Hesitating, my mind reeled at what I could say— how I might somehow slip in where I was.

"Tyler?" Adam watched.

"Yeah?" I turned to look at him.

The room was still dark, silhouetted shadow of the lace mesh curtain creating eery web-like patterns on the far wall and over Adam's face. I had never had a chance like this. This was what I'd been waiting for—*think, Tyler.*

"You do want to try and love me again, don't you?" He was unnervingly still. I forced my uneasiness not to show and smiled.

"Of course."

"Prove it," he said.

"I'm about to," I lifted the phone.

"No, I mean really prove it. You said that you wanted to wait, to kiss me, until it was real. It's real now, isn't it?"

Staring into his steel-blue eyes, shadows along his face, stubble on his chin, desperation rolling off him. Any work that had been achieved with his therapist was down the drain. I'd loved him once. Loved the feeling of his hands on me. I could learn to like it again, at least for now. Couldn't I?

"OK," I whispered.

His eyes widened, a spark lighting in the depths, where thin red veins skirted the pupils. He bit his bottom lip. "Yeah?"

I nodded.

A hand came to my cheek, as tender as the first time he'd kissed me, and I closed my eyes, imagining Ryan in front of me; Ryan's hand on my cheek, Ryan's breath fanning across my face. But the illusion faltered when Adam's ringed tongue pushed its way into my mouth. I stifled a gag. Adam pulled away with a frown.

"I'm sorry," I said quickly. "I'm just hungry, and it's making me tired."

"OK," Adam nodded cautiously. "I'll make some food. But send the message first," he planted another peck on my lips. "I'm so happy you finally see that it's meant to be you and me." Adam's smile was wide and true.

I smiled tightly, sighing as I began to type:

Hey Ryan, sorry I've been MIA for a while…

"Hang on..." Adam pulled the phone from my hands. "I might as well just write it."

Deleting what I'd written, he typed quickly, I read the message over his shoulder.

"There we go," he said triumphantly. "Happy?"

I almost laughed. "Uh, maybe end it with Ty, and an 'x'? Signing it off just 'Tyler' seems a bit... unlike me."

"Fine," he retyped and pressed send.

"Can we get some food now? I'm starving. And I need a shower," I said.

"You go shower. I'll sort the food."

Placing clean clothes in the bathroom, his eyes lingered for a moment on the boxers before flicking to me.

"It drives me crazy, knowing you're wearing my boxers."

This man didn't even look like Adam any more. His feral gaze, hair sicking at angles. And he was too thin, ribs protruding from his chest.

I'd been able to keep the distance between us for a while now, feigning that if we were going to make a real go of things, it needed to be organic... real. We needed to wait until it felt right for both of us, and so far, he had respected that boundary, even if the rage blackouts overstepped others.

I smiled tightly again, he walked towards me, a hand snaking under my shirt to my tummy. He groaned into my hair. "Fuck," he dropped his hand and stepped back. "Don't worry. I'll wait until you ask me to."

Shutting the door behind him, the lock clicked into place, before I let out the breath I'd been holding, sagging to the floor, pulling my knees tightly to my chest.

You can do this, Tyler, I told myself.

The bathroom was nestled on the ground floor, under the stairs, with no windows, and Adam had gone through meticulous effort to remove anything 'unsafe'—as he had called it.

Finishing in the shower, I towel dried my hair, pulled on the clothes, then knocked on the door with a shout that I was done. For dinner, he cuffed me to a tall, heavy floor lamp that sat beside the couch, though never left me alone like that for too long—we both knew that with enough time, I could slide the cuff loose somehow.

The food soaked up a lot of the alcohol in his stomach, and he sat calmly while we watched TV, an arm draped lazily over my shoulders. My phone flashed with a new message from across the room where he'd thrown in on a side table, and Adam frowned, a laugh bubbling through his chest at whatever the message was.

"What?" I asked.

"Nothing," he threw it back on the table.

Before bed, Adam picked the phone up again, typed quickly, then shoved it in a drawer in one of the cabinets. He again cuffed my arm to the headboard, wrapped an arm around my waist, and fell asleep with his body tightly around mine, his breathing heavy in my ear.

****

A loud pounding on the door woke us both, and Adam looked groggily at me, as if I had something to do with it.

"What the fuck?" he shouted, heaving himself out of bed, the clock showing five a.m. Shirtless and wearing only a pair of faded, navy joggers, he stormed downstairs, a stream of curses trailing behind him.

Shifting awkwardly, I blinked away heavy, crusted sleep from my eyes, craning my neck to peek out the window. My stomach dropped, recognising the car parked out front.

Hattie.

The pitch to her voice travelled through the levels, followed by the deep vibration of Adam's.

No, not her. What was she doing here?

I frantically scrambled through thoughts of a way to get her away from here. Adam wasn't thinking straight. If he hurt her…

I could scream. Maybe, in the commotion, she would realise I was here, and get away from Adam. No. What if she hesitated, and he grabbed her? Maybe I could catch her eye out the window as she left?

Their voices grew louder. Hattie was shouting now.

Please don't hurt her.

Looking around the room, hoping Adam had forgotten the cuff keys somewhere close, footsteps sounded on the stairs, and I slumped quickly back against the bed. Adam swung the door open, rage in his eyes.

"It's *Hattie*," he said, as if I couldn't recognise my best friend's voice.

"What does she want?" I smothered any desperation.

"She doesn't believe that you want to be here. She won't leave until she's seen you," he huffed.

"H-how does she know I'm here?"

Sitting on the end of the bed, Adam ran his hands through his hair. My heart ached for him. Here I was, tied to his bed, being kept against my will, and somehow, he thought that Hattie doubting I wanted to be here, was wrong. I used to believe that his over-controlling nature was just a flaw in his personality, but now I knew, there was so much more to it. He needed help, *real* help. He had demons. Demons that taunted and whispered in his ear. He was frantic, pulling fingers through his hair, over and over, sweat glistening on his bare back.

"I said something last night," Adam kicked at the side of the bed, answering my question. "Fuck!"

"What did you say?"

"It doesn't matter. But you have to tell Hattie to leave," he fumbled in his pocket for the key.

336

"What?" My eyes widened; here was my chance.

"She won't leave!" he shouted like a child that wasn't getting his way.

"OK. OK," I tried to calm him. "I'll come and talk to her."

Leaning across my body, slotting the key into the cuffs, he held my freed hands in his, kneeling in front of me.

"Please Tyler," he pleaded. "Just tell her what you told me, OK?" He cupped a hand around my cheek.

The kitchen windows were frosted with morning mist, sun shining hazily through, Hattie's shadow like a statue on the opposite wall. She stared out the window, arms folded over her chest. The sight of her brought water to my eyes that I quickly blinked away.

I needed to convince Hattie in a way that would ease Adam. He was already teetering on the edge, and I was afraid of what he might do if he felt like Hattie and I were against him. I needed to handle the situation gently.

Hattie spun when Adam and I shuffled into the room, eyes wide. "Tyler," she breathed, with a step towards me as if to embrace me, but Adam's body tightened, pulling me protectively behind him.

I let him do it, trying to tell her with my eyes that we needed to calm the situation—we used to be able to understand each other with just a look.

"Tyler," Hattie said again, straightening. "Are you OK?"

"Of course, she's OK," Adam said sternly. Her eyes flicked to his, then back to me. Adam turned. "Tell her."

I cleared my throat. "I'm OK, Hattie," I nodded, pulling my hair over my shoulder.

If she saw the bruise, she didn't so much as flinch. Instead, gathering her composure, she squared her shoulders. "Good. And you're happy here?"

"I am."

"I told you she was," Adam snapped.

He'd gone still. I scrambled through my thoughts. "I'm fine, Hattie. You should go."

She looked at me for a beat before nodding. "OK," she turned to the door.

"Make sure, you tell that nob!" Adam shouted at her back, grabbing the door to slam it shut behind her.

I watched as she got into her car, relief and hope flooding through me when she disappeared down the street, then forced myself to focus on what was happening right now.

Adam paced across the kitchen, heavy breaths making the tattoos on his chest expand, the phoenix on his shoulder looking as if it was ready to take flight.

"What's wrong?" I asked cautiously. I had to stop him from unravelling, stop him and buy Hattie some time.

"Her!" he shouted, pointing to the closed door. "All of them! Why won't they just leave us alone? It's none of their fucking business."

"It's OK, Adam," I placed a hand on his arm, but he flung it away.

"We're the same. You and I, Tyler. Baby, please, you have to see that. Just come back to me. Be with me like you used to."

"Adam…"

"*I'm sorry, OK?*" he boomed suddenly, voice exploding off the walls. "Can't you see that? It's my fault. It's all my fault, and I *know* that. But I'm trying to be better." A fist slammed into the counter, splintering with a deafening crack.

"It's OK," I held my hands in front of me as if taming a wild animal.

"Don't you see it?" he propelled towards me, grabbing my arms, face close to mine. "They don't want us to be together. But you're mine. *Mine*."

"Yes," I nodded, fingers digging painfully into my skin. "Yes, Adam," I repeated, bringing shaking hands to his cheeks. "It's OK," I whispered. "We're OK." Our bodies trembled together. I rubbed a hand across his skin. "It's OK," I said again, his grip loosening. "Shhh," I purred, his eyes relaxing.

Dropping his head against my shoulder, his body sagged, long arms wrapping around my waist, fingers knotting in my shirt. At the window, movement caught my eye, then Hattie's car pulled up again, and out the passenger side, came Ryan.

I could have wept at the sight of him.

But Ryan couldn't come in here. Not with Adam like this.

Ryan's eyes searched the house, but I knew he couldn't see us through the window from where he stood. He began to storm towards the house, Hattie caught his arm, pulling him back.

I gripped Adam's head in the nook of my neck tighter—*please, don't look up.*

As if feeling the change in my body, Adam shifted, lifting his head, eyes puffed, lips swollen.

"Adam," I said quietly—*don't look away, keep looking in my eyes.*

"Yes?"

"Let's… let's go to the lounge? OK?" Wrapping an arm around his back, I guided him away from the window, but the *whoop* of a police siren echoed loudly through the room.

His body went rigid, and he spun. "No, no, no, no, no!" he shouted, taking in the police cars congregating outside, the policemen with their radios and belts of guns. "Why? *Why*?"

He wiped his arms over the kitchen counter, glasses and dishes crashing to the ground.

I tried to dart past him, but his hand caught the end of my shirt, and he tugged, pulling until my hip cracked against the corner of a cabinet. I buckled under the pain.

"I'm sorry," Adam said. "But they're not taking you."

He was searching through the drawers now.

340

"Adam," my voice sputtered around the pain, a blinding ache ripping through my abdomen. "Adam, it's OK." I reached out a hand.

"It's not OK, Tyler! *Stop saying that!*" he turned with a knife in his hand.

"Adam…"

"They can't have you. I won't let him take you from me again."

The wild look in his eyes and the searing pain in my side finally caused tears to spill over my cheeks in heavy droplets.

How did I stop this?

Advancing on me, I scurried backwards along the carpet. A loud knock came at the door.

"Adam Wisely, open up!"

His head whipped between the door and me. "No," he said as if it would stop this. "We can be together, Tyler; I know how we can be together."

With the knife at his side, the other hand grabbed my arm, pulling me from the floor. "We'll be together forever."

CHAPTER TWENTY-TWO
Ryan

I'd taken the bus into town, walking the way Hattie had taken us the day before. She hadn't sent Adam's address yet, but I couldn't just wait. I needed to confront him, even if it was just for closure in knowing that Tyler was OK.

The garage wasn't open yet, so I sat on the cold pavement, cement biting into the back of my jeans. Early morning commuters weaved along the small road, exhaust fumes of passing cars mixing with the ever-present stench of oil heavy in the air. Discarded McDonalds packets, empty bottles, wrappers lined the gutters, decomposing cigarette butts littering the sidewalk. Calls of gulls echoed overhead, and my mind turned to the nearby docks. Perhaps I'd go there after talking to Adam—water always had a way of soothing me.

The morning sun was still weak, a sliver broke through the buildings across the road, sending a strobe of honeyed light across my face. Tendrils of sunlight spread over my skin, pinpricks of warmth exploding where it touched.

I closed my eyes, willing myself to keep it together, to stay calm. I needed the agitation boiling inside of me not to show when talking to Adam. I just wanted answers.

My phone rang, and I dug it out of my pocket, heart in my throat. "Hattie?"

"Ryan," she sounded out of breath. "Where are you?"

"I'm outside Adam's garage. Are you OK?"

"Stay there. I'm coming to get you," she spoke fast.

"What's wrong, Hattie?"

"Just… stay there. I'll explain soon."

Within a few minutes, Hattie's small Toyota Corolla careened around the corner, tires screeching to a stop on the cracked road in front of me. "Get in!"

The inside was cold, both windows down, blowing in cool air as she hit the accelerator before my door was even shut.

"Hattie? What is it?"

"Tyler…" there was fierce determination in her eyes, a pink flush over her cheeks. "She's at Adam's."

So, it was true. "Did you go there?"

She nodded.

"Hattie, please, just tell me."

She jerked the steering wheel to the side, my body thrown this way and that as she zig-zagged between hooting cars. "She's there, Ryan. But it's not good."

I felt sick.

"Adam, he… he was different. And Tyler—"

343

"Is she OK?"

Hattie shook her head. "No."

"What do you mean no? Hattie, tell me." My voice was frantic, verging on shouting.

She lacked her usual flamboyant makeup, making her look young beyond her years. "I can't explain it, Ryan. I just know something is wrong."

Nails digging into the skin of my clenched hand, a roaring inferno built inside my chest. I hadn't allowed the idea that something bad had happened to Tyler to sink in. A part of me had rationalised, that Tyler was gone because she had chosen to, the logical part of my brain trying to prepare me for *that* fall out.

I hadn't prepared for this.

Within minutes, Hattie turned down a cul-de-sac of large, red-bricked houses with conservatories and ample sized gardens. The residents had only just begun to rise, puffs of smoke emerging from chimneys like clouds against the blue sky, children in school uniforms dashing to cars.

At the end of the street was the only house with unruly, tall grass at its front, an untrimmed hedge against a green wooden fence. Hattie bumped the small car onto the sidewalk, stomping on the brake.

"Is this it?"

Hattie nodded, tugging the handbrake.

My hand shook as I grabbed for the handle, pushing open the door to dash across the grass, but Hattie pulled me back with impressive force.

"Wait, Ryan. You can't go in there."

"Why not?" I demanded.

Tyler was meters away, in who knew what kind of trouble, there was no way I was just going to stand outside.

"You can't go in there," Hattie's face was stern.

Before I could pull out of her grip, a police car pulled beside us, another not far behind it. My head whipped around, then back to Hattie. She'd called the police...

"Hattie?" An officer approached.

"That's me," she nodded, finally letting go of me.

"You said that Tyler Blake was in this house and being held against her will?"

My eyes widened.

Hattie nodded.

"OK, you two, wait here," the officer turned to his colleagues, speaking into the radio on his shoulder. Another car arrived, this one with the whoop of a siren, and it was only then that a silhouette within the house moved, and I saw the outline of a person.

The police saw it too, a hush travelling through them as one form became two; Tyler and Adam—Tyler's small frame pushed beside his.

My eyes strained through the darkness, past the shifting net curtain hanging at the window, but they disappeared.

"Adam Wisely, open up," an officer pounded on the door. "Come out with Tyler." The officer stepped back.

Uniformed men and women fanned the front garden, others patrolled the road behind, a few on the sidewalk directing the morning's foot traffic away from the house—I had no idea when they'd all arrived. Minutes felt like days, heart pounding in my ears, it took all my willpower to keep my feet planted where they were. From one agonising breath to the next, my heart felt like it was squeezed in a steel fist, my stomach as if it could empty onto the road at any minute. Hattie's hand slipped gently into mine, fingers squeezing in reassurance.

Finally, the sucking of an opening door sounded, and when Tyler appeared, time stood still.

Her skin was pulled too tightly around sharp bones, the T-shirt she wore hung limply around a meek frame. A purple bruise fanned along her jaw, smaller ones down her arms, tear marks streaking down her cheeks. Even from where I stood, I could see the redness to her eyes. She was limping, and only then did I notice the arm wrapped around her waist, Adam's towering form pushing behind her, and in his other hand, a knife.

The officer who had pounded on the door put out a hand to the unit behind. "Adam," the woman's voice was firm. "Adam, put down the knife, and let's talk."

Adam's hair stood on end, frantic eyes flicking from side to side, until they found mine.

The inferno inside me burned through my skin, melting everything away, until all I felt was anger and hatred for those cold blue eyes.

"She doesn't want you!" Adam shouted. "She's mine!"

"Don't say anything," the officer nearest cautioned.

In his arm, Tyler had gone limp, as if Adam was the only thing keeping her upright, her gaze glazed and defeated.

"Adam, let her go mate, and we'll talk about this," another officer said.

"No!" Adam swung frantically, like a cornered, feral animal, Tyler's body bobbing like a rag doll.

He retreated a step, pulling Tyler closer, head dipping toward her ear. Tyler's eyes lifted with effort, the fog clearing in her gaze, to meet with mine.

Electricity zipped through me, and she finally stood, supporting her weight. Adam's lips moved against her hair. Her eyes turned fierce and full, before widening with a jerk.

Shots sounded. Tyler jerked forward. Adam fell back, and finally, I ran.

"Tyler!" I skidded to stop beside where she lay in the grass, crimson leaking into the earth, staining the green grass.

My world stopped, I touched her cheek, vision marbled, tears leaking into the ground to mix with her blood. "Ty," I breathed.

Her eyelids fluttered gently, though never opened, and paramedics pulled me back, closing around her, a stretcher laid beside her body.

Tearing my eyes away to where Hattie had collapsed over herself, a hand over her mouth, tears raking through her quivering body. Knowing I was no use to Tyler, and better out the way of the paramedics, my legs wobbled over to Hattie, crouching beside her to wrap my arms around her shoulders. She leaned into me with a heaving breath in, a hysterical cry escaping past her hand.

CHAPTER TWENTY-THREE
Tyler

I was dreaming. I knew I must be dreaming because Luke was there.

We were sitting on the edge of the pool by the poolhouse, feet submerged in the crystalline water, humid Jamaican air clinging to my skin. Luke was smiling, like he always was, and I was relaxed, calm, though a nagging feeling in the back of my mind told me that I shouldn't be so tranquil, except I couldn't put a finger on why. Every time I got close, it drifted away like ink in water.

We were talking, though I didn't know what about—it was like watching a movie, being in the character's body, my lips moving on their own. Then Luke laughed, the easy sound reverberating through my bones.

Luke's face morphed into Ryan's, and now we sat in the little shack by the pond, except Ryan was sixteen, skin tanned and golden. His brown eyes watched the dam in front of us, undoubtedly searching the surface for fish. Suddenly, my stomach tightened; *did this Ryan know that we were together? Did he know we were engaged? What if he didn't?*

I felt sick—*this* Ryan wasn't quite *my* Ryan.

How could I live in a world where Ryan and I were apart? Why did I do this? Was there a way to get back?

But everything was so real. Somehow, I'd travelled back in time, and only I knew what we used to be. Birds chirped loudly, wood from the shack scratched under my palms, spiking into the back of my thighs.

There was no going back now.

Tears pricked my eyes—this was it. This was my reality.

How was I supposed to go back to the way we used to be? When now I knew what it was like for those brown eyes to look at me full of love. Know what it felt like to have him touch me, the taste of his skin, the feeling of knowing that he loved me too?

I wanted to say something, to tell this Ryan that one day, he would love me too—but I didn't want to scare him. I didn't want him to think I was crazy. I had to try to win him back. I had to…

A beeping echoed through my head, a ripping ache spreading like lava.

"Tyler?"

A voice… it sounded far away, as if someone was speaking through water.

"Ty?" It came again, except louder.

Mum? *Let me sleep in, please? I'm so tired.*

Wait, where was I? I didn't remember going to bed. When did I go to sleep?

Where was I? In my room in Gloucester?

Adam. Adam. *Adam.*

Adam's house. Adam standing over me with a knife. Adam holding me tightly, police surrounding us.

"It's the only way, Ty. We'll be together. Always and forever. Forgive me, but I promise I'll follow you," the ghost of Adam's voice whispered in my ear.

Always.

Forever.

Noises shifted into blurry focus, voices came as if through the static of a TV. A hand was in mine, I squeezed.

I'm scared—everything's dark.

"Tyler?"

"Ty?"

"Wake up, honey."

"We're here."

"You're OK."

CHAPTER TWENTY-FOUR
Ryan

I shifted uncomfortably in the small hospital chair, mechanical beeping filling the small room. Mel and Jane returned with the smell of coffee drowning the stench of bleach, and Mel handed me a plastic cup without a word, a tender hand on my shoulder. Brenda and Tom were in the hall, talking to a doctor, their soft voices filtering into the room.

Tyler had been out of surgery for a few hours now. The purple marks along her skin stark against the white bedding, and my chest hurt every time I looked at her, thinking of what that psycho did. Praying that if she came back to us, I'd never let her go again.

Each hour that passed was agonising.

A nurse came in regularly to check, assuring that all her vitals were good, she would wake when she was ready.

"When she's ready?" Brenda had asked a doctor an hour earlier, sitting on the side of the bed, Tyler's hand clutched in hers.

"Yes. Physically, she's healing. But mentally," the doctor shook his head. "We don't know what happened these past months. The brain needs time to heal too."

Hattie arrived with a basket full of sandwiches that she passed around, before sitting beside me, head resting on my shoulder.

We waited.

CHAPTER TWENTY-FIVE
Tyler

Pulling my heavy lids open was like wrenching apart Velcro. My mouth achingly dry, everything so bright I could barely make out the blurry forms around me.

"Oh, sweetheart."

"Mum?" I croaked.

"Yes, honey, we're here. You're OK."

I blinked slow and painfully. Finally, everything shifted into focus.

The first thing I noticed was the too white room, and a poster with some words and a picture of a smiling meerkat on the wall. Mum sat beside me, her small hand tucked into mine, dad behind her, a hand on her shoulder. Both their eyes were red. I looked past them to Mel and a girl I didn't recognise at the bottom of the bed, then on my other side to Hattie.

Smiling was like the cracking of cement, I tried my voice again. "Hi."

They smiled around sad faces, mum wept, leaning into my shoulder—how bad was it? Was I paralysed? Had I lost a limb?

Sitting up, a blinding pain ripped through my stomach.

"Don't try to sit," dad pushed me back gently with a warm hand on my shoulder.

"What happened?" I asked, obediently lying back. "Where's Ryan?" I jerked back up. What if the dream was real?

"I'm here," his voice filtered from somewhere in the room.

Standing from behind Hattie, his eyes were red and raw too, wet in the corners from newly formed tears. Swallowing hard, he shoved his hands in his pockets. My chest shuddered at the sight of him, and when I snorted an awful hiccup, tears quickly spilling down my cheeks, Ryan rushed to the bed.

"Oh Ty," he whispered.

Reaching up, I tugged him to me, lifting, ignoring the pain in my stomach. His arms wrapped around me, and in the cocoon of his embrace, I finally felt safe.

When the tears eventually stopped, and I could stand the pain no longer, Ryan carefully lowered me back onto the bed. When I didn't let go of his hand, he shifted to sit on the bed beside me, Hattie moving to stand beside Mel and the other girl.

"How do you feel?" Mel asked.

"Thirsty."

"Here," dad procured an orange plastic cup.

"What happened?" I asked again once I'd gulped down as much water as my tender throat would allow.

Mum and dad looked at one another, it was Hattie who spoke. "Adam… he, well, he stabbed you."

I frowned. Ryan was rubbing the back of my hand in small circles.

"I know," I nodded.

It's the only way, Ty. Then we'll always be together. Forgive me, but I promise I'll follow you.

I shuddered. I knew what he was going to do when he'd said it. I knew what he'd meant.

"What happened to him?" I looked at the faces around the bed.

"They shot him, Ty," Ryan said quietly. "The police, they—"

"They *what*?" I turned quickly. "How could they? Why would they… *why*?"

"He was pronounced DOA, sweetheart," dad said gently.

"No," I shook my head.

Adam was troubled. He needed help. But he didn't deserve that…

"How can you not want him dead?" Mel asked harshly. "After what he did to you?"

"You don't understand…"

How did I explain to people who only ever saw the wrong side of Adam; that he was caring? That he loved me beyond everything. Just because I couldn't reciprocate his love didn't—*never*—meant I didn't care about him.

"Ty, he kidnapped you. He kept you locked up; don't you remember?" Mum asked.

I laughed. "Of course, I remember…"

"She must have that syndrome, what's it called? Where the hostage starts to sympathise with their captor," Mel said.

"No," I shook my head. How could they think that?

I turned to look at Ryan again, searching, hoping he at least understood.

Bringing fingers to my temples, a headache thumped numbingly at the base of my head, a doctor entered the room.

"Ah, I heard she was awake," he said in a loud, self-assured voice.

"Doctor Morley," dad said. "She woke up about twenty minutes ago."

Doctor Morley had brown skin with a bald head, grey hair in an otherwise black moustache, with a pair of square glasses.

"How are you feeling, Tyler?" Doctor Morley asked. "Your family has been waiting very patiently for you to wake up."

"Um, OK, I guess. My head is sore. And my stomach."

The doctor nodded. "I imagine it would be. We'll get you some pain killers. Has your family explained what happened?"

"Yes, I was stabbed, I know that."

357

"But you had to go into surgery," he waited. When I didn't respond, he continued. "Adam stabbed you in the lower abdominal area. The knife missed your stomach but caught the left Fallopian tube. Do you know what that is?"

"It's…" I tried to think past the thumping in my head. "It's where the egg comes from?"

Doctor Morley laughed. "Basically, yes. You have two, one on either side of the uterus, and they both take turns dropping eggs every month. Unfortunately, the knife pierced the left tube. Still, we managed to get you into surgery before there was too much bleeding. However, the tube was too damaged for us to try and save, so we had to remove it."

He waited.

Had to remove it? Did that mean…?

"Does that mean I can't have kids?" My voice was small.

I'd never really thought about having kids. Of course, I wanted them. I always knew I wanted to be a parent, but I never thought I'd consider it for a long while.

"No," the doctor said. "It doesn't mean you can't have kids. You still have the other tube, and the body is a wondrous thing. It just may take a little longer than usual when you're trying."

I didn't want to look at Ryan. Would he still want me if I couldn't have kids?

I nodded when the doctor didn't continue.

"You have some stitches in your stomach, so you'll have to be careful. They'll probably hurt for a while. But we'll give you some painkillers for the time being, OK? Do you have any questions?"

I shook my head, eyes glued to the duvet where my feet created a small summit beneath it.

"OK," Doctor Morley said. "Mr and Mrs Blake, Ryan, can I talk to you for a moment outside?"

Ryan kissed the crown of my head when I squeezed his hand. "I'll be back," he said quietly, pulling free to follow the others out the room.

Hattie quickly grabbed the hand Ryan left. Mel pulled the other girl to my other side.

"By the way," Mel held the girl's hand. "This is Jane."

Jane had soft blonde hair hanging around her shoulders. She was shorter than Mel, her skin a pale pink.

"Nice to finally meet you," I smiled. "Sorry, it's under these circumstances," I joked. A smile tugged at her lips.

"Don't be silly," Jane said kindly. "I'm glad you're OK." She touched my shoulder lightly.

"I'm surprised you're still here," I turned to Hattie, raising my eyebrows. "All this not scared you off yet?"

Hattie laughed. "Almost. I was considering just leaving you there. Cut my losses."

"Uh, we'll grab something from the canteen," Mel and Jane walked to the door.

"Oh, can you get me some food? I'm starving," I said, Mel bobbed her head.

"I'm glad you're OK, Ty," Mel said before they disappeared.

"Oh Ty," Hattie sighed, tenderly brushing hair from my forehead. "When will you stop getting into trouble?"

"Thank you," I smiled. "For coming back for me."

"You don't blame me? For Adam?"

"No! No, it wasn't your fault. How are you doing? He was your friend longer than he was mine, I guess."

"Fine," she shrugged. "It's strange. I never thought he would do something like that. I mean, I didn't know him that well, but I didn't think…"

"It wasn't him. Not really," I said quietly.

CHAPTER TWENTY-SIX

By the time my parents and Ryan returned, I was exhausted and fell asleep quickly with my head resting on Ryan's chest. I'd moved enough so that he could prop his legs up, easily dropping into a deep, dreamless sleep.

When I woke, Ryan was out cold, his head dropped back, mouth slightly agape, breathing deeply. It was late, my room empty, all the lights off except for one filtering in from the hall. A nurse came quietly in, and, seeing me awake, smiled and whispered, "I'm just going to check your vitals, OK honey?"

Gently, she took my arm, checking my blood pressure and writing in a little pad, before checking the drip and jotting more down. Before leaving, she said, "I can bring another blanket and pillow for him if you like?"

"Yes, please. Thank you," I smiled.

When the nurse returned with the pillow and blanket, I poked Ryan awake. He jumped, frantic eyes searching the room before falling on me.

"How are you feeling?" he whispered.

"I'm OK. Thanks for staying with me."

"Of course," he breathed.

We had so much to talk about. I had too much to say, but exhaustion got the better of us both, and we fell asleep again, wrapped in each other. This time, my dreams were plagued with Adam, and I woke every so often with a jump, when the dreams turned to nightmares that reminded me of the times Adam was violent. When the darkness in his eyes consumed him.

I didn't hate Adam; I was afraid of him, I was angry at him for what he'd done, but I couldn't bring myself to hate him the way Mel expected me to. Watching him spiral was like watching a ball of string unravel—no matter how hard I desperately tried to grab it, to put it back together, there was no going back.

Had I done that to him? Was it me that had caused him to break down the way he had? If I hadn't come into his life, would he still be alive now? Maybe I should have said something, done something when I'd seen the darkness descending. When had I first noticed it happening?

I couldn't put my finger on an exact time, the moment when I knew something was wrong. Did I ever really know something was wrong until that final blow? The one that finally made me realise we were toxic for each other.

Was I just as bad as him? Was all this just as much my mess as it was his? I had to take responsibility for my part. How unfair it was that I was here now, heart full, Ryan resting peacefully beside me, the warmth of his body warming mine, whilst Adam was… bile rose in my throat. I twisted, finding a bucket near the bed, heaving the menial bit of food I'd managed to put down earlier into the bottom.

Ryan jerked awake, a hand coming quickly to my back, rubbing soothing strokes down my spine.

My eyes burned, sweat plastered my flushed skin.

The sun was rising gently, rays catching the white blinds hanging over the glass, my stomach clenched and heaved. A few minutes later a nurse came in, handing me a box of tissues and removing the bucket.

I was reluctant to sit back, not wanting to look at Ryan, to let him see me in this way. But when I did, there was only gentle understanding in his eyes.

"How'd you sleep?" I asked, shuffling back.

He smiled tightly, leaning back against the pillow. "You won't believe it, but it's the best I've slept in the last three months."

"Three months? Is that how long it's been?"

He sat up, hair messy and falling across his forehead. "You didn't know?"

I shook my head. "I tried to keep track…"

Ryan was quiet, thinking through his next words. "Ty, I'm here when you're ready to talk about it all, OK?"

I nodded, smiling tightly.

I didn't know what he was expecting to hear, probably some horrible story about how awful Adam was to me. I needed him, of all people, to understand, to *really* understand, how I couldn't hate Adam. But I didn't want Ryan thinking that I loved him any less or to think that I loved Adam more.

"Ty?" Ryan sighed, shifting so he to sat in front of me.

"Mhm?" I swallowed.

"Do you, uh, want some gum?" He pulled a packet from his jeans, sheepish smile pulling at his mouth.

A chuckle rattled through me, I put a hand to my stomach. "Don't make me laugh. It hurts."

He was smiling now, and it was like a breath of fresh air on a hot day, like turning to the sun and letting the rays wash over my face.

"Yes, I really would like some gum," I snagged one from his hand, he popped one in his mouth too.

A moment passed, and then he cleared his throat, saying gently, "I thought—I don't know—a part of me really thought you might have left me for him."

I took his face in my hands, resting my forehead to his, "I'm sorry I did whatever it was that would make you think that."

"It's not really something you did. It's just the way our lives always seem to go. Like we're not meant to be together because we keep getting pulled apart. And I thought, maybe, it had happened again."

Kissing him properly for the first time in months, his lips were like liquid gold across mine; soft and tender. There was pain in the kiss, and I could only imagine what might have been going through his mind all these months.

With a deep breath, I knew I needed to explain things to him, and now was as good a time as any. "I bumped into Adam at the shop…"

"You don't need to do this now," he uttered gently.

"I want to," I nodded, before continuing. "I bumped into him at the shop. He seemed like he was doing well; there was a light about him that I hadn't seen in a while. He said he'd been seeing a therapist and he asked me how I'd been, normal stuff you know? Which for us was a massive leap." Ryan listened cautiously. "At first, I wasn't sure if I should tell him about you. I mean, you know how insecure he was about us from the start, and after seeing all the progress he made, I didn't want to do anything to jeopardise that. But then, I don't know—I just thought rather he finds out from me than from someone else. But also, I thought that if he was over me, he wouldn't mind, right? Maybe it was naïve of me to think that. Anyway, when I told him, that's when, you know…"

Ryan nodded again.

Fiddling with the bed covers, it was easier to tell the story without watching the emotions on his face. It was how he felt at the end that mattered.

"He didn't hurt me while I was at his house. Not really."

"He *did* hurt you, Ty. Haven't you looked in the mirror?" Ryan's voice was wary.

"No, he didn't mean to. He just… lost control sometimes. It was like he was two different people. He got lost inside these rages, and when he was in one, even when I looked in his eyes, it was as if he wasn't there any more. I don't know how to explain it, but I watched as common sense left him. Like he truly believed what he was doing was right. He was so convinced that... that keeping me there was the right thing to do. Like he didn't even realise that he was keeping me there against my will. It was so scary to watch that happen. To watch him spiral further and further." I paused, taking a breath.

"The day he saw you," I continued. "That day, I don't know what happened, he didn't say, but I think it might have jolted him awake. And then because of it, he started to realise what he was doing, and he got angry. He got scared. I'll never forget the look in his eyes when the police showed up. He looked so lost."

"What did he say to you?"

"What do you mean?"

"Before he... before he stabbed you."

Biting my lip to stop it from quivering, I paused. "He said it was the only way for us to be together... It was like he was a child afraid his favourite toy might be taken away from him."

"Ty," Ryan sighed, running a hand through his already messy hair.

"Don't you see?" I asked desperately. "He was battling demons. I tried to help him, but I wasn't good enough. I think I was the trigger. If only we could have got him to someone that could have helped, maybe he would have been all right." My voice hiccupped, Ryan pulled me quickly into his arms. I buried my face in his shirt.

"It isn't your fault, Tyler," Ryan said into my hair, my heart squeezing.

Tears racked through me for Adam, body convulsing so my stomach hurt where the new stitches pulled. Ryan just held me tightly, rubbing my back, placing tender kisses wherever he could. After a few minutes, I noticed Ryan's finger absently running over the bare spot where my ring should be, I squeezed my eyes shut.

How did I tell him?

How did I say that Adam flushed it away? Adam, who I was asking Ryan to forgive.

Was I asking too much of him? Was I being unfair? Was I taking advantage of his kind soul?

He stared absently into space, still rubbing the empty spot, and I forced myself to whisper, "I'm sorry."

Ryan pulled back. His eyes puffed from sleep, crease marks from the pillow still laced across his skin. "Why are you sorry?"

"My ring," I said quietly.

His eyes slowly travelled down to my hand in his, and he swallowed. "It's OK. It's just a thing. It doesn't matter."

"It does, though. I loved it. You picked it out for me, and it reminded me of one of my favourite spots in the world."

"Peru?"

"Our little balcony on the beach of Máncora. In *Peru*," I clarified, managing to tug a smile from his lips.

I wished we could go back.

Back to when we were carelessly happy and in love—experiencing new things, creating new memories, sand crusting our skin and in our hair.

"I'll get you a new one. If that's what you still want?"

I pulled away from him this time, pushing him back with a hand on his shoulder. "You're not serious?" I searched his face.

Looking away, he shrugged, sunlight turning his eyes to molten amber. He *was* serious.

"When I thought you left me. I came to terms with maybe you didn't want to be with me, no matter how much I wanted to be with you. And I realised that above all, I just want you to be happy."

"But what about... what if I can't..." I rubbed a thumb over my stomach.

He shook his head gently. "I don't care. We'll cross that bridge when we need to."

My heart melted, and suddenly I wanted to be as tied to him as I could be. I wanted to give everything I had to him. I didn't ever want to be apart from him again.

"I love you, Ryan. And I want you. Only you. Forever."

CHAPTER TWENTY-SEVEN
Five years later

Standing at the bottom of the garden, I could see the whole creek as it weaved between the trees at the bottom of our land, to where it disappeared into the neighbours. Soft sounds of gurgling water sighing across the field.

It was early, the air still crisp, birds singing so loudly in the trees that my thoughts were lost to their beautiful melodies. Pulling the blue cardigan I'd found on the floor, tighter around my shoulders, I watched the edge of the field for movement. A form appeared wearing a big hat, dirty pair of jeans, and that hideous shirt I couldn't stand.

Twirling the wedding band around my finger, I watched Ryan make his way across the field, still in awe, even after all these years, that I got to call him my husband. That I was the one he came home to every day. It had become a habit, that I ran my fingers over the scar on my stomach, as if in a way, if I could pass enough loving and healing energy through my palms, my insides would recover enough to give us a child.

Ryan and I got married on that beach in Máncora. He surprised me with a trip a year after my surgery, organising for both our parents, Mel and Jane, and even Hattie to join us. We went back to the little store where he had bought my engagement ring, and instead, purchased wedding bands.

"Why wait?" I'd asked. "I'm ready now. I want to marry you, and I don't want anything to get in our way again."

The ceremony was small but perfect.

I bought a dress from a little boutique in town, Ryan wore a pair of beige trousers, with an open-collared shirt. I'll never forget the way he looked; windswept and sun-kissed when he said, 'I do'.

Our engagement and marriage all happened so quickly, though it didn't feel quick. It felt like a lifetime in the making.

It wasn't long afterwards that we decided it was time for us to move back *home*. So instead of buying our first house in England, we took everything we had, and returned to Australia, where it all started. England held too many painful memories, plus, there was a poetic familiarity to returning to the place where we had begun, to begin the rest of our lives.

Maleny was where we called home now. We had a beautiful house nestled amongst the rolling farming hills, gum trees running along the borders of our small piece of land. Ryan was by nature an early riser, I preferred to lie-in, so most mornings, I waited at the edge of the garden for him to come back from whatever errand he'd run off to do.

When I thought about my life—our life—before this, it seemed fractured, like it wasn't whole until we were together. We had a rough start, but everything that happened was meant to happen, to bring us to this moment. To the life we shared now.

Destiny had a way of making things work out. Ryan and I were destined to come together, one way or another, no matter how hard one pushed, or the other pulled.

Sometimes, I thought about what my younger self would say, if she could see her future—married and adored by Ryan Andrews. I wouldn't have believed it. Or I would have laughed in victory, pulling my tongue at Mel and Lilly, "Na, na, na, na, naaaa!" The thought still made me laugh.

I couldn't help comparing Ryan and Adam sometimes. I knew I shouldn't. But where Adam was all prickly shadows and dramatic love, Ryan was the total opposite.

My relationship with Adam was like a storm; sometimes completely calm and beautiful in the eye, until the winds hit, and everything turned upside down. Though I didn't regret it. Ryan made me a better version of myself, and I sometimes wondered what might have become if I had stayed with Adam. If I hadn't somehow found the strength to pull away from his gravitational pull.

My lord of shadow.

And my king of light.

"Good morning," Ryan's soft voice sent goosebumps along my spine, planting a tender kiss on my lips. "Don't get that dirty, I was going to wear it again," he playfully tugged the cardigan I was wearing.

I giggled guiltily, pulling it tighter around me.

At the age of thirty, Ryan's hair already had small flecks of grey scattered here and there, joking that they'd appeared during those months I was missing. An arm draped around my shoulders, mine wrapped around his waist, shoulder nestled under his; we walked arm in arm back to the house. He told me about the fish he'd seen in the stream that morning and about the otter that lived amongst the rocks.

My eyes pulled to the edge of the trees beside the house, where I saw, as I always did, a haunting figure in a black suit—the suit he'd worn to my graduation.

Adam stood under the trees, those piercing blue eyes watching me.

I knew that if I looked away, when I looked back, he would be gone. But for now, his hooded eyes trailed us.

He was as devastatingly beautiful as when we'd first met, and I was no longer shaken at the sight of him as I had been when he'd first appeared.

As if, even in death, Adam waited for me.